THE HIRED MAN

THE HIRED MAN

Aminatta Forna

WINDSOR
PARAGON

First published 2013
by Bloomsbury Publishing
This Large Print edition published 2013
by AudioGO Ltd
by arrangement with
Bloomsbury Publishing PLC

Hardcover ISBN: 978 1 4713 4553 1
Softcover ISBN: 978 1 4713 4554 8

British Library Cataloguing in Publication Data available

Printed and bound in Great Britain by
MPG Books Group Limited

for Mo

1

September 2007

At the time of writing I am forty-six years old. My name is Duro Kolak.

Laura came to Gost in the last week of July. I was the first to see her the morning she drove into town. From the hillside you have a view of the road, one of the three that lead into town: the first comes direct from the north, the second and third from the south-east and the south-west respectively. The car was on the road that comes from the south-west, from the coast. An early sun had burned off most of the mist and on a day like this the deer might be encouraged to leave the woods and come down the hill, so I'd turned back to fetch my rifle even though it was not the season to hunt.

I'd chosen my spot and laid out my breakfast. On the branch of a tree a collared dove rested out of view of the falcon soaring above. I trailed the bird lazily through my rifle sights and that was when I noticed the car. A large, newish four-wheel drive, being driven very slowly down an entirely empty road as though the driver was searching for a concealed entrance. I lowered the gun so that I had the vehicle fully in my sights but the angle and reflection of the sun made it impossible to see who was driving.

An hour later I was on the road home carrying my gun and an empty bag. Instead of cutting through the long field I kept to the road until I reached the blue house. A row of trees grew on the verge in front; over the years I'd watched three of them reach and exceed the height of the roof, the fourth had died some years back. Nobody to cut it down and so it remained standing next to its living companions, branches like bleached bones. The overhang of the roof cast a deep shadow on the walls of the house, stains flowed from the windowsills down the whitewash, buddleia sprouted from a high gutter: a slow slip into decay. Nobody had a reason to go there, not even children for whom there was no shortage of empty houses to play in and anyway this one was too far away, beyond the boundaries of the town.

The door of the house rested upon its hinges, the shutters were pushed back and one of the windows (glass darkened with dirt and crossed with silvery strands) stood open. Parked up with two wheels on the grass was the car I'd seen earlier in the morning. From inside: voices. One, a girl's: young, high, hesitant. The other was older. They spoke in English (from what I understood, it had been a long time since I'd heard English), they were talking about something they'd lost. I was listening to a mother and daughter. The daughter said she'd go and look in the car.

I slipped out of sight around the side of the building where the old ladder hung. I waited, leaning against the wall, and listened to her footsteps, the heft of the car door. Only then did I realise I wasn't alone: a boy of sixteen or seventeen was standing at the other corner of the building. He wore a checked shirt, jeans, black-and-white baseball shoes and stood with his eyes closed and his face tilted up to the sun. He had his hands cupped over his ears as he listened to music through his headphones, lost to the sound and unaware of me. I retreated softly to the road.

At home I considered all the possible meanings of what I'd seen while I did my exercises: twenty-five pull-ups from the bar over the door. Twenty-five squats. Twenty-five crunches. I did press-ups until the muscles in my arms burned. Afterwards I started brewing some coffee. I'd only taken a single cup before I left the house, but then I changed my mind and set the pot back on the stove. I decided to go into town and have coffee at the Zodijak instead.

*　　　*　　　*

Outside the Zodijak the chairs and tables were already out. I nodded at a couple of the guys—one of them worked in the garage next door. Fabjan had hired a new girl for the summer, who smiled at all the customers, which here is as disconcerting as if she walked through the streets singing. She told me Fabjan was on his way in. I ordered a coffee. Someone else called for a Karlovačko. We sat in silence and watched people passing in the street.

It was close to nine by the time Fabjan showed up. Fabjan drives a custom-sprayed BMW, meaning nobody else has one in the same colour and so he doesn't need to bother to lock it. He was wearing a new suede jacket, something like the colour of butter, and freshly laundered jeans, faded and tight around the balls. Fabjan's put on a few kilos over the years and the waistband of his jeans cut into his gut. He wore a year-round tan and the beginning of jowls.

Fabjan joined me. He didn't have much choice;

3

I'd taken his table, which is something I do to annoy him: a small pleasure in a quiet town. He put his car keys and Marlboro Lights on the table, called for a Karlovačko and rummaged in his pocket. Lately he'd been complaining of a toothache, but he hates dentists and so took two pills with his first gulp of beer. Fabjan's gums are receding at the same rate as his hair, one of his front teeth is broken. I knew how he'd broken it and when; in all that time he'd never had it fixed. A gold glint in the back of his mouth provided the sole evidence of dental work. I wondered if Fabjan was sleeping with the new girl.

'What's up?' I said.

Fabjan shrugged and sipped his beer.

We sat. I finished my coffee and called for another. The postman arrived, climbed off his bike and leant it against the railing at the front of the café. '*Dobar dan,*' he said.

We nodded. I said hello. My father used to work at the post office and I knew a few of this man's colleagues, even if he himself had only arrived ten years ago or less by which time my father was dead. The girl came from inside to take the mail and smiled at him. The postman cycled away. Minutes passed, but I am a patient man. I ordered a third coffee. Eventually someone spoke and it was what I'd come for.

'New people in the old Pavić house.' It was the guy sitting with the one who worked in the garage. He was jug-eared and fat.

Fabjan grunted, cleared his throat and sucked his teeth. Nobody spoke.

After a minute or two the same man spoke again. 'English. English.' And because he knew he had our attention, he continued, 'Not visitors. They've

4

bought it.'

The man worked in the municipal offices. I'd dealt with him a few times when I went in to pick up building permissions. Fabjan stared ahead of him into the street and cracked his knuckles as if the news was of no interest to him. He called for the girl to bring over the post and made a show of being busy. I waited to see if the man had any more to add and, when I decided he didn't, I paid my bill and left for home.

* * *

Next morning I woke before sunrise. I worked through my exercises and since it was still early I drank a coffee and waited. At eight thirty I went out. I let the dogs out of the pen so they could come with me. They ran ahead, noses to the ground. We walked in the direction of the blue house.

In the road stood a woman. She wore a denim skirt and espadrilles, her face was hidden by her hair which fell loose either side. She was bent double, inspecting something at the side of the road. I whistled for the dogs to return to me and at the sound she straightened and raised one hand to shield her eyes from the sun. She looked directly at me and gave me so welcoming a smile that for a moment I thought she'd mistaken me for somebody else. I saw that she'd been looking into the depths of a drain. 'Hello,' she said.

I replied.

She pushed her hair back and dropped her hand. The dogs ran forward. I whistled, but she said, 'It's OK,' and held out her hand to let them smell her and when they were satisfied she patted each dog

5

on the head and fondled its muzzle. 'They're lovely,' she said. 'What are their names?'

'Kos. Zeka.'

She repeated the words as she petted the dogs. 'Which is which?'

'Zeka.' I pointed. 'He is younger. She is Kos.' I indicated the bitch on whose head the woman's hand rested.

'Zeka,' she repeated. 'Does it mean anything?' She was older than she appeared from a distance. Attractive.

'It means rabbit.'

'And Kos?'

'Blackbird.'

The woman laughed. Because I didn't know what was so funny I looked away from her and towards the open drain. Her eyes followed mine and she laughed again (she had a sense of humour, this one) and shrugged. 'I'm looking for the water mains.'

'This is a drain,' I told her. 'For rainwater.'

'Yes. I mean I realise that now. I thought it might be a manhole. In England you often find the stopcock under the pavement in front of the house.' I should mention that she'd greeted me in English and now we spoke in English. My English is imperfect, it had been a long time. I wondered what kind of assurance she possessed to speak to a stranger in a foreign land in her own tongue and expect to be understood. Clearly she enjoyed the luck of the innocent.

'Here,' I said. I walked to the back of the blue house. We reached the well and I pointed. She looked at it and then at me, she frowned.

'No mains water?'

I shook my head. 'We are a little far from town

6

here.' I showed her how the pump worked and it did, still, after so long. I levered it a good few times.

'You mean I'm going to have to do that every day?'

I pointed to the roof of the house. 'There's a tank. And soon you will get an electric pump fitted. After that—easy.' I walked to the back door and was about to step inside when I remembered myself. 'OK?' The woman nodded. I told Kos and Zeka to wait. Inside I went to the kitchen sink and turned on the tap. 'See?' I held my fingers under the water, which was clear and good. The woman did the same and seemed excited by the water. She shook the drops from her hand and stuck it out at me.

'Laura.'

'Duro,' I said and took her hand. Slim fingers. A wedding band.

'I can't thank you enough. We had to use the water in the rain barrel yesterday and this morning. Thank goodness you were passing by at just the right time. You must have thought me very silly. Would you like a cup of coffee? I'm about to make some. You can tell me about the place.'

'What place?'

Laura laughed. She said, 'Here of course. I mean Gost, the town, the area.'

'Gost?'

'Yes.'

'There's nothing to tell.'

She put her hands on her hips and tilted her head on one side. Still smiling she said, 'You've lived here all your life?'

'Yes.' Almost.

'So you take it all for granted.' She went to the window where the breeze had blown the shutter

7

closed and pushed it open. 'Well this is one of the most beautiful places I've ever been. You don't notice it any more, but you don't know how lucky you are.'

I crossed the room to the window, leaned past her and fixed the shutter to the latch on the outside wall. A row of flycatchers balanced on a high wire. The field that had lain fallow for some time was full of long grass and purple aster as well as some kind of yellow flower, fleabane, I think it's called. My father was generally good at the names of plants and flowers. Fleabane is a weed and grows just about everywhere, especially rubbish dumps and at the side of the road. It meant the soil in the field was probably not so good.

Laura started making coffee and I looked about the room. I'd been mistaken in thinking nobody had been here: the whole place had been swept out, the walls had a new coat of paint. I wondered when the work had been done. I'd always kept an eye on the house, I don't mean doing repairs, for as the house didn't belong to me that was not my place, but rather I'd kept watch over its decline. The changes come slowly, like watching a woman age: another line, the spread of crow's feet, age spots rising slowly to the surface. One day the face you knew is ravaged.

A stain in the top corner of the room spoke of a leak in the roof. Some of the plaster had broken away and a patch of lath showed. By the door, a box of junk ready to be taken out: some crockery, an old plate rack, empty bottles. The grate in the hearth carried the cinders of a long-ago fire, hardened and splashed with bird droppings from the chimney. Though the walls had been done, the blue paintwork of the windows was crazed and flaking. The tendril of a vine crept over the boundary of the frame. I brushed the surface of the table in front of me with fingertips feeling for the grooves of the grain, the dip and incline of the warp. Laura came with the coffee and cups. A young girl appeared at the back door. 'There's a pair of dogs out there.'

'They belong to Duro here,' said Laura. 'Come and say hello. Duro, this is my daughter, Grace.'

'Hello, Grace.'

The girl's eyes ranged over me and saw nothing of interest. 'Hi,' she said.

'Come and join us.'

'No thanks.'

'Duro helped me with the water.'

'Awesome. Does that mean I can have a bath?'

'You'll need to wait for it to heat up. What are you doing?'

'I want to go for a walk. Are those OK? They look kind of wild.'

I told her they were good dogs. Grace was fifteen, plump and plain; a dusting of pale hairs across her upper lip made it look as though she had a permanent milk moustache. She wasn't nervous of the dogs, just attracting and deflecting interest the way teenage girls somehow learn to do.

The daughter gone, Laura poured the coffee.

'You have a leak,' I said.

'I know. I spotted that. I'll have to find somebody to fix it.'

'You can let me take a look. Maybe it's a roof tile or maybe the gutter needs clearing.'

'Really? That would be a big help.'

'No trouble.'

She twisted her wedding ring. 'My husband's stayed behind to work, he'll be coming out later. My son's asleep. Can you imagine? I expect you're an early riser.'

I nodded. Her eyes were narrow, slanted slightly upward, more so when she smiled. A broad forehead: a mole above her left eyebrow.

'London?' I asked.

She blinked before she cottoned on. 'No.' She shook her head.

'Manchester?'

'No, not Manchester either. What makes you ask that?'

'Manchester is the most important city in England.'

'Is it?'

'Yes,' I said. 'Man U. Manchester United. The world's greatest team.'

She laughed and when she stopped laughing and closed her mouth her lip caught on an eye tooth in a way that made me want to look at her more.

'No, we live near Bristol. A place called Bath. Have you heard of it?'

'*Pride and Prejudice. Sense and Sensibility*,' I said, so that she would laugh again.

'Exactly!'

I watched her and then I said, 'Let me check your roof and then tomorrow I'll know which tools to bring. Do you have a ladder?'

She looked around the room as though in search of a ladder she might somehow have overlooked.

'Perhaps in the outbuildings?' I said.

'I haven't dared look in them yet.'

Pigeons had done their dirty work from the rafters and the first thing I did was tread on a dead bird,

10

the bones crunching underfoot. I kicked the carcass aside. Rolls of rusted wire, a wheelbarrow, an apple press, brittle and broken, stacks of paint cans. In the corner the shape of a car hidden under a plastic cover. 'I wonder what that is,' said Laura, pointing at a row of dust-covered bottles on a shelf.

'*Rakija*,' I replied.

'What's that?'

'Like brandy, home-made.'

A shopping bag stuffed full of papers. Two boxes of paperbacks, their spines broken and their pages splayed or else stuck together in a stiff wave. Cassettes. A box full of household ornaments and an old kitchen clock. A blue-glazed bowl. I picked it up and it fell in two. 'What a shame,' said Laura. 'It's rather pretty.' She held out her hand for the pieces but I tossed them aside. I lifted the corner of the car cover. Laura came over. 'It's an old Cinquecento,' she said. 'I had one once, a long time ago. I had to sell it. I still miss it. How amazing to find one here. Mine was white, but I always really wanted a red one like this.'

'This is like the Cinquecento, but different,' I told her. 'Smaller car, bigger engine. More like the Fiat 600, but this one has a 750 engine. Made here under licence. For a long time it was the only car people could buy. We called it a Fićo, because there was a cartoon and the character drove this car.' Every year you'd see families going on holiday with them, suitcases strapped to the roof, driving over the mountains on their way to the coast. They could pull a caravan, I told Laura, if it was a small one. Hereabouts people often used them to tow farm equipment; more than once I'd seen two of them driving side by side along the road, pulling a potato

11

digger or something else, like a pair of harnessed horses. Then the factory stopped making them and for a long time nobody wanted the cars; they carried too much of the shame of the past, the smell of poverty. Everybody wanted a Golf or a BMW. Now though I'd heard the young people in the cities were crazy for Fićos, young people with money and no memories. I said to Laura, 'I read in the newspaper people want them again.' I pulled the cover away entirely. The car was intact, the tyres flat, naturally; the rubber cracked. I opened the boot to look at the engine.

'I'd forgotten the engine was in the back,' said Laura.

I unscrewed the radiator cap. There was liquid still inside.

'I wonder if we could get it working.' Laura peered over my shoulder.

'Maybe,' I said. I replaced the cap and the cover. 'There's no ladder here,' I said. I pushed the heavy wooden doors back into place and slid the metal bolt. We walked around the house back towards the road and the front door. As we passed the ladder I said, 'Ah,' and lifted it off the hooks by which it hung on the wall.

The gutters were thick with composted leaves in which the buddleia had rooted. Some tiles had worked their way loose or were broken, twelve by my count. A simple job. After the building boom a decade ago there hadn't been too much work around. Some houses had been fixed up fast, but others, abandoned and left to the elements, were in a much worse state than this. People stole the roof tiles. I climbed down the ladder and told Laura I'd be back the next day. She was so grateful she didn't

12

even bring up the question of the price. At the door I picked up the cardboard box of junk. 'Shall I get rid of this for you?'

'Thank you. You'll have to show me where the dump is.'

'No problem.'

'See you tomorrow,' she said.

'Yes, tomorrow.' I whistled for Kos and Zeka and we walked down the road. Laura stood at the door of the blue house and watched us. I knew this without looking round, just as I knew the exact moment she ducked back inside.

At home I reviewed the contents of the box: most of it was indeed junk. Bottles and jars were always useful, I rinsed them and set them aside. At the bottom of the box I found a small number of blue and green mosaic tiles. I turned each one over in my fingers, relishing the contrasting textures: the rough edges of the clay, the slippery glass. I placed them in a line on my windowsill.

*　　　*　　　*

That evening I went into town for a drink, now with the prospect of several weeks of paid work to look forward to. The air was dense with the heat of unbroken storms. Zeka and Kos accompanied me. I bought a glass of wine at the bar and took a seat outside. Though it was Sunday the streets were more or less empty. People had lost the habit of walking at that hour, to exchange gossip, the men to covet the pretty wives of their neighbours, their wives to cold-shoulder those same women. People stay home, they say it's the same everywhere. The sky was full of starlings, carving their speckled

13

shapes in the sky. There must have been a hawk or a kestrel about and sure enough as I watched I caught a glimpse of her sweeping into the flock. It seemed impossible for her to miss and yet the starlings, thousands of them, seemed effortlessly to reshape around her.

I watched the birds for a minute or two and when I looked back at the street—there was Krešimir. Mostly he keeps himself to himself and so do I, so it had been some months since I'd seen him. Gost is neither so large nor so small that his being there was anything more than an ordinary occurrence, I mean you might see the same person twice in one day or hardly lay eyes on them in a year. It is the way of things. This is not the metropolis, but a small country town. All the same it was a coincidence, on this of all days. He'd begun to walk with a stoop, I noticed. It made him look like he was searching for coins on the ground. We'd both held onto our hair, though Krešimir wears his swept back; it reaches his collar and is run through with streaks of grey. Mine is short and black. He wore his shirt tightly buttoned to the neck and at the cuffs. He always dressed carefully, for example he'd never wear anything the least bit scuffed, stained or frayed. Krešimir was especially particular about his clothes and his family were a good bit wealthier than mine. He looked neither left nor right, but walked deliberately along the street, more slowly now than he used to. He didn't see me. As I watched him I had a sense of déjà vu, of having been in this exact place before, starlings in the sky and Krešimir, my old adversary, in my sights.

We used to hunt for birds together, Krešimir and I: many, many years ago.

Krešimir, Anka and I: out shooting pigeons before school. Walking home once, Krešimir inexplicably furious as he so often was. It is raining and only just light. We are coming from the back fields where there wasn't a bird in sight. After forty minutes we have returned home.

Krešimir doesn't like it when things go badly. He has a temper, and when he has a temper on he walks very fast and his arse sticks out and sometimes I laugh, which only makes him angrier. This time Anka and I are not laughing; though we are walking at our own pace, we've stopped trying to keep up with him, which is not what Krešimir wants. Walking fast is his way of humiliating us because I am so much smaller than he and Anka is a girl and younger. Krešimir's walk and his swift, unexpected movements are some of the ways he demonstrates his physical superiority. I don't know what's making him so angry this morning, because it's not as though we haven't come home empty-handed before. We've always enjoyed the hunts for their own sake, but not today. Something about the whole enterprise has served to enrage Krešimir.

At the corner by the bakery I peel off to go home and change my soaked clothes before school. At the corner I turn to wave, but no one is looking. Anka is running to catch up with Krešimir, wiping rain and hair from her face and calling his name. Her voice is high and bright, it carries on the wind, but her brother acts as though he is deaf.

The memory came to me with the wine and the starlings, the sight of Krešimir who can no longer walk as fast and the darkening sky and the chill of unfinished business. On a sudden whim I stood up and called his name and watched him turn

15

unhurriedly, with a deliberate lack of surprise. Krešimir never likes to be caught out and has trained his responses accordingly. I called for him to join me for a drink, though the truth is I didn't think for a moment he would say yes, and yet he came over, marking a semicircle around the dogs. Kos caught a scent of him and lifted a lip. 'She's just smiling at you,' I told Krešimir. Krešimir had a dislike of dogs, of all animals actually—it was one of the reasons he hunted.

Krešimir accepted a glass of wine without thanking me and sat behind his glass, his eyes roaming the street. He picked up the glass, drained half the contents and set it back on the table. He said nothing. Krešimir never bought a round of drinks himself and was disdainful of other people's hospitality. He acted as though it was *he* doing *me* the favour. I had the desire to tease him, all the more for knowing how much he disliked it. 'So what's new?' I asked.

Krešimir did not look at me. 'Same, same.'

'You think it will rain?'

Krešimir looked in the direction of the ravine, where a mass of cloud welled behind the hills. 'Maybe,' he said. 'Maybe tonight. Maybe tomorrow.'

I indicated to the waitress to bring two more glasses of wine. A drop of rain fell onto the table in front of me.

'I need to go,' said Krešimir.

'It's nothing.' I told the waitress to set the wine upon the table. Unlike, say Fabjan, or even myself— Krešimir didn't hold his drink so well. 'So the old house is sold.'

'Who told you?'

I told him I'd overheard it at the Zodijak.

16

He snorted faintly. 'People talk too much.'

'Then it's true?'

Krešimir waved a hand. 'It was going to ruin.' Then he smiled nastily and asked me about work. He did it to switch the subject, not knowing my luck had just changed. Krešimir's job at the fertiliser factory here in Gost is considered a good job for these parts because he works in the offices as a salesman. I am a builder, I work with my hands and find work where I can and not always easily. Krešimir went to college, whereas I never finished technical school. He enjoyed the advantage this gave him over me.

I told him work was fine. It rained faster, still I made no move, watching the drops land on Krešimir's head. As I said, he has quite luxurious hair but which, as well as greying, has receded quite considerably above the temples. By way of compensation he seemed to be wearing it longer, as though nobody would notice the front for being so astonished by the miracle that was the back of his head. I said, 'What will you do now?'

'About what?'

'After you sell the house.'

'Must I do something?'

'People generally do—something, that is.'

'Is that so?'

'Yes,' I said. 'They do.'

'Well since you ask, I am thinking of going away.'

'Away from Gost?'

'Yes.'

'Where would you go?'

'The coast, perhaps. The islands. I've heard the living there is good. People have moved on, Duro. Maybe you should, too. The tourists are back. And now I must go home, I have things to do.' Krešimir stood up and drained his glass.

'Good luck,' I said.

'Good luck with what?'

'With the move.'

'Thank you.' Krešimir gathered up his bags of groceries. Krešimir married later in life. His wife, who started out as a pretty blonde thing, full of ideas, even if they were not particularly good ones, now rarely left the house except when she went to visit her relatives, which she did for months at a time, lacking the nerve either to confront her husband or leave him. Maybe she was away visiting now, or equally likely Krešimir had decided to do the grocery shopping himself. Perhaps she had bought the wrong item once too often, or gone over budget. Krešimir was something of a miser, did I mention that? He circled the dogs—and was gone.

I stayed for a few minutes more to finish my wine, called to Kos and Zeka and started home. It was raining hard: a summer shower. It would be over by the time I reached the edge of town. I thought about the blue house and the new people there. I thought about the leak in the roof. Tomorrow was Monday, a working day. I would go round there first thing in the morning and get started. I looked at the sky, the starlings were gone.

I walked, I thought: So Krešimir is leaving Gost.

2

The buddleia had taken hold both in the guttering and in the pointing. It came free with a shower of powder masonry. Laura, standing at the bottom of the ladder, applauded. I threw the buddleia to the ground and climbed down the ladder.

'Do you have a bucket?' I asked. 'Two even better.'

She disappeared and returned with a pair of old metal pails. I climbed back up and began to clear the guttering.

I'd arrived early in the morning and ready for work, but Laura had made coffee and offered me a pastry. The pastry was stale and Laura apologised. 'I need to get to the supermarket.'

'There's a baker. They make pastries of all kinds. I'll show you.' I had finished my coffee and rose. 'I'll get started.'

Now she stood below, watching me as I ladled rotten leaves and twigs into the bucket. When the first bucket was full I climbed down and exchanged it for the empty one. In this way and with her help I worked my way from left to right across the front of the house, repositioning the ladder every metre or so. Once I looked through one of the upper windows: there were no curtains—and saw asleep on the bed the boy I'd seen two days before. He was naked, lying on his back with one hand on his chest and the other holding his dick. Nothing, not the sound of our talk, nor the scrape and clang of the ladder, had interrupted his sleep.

Around eleven with the job finished Laura made

us both another cup of coffee. I said I wanted to fix the tiles next and, since people often kept a stack of spares, I'd take a look, if that was OK, otherwise we'd have to buy them. Laura's son appeared, wearing only a towel about his waist, his eyes slitty with sleep. In silence he went to the sink and poured himself a glass of water. Laura stood up and kissed him on the cheek. 'Good morning, darling.' He put his glass in the sink and Laura picked it up and rinsed it. He opened a cupboard and looked inside and she asked if he was hungry. When he took down a packet of cereal, she fetched a bowl and a spoon and the milk from the fridge. I saw our conversation was over and stood up. Laura turned. 'Thanks, Duro. Let me know about the tiles.'

I stood on the slope at the back of the house and surveyed the roof. Typically steeply pitched, for the snow as I expect you know. From where I stood I had a decent view of the damage: worse than I thought, but not much more so. Heavy snow and frost take their toll and six months ago we were in the depths of winter. Lichen and moss had a hold. Fixing roofs is a year-round job, as I told Laura. An overgrown hawthorn hedge bordered the courtyard on one side, on the other three: the house and outbuildings. A walnut tree had cast two decades of its offspring on the ground. The grass had grown and fallen for sixteen summers. An old sink, a rusted rat trap and a small wagon: flotsam pulled down into it. In one corner, the outline of several raised beds, where I found rocket, flowering yellow and black-striped blooms. Fennel, grown taller than I stood. Loops of raspberry canes. A parsley pot had overturned and its spilled contents grew in a puddle of bright green. I picked up the pot and placed it upon a windowsill. Against the wall of the house I found a pile of bricks but no tiles. The door of the second outbuilding was wedged shut and I gave it a kick. Again no tiles but a quantity of tools which I sorted through for anything that looked useful. I came out and stood in the sun.

The blue house: I wonder if anyone but me called it that. To most people it was the Pavić house, the first Pavić house, because later they moved to a house in town. I circled it with a critical eye, ticked the jobs off on my fingers: gutters, roof, paintwork: the woodwork of the windows was in a poor state, the stonework needed whitewashing. The building was in reasonable structural shape. The dead tree of course, it needed to be taken down, and there was everything to be done inside, starting with the wall of the front room. I took a trowel to a windowsill where the wood was soft and splintered, I checked another and found it sound. I went back inside and said to Laura, 'We'll need to get some tiles, wood filler and paint, a blow torch.'

She blinked. I added, 'For the windows. The wood is rotten. A few more winters and you'll have to replace them all.' I turned and addressed myself to the boy, who was eating at the table. 'Duro. Pleased to meet you.' I put my hand out.

Laura covered her mouth. 'I'm so sorry. I forgot to introduce you.'

The boy looked up and seeing my hand offered his own, though his grip lacked any kind of enthusiasm. 'Hi,' he said, withdrew his hand and dropped his gaze back to his bowl.

We drove into town in Laura's car. Outside the bakery was a queue, the latecomers getting in before lunchtime closing. 'You need to come into town early for the best bread,' I told Laura.

She craned her neck to see beyond the line of people. 'There's hardly anything left,' she said. 'Let's go to another shop.'

'This is the only one.'

She looked at me and laughed. 'Really? Somebody needs to open another one. They'd make a fortune.'

'There used to be another one.'

'Don't tell me it closed for lack of business.'

'The people went away.'

She glanced at me and shrugged. 'Oh well, nothing to do but wait. I expect you have things you need to do.'

In the Zodijak I drank an espresso. No Fabjan. After fifteen minutes I returned to the bakery where I found Laura at the counter talking loudly and pointing with fluttering hands. The woman behind the counter faced her squarely, blankly refusing to join in the game of sign language. I stepped past the waiting people.

'Duro. Thank goodness.'

'What would you like?'

'I'd like a loaf of bread. Can you ask if there is any wholemeal?'

I doubted there would be such a thing but I translated anyway. The woman, who had been married to a cousin of mine for a while, replied in Cro. 'No.'

'No,' I repeated. 'There is only white bread.'

'Can I order some wholemeal, maybe for tomorrow?'

I translated.

'What do you think?' replied my cousin's ex-wife,

22

again in Cro, which of course was all she spoke.

'She apologises,' I said to Laura. 'Unfortunately they're too busy to take special orders. You can only have what's here. As you see, they have a lot of customers.'

'OK, well I'll take one of those.' Laura pointed at a large loaf and the woman put it into a bag. 'What's in those pastries? Is it jam or chocolate?'

'Gold coins,' replied the woman. She pointed at the three types of pastries. 'Gold coins in here. Lost treasure in this one. The last one's chocolate, we ran out of treasure.'

Somebody behind tittered.

'Custard,' I told Laura. 'Like sort of crème patissière. Not so good. The last one is chocolate. They're the best.'

'Then I'll have three chocolate. What would you like, Duro? Have one on me.'

'Thank you.' I gave the order.

'Lucky you,' said the ex-wife. She raised an eyebrow. I ignored her.

'How much?' Laura asked, glancing between me and the woman.

'800 kunas.'

Laura turned to me and shook her head slightly. 'Sorry, what did she say?'

'8 kunas,' I said, and helped her with the coins.

We were back in the car. Laura apologised. 'Thanks, Duro. I don't think she was being very friendly.'

'It's just her way.'

'I thought I'd offended her.'

I said, 'She is an angry person; her husband left her.'

'I'm not surprised. Is that the hardware shop?'

23

She slowed the car.

'No, there's another shop where the prices are better. Turn left here.'

We entered the shop and went to the back where the tiles were stored. I picked up two packs of ten. The prices in both shops were much the same, but Fabjan was part-owner of the other one and I had no interest in making any more money for him. I took a few other things we needed and said to Laura, 'What colour paint do you want—for the windows and the door?' When Laura hesitated I said, 'Can I make a suggestion?'

'Of course.'

'Simplest if you choose the same colour. Makes the job easier. Where the wood is sound I rub it down, no need to burn the paint off.'

'OK,' agreed Laura. 'It's a beautiful colour. Almost the colour of cornflowers. You never see it in England, the sky's too grey, I suppose. You need the sun to bring out hues like that.'

'People say the colour keeps insects away, mosquitoes especially.'

'That's the second time I've heard that. In the southern states of America they have a very similar shade of blue, haint blue, it's called. You see it everywhere, especially on verandas and porches. They say exactly the same thing, that it repels mosquitoes. Then in Savannah somebody told us that the real reason for the blue was that it kept away restless ghosts and spirits, an old slave superstition, apparently. That's why it's always on the outside of the house.' She laughed.

I said, 'Here in many villages we have a festival where the men dress up in masks and animal skins to chase the evil spirits from the woods. If you are here in February, you will be able to see it.'

Back at the house I spent twenty minutes sorting the tool shed and storing the things we had bought. When I went back inside Laura's daughter Grace was cleaning the windows. '*Dobar dan*,' I said and startled her. Her head jerked up, she glanced at me and quickly away.

'Hi,' she said. A tiny squeak accompanied the word and an odd little humming, like the sound of a tuning fork.

Outside I heaved the ladder into position and climbed onto the roof. To make each repair I had to slide the flat bars into position, descend to fetch a tile, climb back up to fit it. I threw the broken tiles down. It would have been a help to have somebody with me, to pass me the tiles, and the obvious candidate was Laura's son, of whom there was no sign. Even with the hindrance of going up and down the ladder, I got on with the job. Solitude suits me. I am not given to the camaraderie of the building site with its undercurrent of aggression and where, if you choose to work rather than shirk, you are asking to be picked on by the others. I'd worked enough sites not to let it bother me; I got on with the job and I could take care of myself. But given the choice I'd rather work alone. I often thought I would like to be a writer, alone in a room. But for that I would have needed to go to college. I was good at history, languages. But my father dissuaded me: no jobs, unless you came from certain families and even then—did I know how people lived in the cities? So-called professionals, three generations in the same small apartment, endlessly partitioning rooms into smaller and smaller spaces. Work with your hands, he said. That way you will be your

own master, hold onto your destiny and always eat.
My father was right.

*　　　　*　　　　*

'Where did you learn to speak such good English,
Duro?' Laura asked while we sat together over the
kitchen table. She handed me a beer. Earlier in
the afternoon a fridge had been delivered and now
it was the end of the day the beer was almost cold
enough.

'I worked for a while on the coast,' I said.

'What did you do there?'

'Many things. I was a waiter. Once I was a
handyman in a hotel. Mostly I worked the boats.'

'Did you travel?'

'No,' I said. 'It was not so easy then as it is now.
And besides I had little money. What of you?'

'A bit, yes—on holiday mostly. The furthest I
ever went was to Pakistan, to visit a friend who was
working there. People stared at me the whole time.
We went to a restaurant one evening and I was the
only woman in the whole place. Their women aren't
allowed out, and then even when they are they have
to be covered, you know, their faces. White women
attract a lot of attention.'

I didn't know about Pakistan. I asked, 'Is this your
first time here?'

'I came here when I was little. It must have been
the late '60s or maybe early '70s. I came with my
parents. I fell in love for the first time.'

I told Laura she looked too young to have been in
love as long ago as that.

Laura laughed, a proper laugh, not the titter
women give when they think they're being flattered

26

and which Laura produced every time she felt awkward. 'I was just a kid. Not much more than five or so. I know it sounds ridiculous, and of course it wasn't really love—but it was the first time I felt that kind of emotion, something that was different from the way I loved my parents or my sister, something far more thrilling. I can remember the exact moment, the place, what it looked like, smelt like . . . rosemary, lavender and thyme—all those herbs that grow wild, mixed with dust and salt from the sea. The heat. Even what I was wearing, which was a swimsuit with a big yellow sun on it. I was standing on a beach with my sister, my parents were in a boat offshore. I don't know how we came to be separated like that, but we were and probably it wasn't that far to swim, but to me it seemed a very long way. Everyone in the boat was calling to me, even my sister tried to encourage me into the water, but I panicked and started crying. I'd only just learned to swim and I still used my rubber ring; trouble was the rubber ring was on the boat. I refused to get into the water without it.'

'Didn't one of your parents bring it to you?'

'No. The boat boy, the son or nephew of the man who owned the boat, he'd come with us to help out for the day and was completely at one with the water, he grabbed it and dived in. I worshipped him for the rest of the holiday. I guess he'd have been about nine. I still remember the sight of him diving from the prow of the boat. It made me feel special. He was my hero.' Laura laughed again, softly.

*   *   *

At sundown I walked the dogs on the hills. The

27

lights of Gost separated me from a vast darkness: the sea, two hours' drive away. Zeka picked up a scent and ran ahead with her nose to the ground, Kos behind. I left them for a short while, to see where they were headed, and then called them to heel before they could disappear into the pine plantation. Together we entered the trees. Inside it was closer to night. The pine needles were soft underfoot, soundless. There is a place where the deer gather on the other side of the plantation and the trees give way to a clearing. At about fifty metres from our destination I told the dogs to go down and wait for me, which they did, sinking slowly to their haunches. They liked to pretend they didn't care, Kos and Zeka, but under the skin every nerve and muscle twitched. I moved slowly forward, balancing my weight on the outside edges of my feet; every ten steps I stopped and listened. In the silence of the forest I counted on hearing the deer before I saw them and so it happened: a group of eight grazing at the edge of the clearing. A young doe lifted her head at my approach. I froze. She glanced about nervously before she lowered her head again. Seven does, two bucks. The bucks were younger, less than a year old, probably. The doe who'd raised her head was closest to me and perhaps three years old. I lifted my rifle, set my sights on her and released the safety catch. She grazed on, her body angled away from me. I watched and waited. She might have sensed me, for she lifted her head a second time and looked to the left and right and then in my direction. An ear twitched. Neither of us moved. Then she relaxed and lowered her head; reaching for another morsel she shifted her footing and presented her broadside to me. I placed the

28

cross hair at her temple, took a breath, exhaled, squeezed the trigger and watched her drop.

At the sound of the gun the rest of the deer fled. Kos and Zeka were at my side, ready to follow the blood trail if there was one. But I didn't need them today: she'd fallen exactly where she'd stood. The sky had turned to a deep blue and it was too dark now to dress her in the woods, so I hoisted her onto my shoulder and headed in the direction of home. For two days my thoughts had been crowded by memories of Krešimir and of Anka. It felt as though I had been lifted up and set back in that time, the events of which I'd found a way to live with. I'd had no choice, none of us had, though some were better at it than others. Now I remembered how here, where the ravine meets the pine trees, we'd seen our first boar.

Anka, wearing yellow pop sox, stands upon a rock, showing off her balance: on tiptoe, her arms above her head, like a dancer in a musical box. Slowly she extends one leg behind her, an arm in front. She is wearing a yellow skirt which matches her socks and it ruffles in the breeze; otherwise she is impressively still. I have opened my mouth to cheer, when I see her expression and follow her line of sight to the first row of trees. There, in the no man's land of shadows and sunlight, a boar: huge. Slowly I raise my gun and take aim. I miss, thank God, because the gun is a pea shooter and would doubtless only have made him mad. The bullet ricochets off a tree. The great beast shudders, regards us a moment longer and is gone. Anka jumps off the rock and into my arms.

We walk home exultant. Nobody bothers to mention that I really shot a tree and not a boar.

Krešimir and I are fourteen and Anka is ten. The year is 1975.

I stood and inhaled the cold scent of the pine, the base note of leaf mould, made all the more powerful by the darkness. I closed my eyes and tried to imagine 1975 and then opened them before a picture could come. I whistled for Kos and Zeka and we returned by way of the road. Light flared between the shutters of the blue house. I stood on the road facing the house, the warm corpse of the deer over my shoulder, the dogs silent by my side. Somebody (Laura?) crossed in front of an upstairs window. I stood there for some minutes more until Kos spoke, a soft whine, and we turned towards home.

I lay awake, thinking about the past, things I hadn't thought about for years. Somewhere nearby the vixen called, an awful sound. I'd seen her, she came some nights, circling the houses to search for scraps to take back to her half-grown cubs and drawn that night by the scent of the deer I'd dressed in the yard a couple of hours before. She taunted the dogs and the dogs answered, racing up and down their pen, barking and howling, clawing the wire mesh.

Next morning, the Tuesday, I arrived early at the blue house. In my hand I held a chisel. A few years after the house first became empty somebody had plastered and whitewashed a section of the façade. The job had been hastily done. I checked nobody was around and then I scraped at a layer of the plaster, loosening a portion, which I pulled away with my fingers. I stood there for a few minutes scraping and tossing lumps of plaster into the tall grass. I stopped and stood back. Now you could see

30

a part of what lay beneath: a patchwork of small blue and green tiles made of glass and clay, the same as the ones lying on my windowsill.

Inside Laura was talking on her mobile phone. The day was clear and the sky pale blue. On many days the mountains blocked the reach of the mobile networks, but that day the invisible force field that seemed to surround Gost so much of the time had lifted. Laura pointed to the phone in her hand and mouthed something to me, then waved a hand at the coffee pot on the table next to a single cup. She left to finish her call upstairs. No sign of either the son or the daughter. I carried my coffee outside and set to work removing paint from the windowsills.

An hour on Laura came out to see how I was doing, then left to go into town. When she came back I set down my tools to help carry the groceries from the car. More coffee, which we carried outside again. Laura turned her face to the sun, closed her eyes for a few seconds and then opened them again to take a sip of her coffee; her eyes roamed the front of the house. When she noticed the place on the wall where I had scraped away the plaster she stood up and went over to inspect it, running her fingertips across the tiles. I watched her for a bit and then I said, 'What is it?'

'There's something under here,' she replied. 'It looks like a mosaic.'

3

Gost lies upon a polje of karst limestone. Thousands of years of sediment made for good farming, and the soil is what kept Gost rich in grain all those years. They say that there are lost rivers, limestone caves and sink holes. I don't know about that; I can only tell you that if you stand in the middle of Gost facing north and raise your head to look up into the hills, you will see how the river banks more steeply on one side than the other. The river starts as a spring outside a hamlet a few kilometres from Gost and it flows north, away from the sea, through our town, passing the old mills of Gost, cuts through the hills and eventually flows into a large lake some several hundred kilometres north-west of here. Visible from Gost is a scar of grey rock running through the green before the river divides into tributaries somewhere above the swimming hole: that is the ravine Gudura Uspomena.

Gudura Uspomena is Krešimir's and my favourite place. The ravine is deep and we dare ourselves to climb down where the sides slope. A rock projects out beyond the others; we inch along it and lie on our bellies, peer over the edge at the dizzying drop, grow weak resisting the pull of the fall. We might climb down the slope and stay in the ravine for hours, a place nobody can find us. In the summer we swim in the swimming hole, leave our clothes in bundles to hop across the rocks, skinny and pale, and dive into the water, which is freezing all year round and leaves us gasping and winded. We dry off in the sun and then leap back into the water. Later we climb down to the waterfall below the swimming hole and hold our hairless dicks under the rushing water until our stomachs convulse with a strange new pleasure.

Other times we build encampments in the perpetual twilight of the pine forest, where we hoard stolen food and puff on cigarettes and later take turns drinking from bottles of *rakija*, with grimaces and coughs. Once we turn to alchemy and make our own: cheap grappa into which we stuff wild fennel, thyme and unknown berries we find in the ravine and which may or may not be poisonous. We bury the bottles and dig them up too soon and spend a night puking.

Once, under the influence, I challenge Krešimir to a dare. Stripped naked and on the count of three we race through the trees. You see we are hunters, fascinated by night vision, to which we attach great importance and as a consequence manliness. The naked race is to determine who possesses the greater night vision; the winner isn't the fastest runner, although the whole point is to run as fast as you can, but rather the one who suffers the least damage: scratches, cuts and bruises, in other words who smashes into the fewest trees.

At other times we climb the hill to play in the old bunker, just above the tree line. Of course we're not supposed to, the bunkers are there in case of a Soviet strike. Ours is cracked and covered in moss and the inside is dark and dank, with a dripping roof and smells of rot and pee, though who exactly would climb up there to empty their bladder, God only knows.

We are twelve years old, maybe eleven. A night in the summer we persuade our fathers to allow us to sleep in the woods. My father believes all boys should be toughened up, especially me because I have two older sisters and am small for my age. Krešimir's father hasn't died yet and he says OK. But the pine forest is alive with activity all night and it isn't the cry of the animals that frightens us, but the sound of car engines, the glimmer of headlights, the tramp of boots and the sound of voices.

The next day my father looks at our sorrowful faces and tells me they are most likely black-marketeers, smugglers. He asks me whether any of the men saw us. I say no. Good, he says, and he pats me on the head. Krešimir and I add our brush with the smugglers to the repertoire of happenings that will one day make us men. In the market for the first time I notice men in leather jackets who stand together in groups as though they are waiting for something. They light cigarettes and exhale smoke and frozen vapours into the air and then throw the stubs onto the ground. Better mind your own business, chief, says my father (in those days he always called me chief). He gave me a shove. Don't forget, chief, never ask a question you don't have to, that way you'll live a lot longer.

Charlie, Revlon, leather jackets, videos, second-hand jeans, American tobacco, Pino Silverstre aftershave from Italy, pirated pop cassettes, chewing gum and tampons, and in the years to come: Asian porn and disposable nappies and when things get really bad: toilet paper. Some days my father brings gifts for my mother and sisters: Eve roll-on deodorant, one for my mother and another for my sisters to share, a tiny jar of night cream with a red lid and the words Elizabeth Arden for my mother. My mother puts the jar away along with all the other things she never opens. My sisters smile and kiss him. My father blushes, and escapes by slipping on his clogs saying he has things to do; he goes to his shed at the bottom of the garden where I know he reads the newspaper and smokes. Another day he and I share a bunch of bananas. When I ask him where they come from he tugs my nose and winks.

* * *

Laura worked on rescuing the mosaic. At times we worked side by side, I on the windows, she on the mosaic. She drove into town to buy a small brush and tools better suited to the job: she was curious to know what lay beneath the layer of plaster. There was plenty to do on the house, but now she had me to take care of things. We passed several hours in each other's company, often in silence, though from time to time Laura asked me a question. 'Are you married?'

'No.'

'Oh, I'm sorry.'

I asked her why she was sorry. She told me she hadn't meant to pry. I replied that she wasn't prying. She asked, 'Were you ever married?'

'No.'

'I suppose you enjoy the freedom.'

I didn't say anything because I didn't know what else to say. My father and one of my sisters were dead. My mother and my eldest sister lived two hundred kilometres away, never came back to Gost and constantly urged me to move to be with them. Here I had Zeka and Kos, nobody else. I wondered if this was the freedom Laura was talking about.

35

Laura apologised again. 'I hope you don't mind me saying that.'

'It's OK.'

'I was just wondering, that's all.' Laura who speaks in English to strangers in a foreign land, but hates to be misunderstood.

Another time she asked, 'Did you never want to marry?'

'I never had the chance.'

'What do you mean?'

'I mean things never worked out that way, but yes, why not?'

Laura told me her husband needed to stay behind in England to continue running his business and because he had meetings somewhere overseas to attend, otherwise he would have come with them. She'd headed out with the children to begin putting the house in order. Her husband would follow in a week or so. After that we were quiet for a while until Laura said, 'I think it's a hand.' She stood back a metre from the wall with her head on one side, one arm wrapped around her waist, the elbow of the other arm cupped by her hand. Between the thumb and forefinger of the other hand, which rested against her cheek, she held the brush. I climbed down from the ladder. The mosaic had begun to emerge. Now visible against a background of chalky white tiles were what may very well have been three fingers. These were made of green tiles. Above the hand—if that is what it was—was a row of pointed shapes composed of deep blue tiles.

'It could be a hand,' I said. 'It's hard to tell.'

'Only one way to find out,' said Laura.

At that moment Laura's son appeared. I say Laura's son, his name was Matthew. Laura called

36

him Matt or Mattie. Matthew seemed to spend the large part of the day asleep or else listening to his music with his eyes shut. Laura waved and said, 'Matt, come and look at this.' He ambled over without removing his earphones, inspected Laura's work and gave a thumbs-up. 'Ace.'

I watched him go. He walked with his hands shoved into his pockets, long and loose-limbed, his hair curled at the back of his neck and around his ears, pale blue eyes with heavy lids which added to the general air of listlessness. Laura watched him too with a slight smile and a look of something like longing, if that doesn't sound strange, as if she wanted to run after him and touch him. She sighed and turned away.

'Perhaps your son can help?' I said.

Laura wrinkled her nose and shook her head. 'You know boys. I'd never get him to, but Grace will. Grace!' Grace appeared a few seconds later and Laura said, 'Come and lend us a hand?'

Grace shrugged. 'Sure.'

Laura went into the house and left Grace with the tools and the brush. Grace began to pick at the plaster. I climbed down the ladder. 'Here,' I said. I showed her how to fracture the plaster with the small hammer, and prise away the pieces with the pick.

'Thanks,' she said from beneath her fringe, following the word with the odd little habit she had: the curious apparently involuntary humming.

I climbed back up the ladder. 'Do you like it here?'

Grace shrugged, hummed, blinked and then nodded. 'We only just got here. I guess it's pretty.' She hummed. 'There's not that much to do.'

I said, 'There's plenty to do once you get to know the place.' City kids like her brother didn't understand entertainment unless it came with batteries.

'There's not even a cinema, and even if there was I wouldn't understand.'

'No, there's no cinema. But there is a waterfall and a swimming hole up in the hills.'

'Really?' She was so surprised she actually looked directly at me.

'Yes,' I said. 'I will show it to you one day. You will have it entirely to yourself if you want. Nobody goes there.'

'Where?'

'Up there.' I pointed. 'We will go at the weekend, if you want.'

'I'd have to ask Mum,' she said. 'But I think that would be really cool.' Then the shyness overcame her like an allergic reaction; she gave a series of tiny dormouse sneezes and returned hot-faced to her task.

*   *   *

Early afternoon a car came down the lane and slowed as it passed the house. The driver craned forward and peered out of the windscreen. From the top of the ladder I saw it was a woman from Gost who worked in the supermarket.

Later the same day we went to the outbuildings with a view to seeing what we could salvage and what we needed to take to the dump. 'What *is* all this stuff?' said Laura as she looked around her.

'Crumbs,' said Grace, bent over the box of books; she pulled out a paperback and shook it, creating a swirl of dust, and flicked through the pages, turned

38

it around to look at the back and front covers. 'I think this is Anne Rice. What does this say, Duro?'

'*The Queen of the Damned,*' I said.

She began to pull books out of the box. 'Gross silverfish! This must be *The Witching Hour*, the cover is the same. Too bad I can't understand any of it, I need something to read. Look at this cassette cover! Look at what they're wearing!'

Laura was on the other side of the space standing near the back wall. 'What's this? It looks like a bread oven.'

'It's a kiln,' I said. I moved next to Laura and opened the door. It was heavy and resisted for a moment: inside the kiln was empty.

Against the wall stood a dozen or so pots layered with dust and a stack of boxes. Inside one Laura found tiles in assorted shapes and colours, many of which matched the tiles in the mosaic. She blew the dust from a few and replaced them, carried the boxes to the door to take into the house. The pots pleased her. One by one she lifted them to the light.

Time and rats had got to most of the stuff. We shouldered what we could outside and made a pile in the courtyard: several old suitcases, a large metal basin, an old canvas tent, a clothes horse, baskets— the wicker gnawed in several places, a coffee table with a smoked-glass top, blankets: swollen and stiff, quilts: powdery with mould, a box of plastic-handled cutlery, a bag of unopened envelopes, car magazines: rippled and sealed by damp, plastic sacks of clothing. Some rolls of fibreglass insulation-matting had survived. A container of petrol, half full. Laura took a liking to the old apple press, but it proved not worth saving. Stacks of empty preserving jars and others, a few, filled with bottled fruit, plums. And the *rakija*. Along with a wooden chair, Laura saved the metal basin in which she said she planned to grow herbs.

When we had cleared—or at least sorted—the outbuilding we carried the *rakija* and fruit into the house. 'I'm not at all sure about this.' Laura held a bottle of fruit up to the light.

'It will be fine.'

She wrinkled her nose. 'You're welcome to it.'

'I'll take it if you don't want it.'

'Have it as a thank-you. Have the other stuff too, the ra . . .'

'*Rakija*. OK, but you must try some first.'

I took one of the bottles and twisted the cork. Laura fetched a pair of glasses, I poured some into each. Laura sniffed the contents of her glass and swirled the liquid around the bottom, gazing at it deeply but without confidence.

'Let's sit outside,' I said. I took the glass from her hand and walked down the steps at the front of the house where the sun was low in the sky. On days such as these it was hard to believe in the existence of winter, when frozen snow covers the fields and the hills and the only people who use the roads are the farmers on their tractors. In winter I set traps and occasionally hunt. Days pass when I don't see another person. In winter Gost is a sleeping beast, which breathes but doesn't move. People stay burrowed, unwashed, and eventually emerge pale and fleshy, blinking in the light. Then the beast is roused and stretches itself. Come the spring it shakes, and settles. Then summer.

It was the blue hour. Streaks of cloud across a lapis lazuli sky. The hills: three shades of purple, the deepest, a black purple, to the fore, and the

40

palest, almost lilac, to the back with the last of the light behind them. The blue paint of the house shone as did the blue tiles of the partly uncovered mosaic, two blue hands reaching for the sky. In the blue hour things happen. Some creatures prepare to sleep, others awaken. Up at the swimming hole at this time the house martins swoop down out of the sky to dip their breasts in the water. The bats begin to leave the hills. Through the trees the houses of Gost were just visible, no lights for at least an hour; many older people had grown up without electricity and regarded it as unnecessary while there was still a glimmer of light by which to move around. As for the other inhabitants of Gost, they'd still be on their way home. The men would have stopped off at the Zodijak or one of the other bars, the youths convened in the car park of the supermarket, where in the hours between work and sleep they tinkered with apparent endless fascination with the engines of their motorbikes.

I raised my glass to Laura and drank.

Laura did the same, but coughed and pulled a face. It was the same for everyone, you got used to the taste, I told her. Laura took another sip and shook her head. 'I think I prefer wine.'

Laura gave me all the plums and the *rakija*, just as she said she would. I left her the opened bottle. There was more than I could carry so in the end I made two trips. The second time I stopped by the pile we had made in the yard and helped myself to several of the cassettes. At the last minute I took the bag of post as well.

At home I dropped a fork into the jar of plums, speared them one at a time and ate them whole. They tasted of all those winters when we ate food

41

pickled and preserved in those months of heat gone by that you could neither recall nor imagine. I ate one jar and began on another. I drank the *rakija* straight from the bottle. Outside Kos barked at something in the night. I went outside and slipped the bolt of the dogs' pen and let them follow me inside where they quickly chose a comfortable spot to lie down, in case I changed my mind.

The truth is, like the old folk of Gost, I'm not much given to the use of electric light either. Those races against Krešimir—I usually won them, I'm perfectly comfortable in the dark.

I looked at the cassettes. The Beatles. *Sergeant Pepper*. *Rubber Soul*. Supertramp's *Breakfast in America*. Electric Light Orchestra. One by a band from here. I still had a cassette player for all the cassettes I owned and had never replaced with CDs. I put the tape in the slot, turned the volume up and sat back in my chair.

The music was terrible. The band was a rock band from the coast who lasted about three years before they broke up. Never my kind of thing, I prefer Roy Orbison, Johnny Cash. Fifteen years on, two of them reformed the band hoping to cash in on their past success, but in that time a lot had changed including the people who'd once been their fans and nobody wanted to know. Nostalgia interested no one, except perhaps the very young. The band released a second album, I think, and then dropped out of sight.

I ejected the tape and put in one by the Beatles. 'Lucy In The Sky With Diamonds'. My heart quickened and drained as I listened to the familiar vibrating notes of the organ. I rewound and listened to it three more times; gradually I raised the volume

42

and hoped they could hear it in Gost.

At two in the morning I was drunker than I'd been in years. I remembered Krešimir and his shopping bags and the rain on his head and thought it was funny. I must have laughed aloud because the dogs came over and nuzzled me. After I petted them Kos returned to her place, but Zeka, who is more anxious and less confident, lay down close to me. When I woke, several hours had passed, it was dawn and I was curled up on the floor, my face pressed into Zeka's fur. Kos was at the door waiting to be let out. The room smelled of spirits and when I stood up I noticed the broken *rakija* bottle in the corner of the room. I must have thrown it there; I didn't remember that at all.

* * *

Pots from the shed washed and arranged in a row upon a windowsill. Laura, coming from the field opposite, a bunch of wild flowers in her hand, said in a tight voice, 'We missed you yesterday.'

'I had some business to deal with.'

She passed me and went into the house without meeting my eye. I realised I'd upset the balance of things. That I was a hired man and she was my employer made Laura relaxed in having me around the house. A mistake to take a day away without explanation: it made her feel she wasn't the boss. I followed her into the house and watched her put the flowers in a vase and set them on the kitchen table. I put the things I was carrying, a car battery and a can of motor oil, on the floor.

'What are those for?'

'The car. I'd like to see if I can get it started. If

43

that's OK.'

I went to work at the back of the house, stripping the paint from the windows. The day was sulphurously hot, the smell of melting tar in the air. I took off my shirt and felt the sun on my back. The work and the heat brought me back to a sense of well-being, to a time I spent working on the tourist boats on the coast—some of the best months of my life. Often I did nothing more than ferry folk to and from the beaches and the islets. One summer I worked on board a ketch. We'd load up in the morning, sail for an hour and drop anchor in a small cove where we'd hand out masks and snorkels and herd the day trippers out from under the shade of the canopy and into the sea. The point was to get everybody off the boat so we could relax among ourselves. For some of the guys it became a game and sometimes they even laid bets. No matter how old or young, they all had to get into the water. Once there was a shoal of jellyfish beneath and another time an old guy with a stick; his daughter went to the captain to say her father didn't want to swim. But even he went in, protesting to the end. I remember the bump on his chest made by his pacemaker. The only exceptions they made were for the prettiest girls.

While they were at it I dived from the other side of the boat and swam to a place on the shore: a flat slab of rock, which caught the sun in the late morning. I'd climb over the other rocks to reach it and for nearly an hour I'd lie there, doing nothing but watching the horizon, which shimmered and shook, a tightrope between sky and earth. The rock was warm, blood temperature, as if during the day it drew life from the sun. It even had a feral, animal kind of odour, of salt, fish and dried seaweed. After exactly fifty minutes I swam back to the boat underwater, passing the tourists unnoticed, and climbed up the rope.

Laura appeared at the bottom of the ladder. Perhaps she'd called my name and I hadn't heard. I'd been back on the islands. She said, 'We're going off to explore. We'll be home in a few hours.'

'Be careful,' I said.

Laura raised her eyebrows and gave a little laugh. 'Of what?'

I had spoken without thinking, living too much in the past. I smiled and started to come down the ladder. 'Of the roads, of course. There are madmen in their cars at this time of year, during the holidays.'

I gave her directions for a drive I said would take her past some pleasant views and through a couple of villages. Forty minutes later and I was still up the ladder when Matthew came out of the back of the house and picked his way through the yard out into the field. The pace of his walk, the rounded back and shoulders, the trousers hanging low on his hips, the thumb of his left hand hooked into his front pocket and the way his skull rocked slightly back in the cradle of his top vertebrae, all advertised his utter boredom. Where he was going I didn't know, but I knew what he was going to do because he was carrying a wine bottle in his right hand.

In the evening I fried sausages, peeled and boiled potatoes and chopped some chard, which I'd pulled from the neglected vegetable beds at the blue house. I poured a glass of wine (enough *rakija*!) and carried my plate of food into the main room where I set it on the table. I fetched the bag of mail I had taken from the outbuilding and began to sift through the contents as I ate.

Utility bills. I opened one at random. A demand for payment of several hundred dinara for electricity and warning of the consequences of non-payment. The next bill, dated a few months later, had been adjusted by the addition of several noughts. There was a time inflation ran wild. A letter from the publisher of the car magazine regretted the non-renewal of a subscription. Several copies of the same magazine still inside their plastic covers. There were no letters or postcards, no envelopes full of old photographs, not even a shopping list or an old chequebook bristling with scribbled stubs, no note left for the plumber, no scrap of paper bearing a scrawled address, directions. There was nothing except official letters and circulars. It was as though somebody had been through all of it before me and removed anything personal. I stuffed everything back into the bag and slung it aside. I thought: Is this all that remains? When I look back to that night I see that the idea for writing this seeded then. Would I take it all with me? Who would tell my story? So many people have left Gost, not like the old days when they stayed away for a few years and came back wearing Italian clothes and carting German fridges. Now they never come back. Of the old crowd, there are just three of us left: Krešimir, Fabjan and me.

Laura arrived and took over the blue house and things began to change. In a very short time it seemed certain people forgot what had been agreed for so long, or perhaps they thought it no longer applied, or no longer applied to them, that the pact we had held to for sixteen years was somehow over.

Some days I wondered what would happen to my own house when I was gone. I've lived here for eighteen years, and maybe with luck I'll live twice as long again. More than likely I shall die alone, as I live now, and as I have no executor a person or persons will be appointed to come and deal with my estates, sort my belongings into piles to sell and throw. They will go through my papers and when they do they will find this.

Maybe that person is you. Or at least, I have to tell this story and I must tell it to somebody, so it may as well be you, come to sort through my belongings. You are young and you don't know or don't remember the things that happened. Nobody seems to remember, even those who are old enough, those who were there. But I remember it all, every grinding minute, hour and day, how things unfolded.

Our story doesn't show us in a very good light. I wish it were different, but there it is. This story is not the story of the whole of the past, just the story of a single summer.

As I said, somebody must stand guard over the past.

In Gost, that somebody is me.

The only person I can trust.

*   *   *

I imagine myself with the body of a bird, a raven. Outstretched wings and neck, rigid beak and shining eye, I swoop over the ravine and hover over the town. Turning my head from side to side, I follow the pattern of the roads, left and right until I find

47

the house. Hop through an open window, a dark shadow moving up the stairs and into the bedroom where a couple sleep without touching each other. The woman opens her eyes and looks straight at me, but she sees nothing except a shadow in the shape of a cross. A silent wing beat. In the room next door a stinking old woman breathes the same foul air over and over. Back in the sky, following the streets. A second house where the window is left open on a hot summer's night. A man and a woman and two strong boys. House to house. Room to room. Night upon night.

4

The next day I arrived at the blue house wearing a pair of overalls I'd kept from the days I worked at the timber yard. I'd been hired as casual labour and though the work didn't last for more than a few months they let us keep the overalls. Dressed like this I looked more like the hired man I was and sure enough Laura soon relaxed back into the same degree of informality we'd shared only a few days ago.

Meanwhile more of the mosaic was being revealed. Grace had brought a combination of zeal and patience to the job. She smiled when I complimented her on her handiwork and then looked down quickly, as if surprised by the sight of her own feet.

A green hand, reaching upwards. Two lines of yellow tiles either side of a single, narrow line of red tiles: deep, dark red tiles. These tiles were made of

48

glass. On the far right of the mosaic the thumb and forefinger of another hand was in the process of being uncovered to match the one on the left; they were two hands reaching into the air. The three downward-pointed blue shapes remained as they had been. All of this against a white background. The tiles were different shapes and sizes, fitted each to the other accordingly. Here and there were gaps where tiles had been lost, some in the process of the mosaic being uncovered. Grace had saved them in a bowl.

'Plus we've got the ones we found in the outbuilding,' she said. 'I'm going to put them back. Like, restore it.'

'Good,' I replied.

'Hey, Duro, can I show you something?' She led me a short distance to an indentation in the ground, obviously the outline of a shallow pond, up to this point concealed by the long grass. An edging of concrete gave way to tiled sides and a tiled base: a second mosaic. Grace crouched down and pulled at the grass to reveal more. 'I think it's an old fountain.'

I squatted down next to her and felt around for the water pipe that had once fed it. 'You're right,' I said.

'Do you think you can help me get it going? If I clean it out, that is?'

'Why not? I think it will be simple.'

'Awesome,' said Grace. She chewed her bottom lip as though she had something else to say. In the end she said, 'Do you think we can go to the place you told me about, the swimming hole?'

'Sure. When do you want to go?'

At that Grace's eyes widened slightly. 'Like maybe

this weekend?'

'Fine.'

'That would be cool.'

*   *   *

My life has been a sequence of temporary jobs and I enjoyed the sense of independence that came from it. Work is harder to come by in these parts but gratitude made Laura generous and we settled on a weekly sum. I considered what to do with the money. My house didn't need any repairs as I was always there to do whatever was needed. I didn't want to travel. My needs, which had always been few, were even fewer now. Perhaps I could go away for a weekend, meet a girl in a bar, one who'd agree to spend a night with me. How long since I spent the night with a woman? Nobody here in Gost, the town was too small. There were bars you could go to in some of the larger towns, and from time to time I'd visited them. But even then I'd never let myself stay the night; at some point before the light came up, and usually while the woman was sleeping, I'd slip out of the bed, pull my trousers on and leave quietly. There were times I would have liked to wake up next to a warm body, in a bed smelling of sex, fuck again and then fall into the streets looking for something to eat. But these things didn't happen that way any more. These days the women clung to you and cried in their sleep; some were angry with you in the morning. And so I left.

One night I picked up a working girl; I didn't know it at the time. Whores never sleep, they keep one eye on the clock and the other alert to the possibility of a dishonest customer. At the door she

50

leapt spitting onto my back. I explained my mistake, that I hadn't realised her profession. Immediately I offered to pay. Her face grew soft and she sighed. She took my cash, counted it, kissed a 100 kuna note and handed it back to me. She told me Monday was her day off. I walked away through the emptied streets. Bar owners were hosing down the pavements. Cats everywhere, glinting eyes watching the barmen and me, waiting for us to go so that they could claim the night for themselves. With every step I wondered if I should return to her.

I applied the first layers of new paint to the windowsills; nurturing the house back into being gave me pleasure. With these old buildings you can't be too careful: few builders are up to the task. Owners prefer to knock them down and use their government grants to put up modern chalets: everywhere now, most of them less than ten years old. Yellow-painted stucco fronts are all the fashion, with wooden balustrades. It makes the place look like a ski resort. In some countries people love the past. I guessed Laura loved the past, one because she bought this house and two because the English love the past more than anyone else. To Laura's way of thinking the past is a place of happiness, of safety and order, where fires, floods and wars were only ever sent to challenge the human spirit. There the sun shines when it should and the fields are full of wheat, in winter comes the snow. I know because of the tourists who came to stay in the hotel I once worked in, some of whom liked to talk to me while I fixed the shower or the cistern and in turn I'd ask them questions about where they were from and they'd tell me about their country, how it used to be and how it was now. The way the English saw it, the past was always better. But in this country our love of the past is a great deal less, unless it is a very distant past indeed, the kind nobody alive can remember, a past transformed into a song or a poem. We tolerate the present, but what we love is the future, which is about as far away from the past as it is possible to be.

By the middle of the day Grace had uncovered most of the mosaic. She showed me her work and I, in turn, made a show of being impressed. 'It's a bird,' said Grace, unnecessarily.

The bird rose, neck outstretched, trailing a tail of red and yellow. The body of the bird was red, the outspread wings were blue, very close to the blue of the paintwork of the house, except for the feathered ends which were the blue of azure, like the sky an evening before. The bird wore a crown of gold, and from its uplifted beak came curls of gold breath. It flew straight upwards into a white sky, the tiles arranged in cloud-like whorls. And below the bird, two hands outstretched. They might be trying vainly to touch the beautiful bird, or equally they could belong to the person who had just released it.

'I think it's beautiful,' said Grace.

I said, 'It is.'

'Weird that someone would cover it up.'

'Maybe they thought it wouldn't appeal to everyone and they wanted to sell the house.'

'There's more on the bottom of the fountain.'

Just as I had returned to work at the back of the house a car came down the lane. The road led to nothing except a collection of farm buildings a half-kilometre or so on and it could also be used as a cut through to a small hamlet four or five kilometres away, but that was it. Have I mentioned that? I don't think so. The point is that there was very little traffic down it and the few cars there were tended to speed. This one, an old Vauxhall, cruised slowly past much as the car driven by the woman who worked in the supermarket had the day before.

*   *   *

I finished work, stowed my brushes and stood before the pile of things pulled from the outbuilding. This time I helped myself to two of the paperbacks. I tend to eat early and after I'd cooked I settled down with the remainder of the bottle of wine. Reading has always been a pleasure, but after the first few pages I felt the wind change and got up to close the shutters just as the rain started. It rained hard for twenty minutes and then stopped and when it did some of the light had returned to the day. My mood had changed with the wind: a restlessness. I collected my shotgun, called the dogs and set off to the hills to scout for rabbits.

Whenever I think back to that time it is with the taste of rabbit flesh in my mouth. Anka must have been about eight years old when she first started to come with us. She was impressive from the start with none of the squeamishness, real or fake, of girls of our own age, nor though did she have any of the fascination with death which Krešimir and I shared. We would return to the scene of a carcass over and over again, watching as it dropped through the stages from rigor mortis to bones, the sweet stink of putrefaction. I remember once deformed piglets born to one of the farmers: Siamese twins, they didn't live long, but every day they lived we ran straight from school to see them. They were joined

53

at the belly and the chest and looked like they were dancing. They snuffled around, the stronger one unable to right itself because of the weaker sibling attached to it. The farmer sometimes helped them onto the teat, prodding them with a stick; he had no intention of keeping them alive but was enjoying the attention for a while. I remember the thrill it gave me to see them: a tightening in my balls.

By then Anka was ten and we tolerated her on our expeditions knowing it was the only way she could escape the eye of her mother, a chain-smoking beauty who'd outgrown her husband and viewed Anka not as a child but a miniature version of herself: a miniature, slower, stupider version of herself.

Anka liked to carry Krešimir's gun. Normally Krešimir didn't like anyone to touch his gun (any of his belongings), but he enjoyed her devotion. When he was ready, he'd silently extend his arm behind him and snap his fingers. Anka would run quickly forward and lay the gun across his palm.

Twenty minutes we'd been out, climbing the slope above the tree line below the old bunker, where that year we'd had most success. A rabbit broke cover fifty metres or so ahead of us. Anka, carrying Krešimir's gun, lifted it to her shoulder and fired. The animal tumbled twice and lay still. Krešimir and I stopped talking mid-sentence and stood with our mouths hanging open. The shot had practically whistled through our hair. Krešimir was proud of her, you could see it in his face. Anka's father bought her a shotgun of her own against the wishes of his wife. A 410 with a clover leaf engraved on the stock.

I was fourteen that year and had taught myself

54

how to cure rabbit skins. In the loft at home I had eight or ten skins, from which I'd scraped the fat and which I had stretched out on wooden frames. When the skins were ready I made them into hats like the ones Canadian trappers wore. I made quite a bit of money that way. So Anka's first rabbit I turned into a hat for her and that winter she wore it all the time, though Krešimir told her she'd catch fleas from it.

*   *   *

'He seemed very excitable,' Laura told me. 'At first I had no idea who he was, then I recognised him as the man we collected the keys from the day we arrived. He parked on the other side of the road and Grace said he gave her the fright of her life coming right up behind her. He seemed to be saying something about the mosaic. She started to call for me, but he banged on the door so I invited him in for a cup of coffee. I assumed he'd come to see how we'd settled in, but the next time I looked round he wasn't there. He was outside standing in front of the mosaic, waving his arms about. I couldn't understand a word he was saying. I almost sent Grace to run and fetch you.' I imagined Laura smiling at Krešimir, a smile full of warmth, as though she was waiting, with immense patience, for him to learn to speak English. 'I tried to explain how delighted we'd been to find it. It's a beautiful mosaic. Then suddenly he calmed down and we shook hands, he climbed back into his car and that was it. Do you have any idea what it might have been about?'

'No,' I said. 'Perhaps it's very valuable and he

didn't know it was there, so now he wants the house back.'

Grace snorted and Laura laughed and looked at me in surprise. 'Dear Duro, I do believe that's the first time I've heard you tell a joke.'

After that Laura seemed to forget about Krešimir. His visit had taken place on Friday evening. I'd not been expected to work at Laura's house on Saturday, but I'd promised Grace I would show her the swimming hole. Laura said she would come too and told me Matthew was certain to want to join us. I brought Kos and Zeka because they have a love of the water and I'd neglected them this past week.

'Will we really have it all to ourselves?' asked Grace.

'Yes.'

'How come?'

'Most people don't know the swimming hole is there. Those who did have forgotten.'

'Why would they forget?'

'My English is very bad, forgive me. What I mean is that we went to this place as children. That was a long time ago. The children of Gost no longer go there. Times are different and it is a long way to walk, maybe thirty minutes.'

*   *   *

In the event it took us nearly an hour. I'd measured the time according to my own pace. Laura brought towels, an ice box of drinks and a basket full of sun-creams and magazines. We followed the marks of a tractor through the grass: sun-hardened chevrons of soil, and when the tracks ended we fanned out, sending up small clouds of butterflies

56

from the flowers. Ahead of us stood a single row of trees: sentries to the hills, behind the trees a solitary hill stood to the fore, tightly forested with steep, sloping and almost perfectly symmetrical sides, which coupled with its isolation made it look almost man-made. We reached it in twenty minutes, skirted the base and entered the woods beyond and began to climb. Laura and Grace kept up the conversation most of the way, though with the uphill work the silences grew. Matthew had come along, though he walked a little apart from the rest of us, minding his own business. Zeka and Kos ran ahead, seeking quarry but noisily, without any real conviction because we never hunted at this time of day.

The route we followed meant we would reach the ravine at a point a little higher up and climb down into it, the only other way being to follow the river from Gost. Briefly we joined a dirt road which led to a place where attempts had recently been made to encourage visitors: a parking place, a wooden bench. To my knowledge no visitors came except the youth of Gost who gathered in the car park and held dirt bike races along the track: a scattering of crushed beer cans and cigarette ends evidence of their activities. Here was the tail of the ravine, everything lay ahead.

The sides rose steeply either side of us. Zeka and Kos returned to my heel. I knew this landscape, every rock, tree and shrub, and I took it for granted, but for the first time in many years, decades, I saw myself in it, as I had when I was a child and coming here, everything we did, was an adventure. I expect it was the presence of others and their reactions to the surroundings.

The sun bore down and on the floor of the ravine

there was no shade. We reached the waterfall some twenty minutes later. 'Can we swim here?' Grace was red-faced and panting.

'A bit further.'

'You mean we haven't even got there yet?' Matthew put down the basket he was carrying, took off his baseball cap and wiped his forehead.

'Just fifteen more minutes,' I assured them. 'And then you'll see.'

'But this is beautiful,' said Laura.

I explained there was little depth to the water, except directly under the fall, which made swimming unsatisfactory. They'd like the place I was taking them to better, I promised. We pressed on. I hoped I was still right. Many years had passed. Obvious from the state of the track nobody had been here recently. The worst that could happen would be that the water had succumbed to weed. The swimming hole was above the waterfall and the climb was a reasonably steep one, but then the ravine bed opened out into a small area of grass and wild flowers and the swimming hole: deep turquoise water, the loose forms of the rocks visible below; purple-black damselflies darted over a glinting surface.

'Holy fuck,' said Matthew.

Suddenly I was in a hurry to be in the water. I excused myself, pulled off my T-shirt and shed my jeans and ran the three or four strides to the pool, launched myself head first into it. After the heat of the sun, the shock of the drenching felt better than anything I'd felt for years. Under the water I opened my eyes and swam to the wall of rock at the opposite end, held my breath until dizziness set in. Just as I surfaced, a splash and Grace entered the

58

water. Matthew was already in. Laura was picking her way from rock to rock to the water's edge until she had positioned herself on the last and highest, with a clear path to the water.

'Come on,' I called.

'It looks very cold.'

'It's lovely,' said Grace.

Still Laura hesitated, edging forward and adjusting her balance on the rock.

Finally Matthew called, 'For God's sake, Ma, go for it!'

At the sound of her son's voice Laura pinched her nose between finger and thumb and leapt to rise a moment later, shaking her head to release silvery arcs of water from her hair. She squealed and gasped and like a young girl swam towards her son.

Twenty minutes later Laura and I lay on the opposite side of the swimming hole where, when the summer was at its height and the water at its lowest, the shallow bank formed a small, stony beach. From there we watched Matthew execute dives from the high rock. With each dive he positioned his feet on the rock, the sun behind his body. His chest was virtually hairless, his limbs long and luminously pale, slim to the point of thinness: neither boy nor man, but something in-between. Laura applauded each dive. Grace was in the water, turning circles with a stick in her hand, encouraging the dogs to swim after it. Watching Matthew and Laura I felt like an intruder, as though I had opened a closed door and found two people stepping away from each other. Laura's shining eyes as she looked at Matthew: enough to please any man. I wondered what was in her mind, what unformed, unspoken, perhaps unspeakable thoughts. He is perfect, she might well think. I made him and he is perfect. Or perhaps: He is perfect *because* I made him. When Laura looked at Matthew did she see herself in male form? I told you already that Laura had a slightly prominent canine on one side; occasionally her upper lip caught on it. For the first time that day I noticed Matthew had it too.

I left Laura's side and walked to where the tall grass, wolfen spurge and wild fennel grew. I pulled some fennel from the ground, shook the earth from it and brought it back to Laura. Fennel grows everywhere, on the borders of the roads around the blue house, a few metres from her own doorstep. But Laura didn't know this. She asked if she could cook with it, I said yes. I picked some leaves of wild garlic, tore them and rubbed them between my fingers, then held them under her nose to smell. I showed her a caterpillar clinging to the underside of a leaf. I told her how for a few hours every summer the mayflies mate on the surface of the water here and that the sand martins go mad darting and swooping, feeding their young and gorging on creatures who have become sated and slow, die in the act of copulating. Anything to draw her gaze away from Matthew, who performed his last two dives unnoticed and withdrew to sit on his towel in the sun.

I had an uncle and aunt who lived on the coast. Many years ago we visited them with my parents on holiday. My uncle would take tourists out fishing on his boat and encourage me to come along: it was useful to have a young lad about in case the anchor snagged. I taught myself to swim with my eyes open underwater. Once, following the line of the anchor chain, I saw a sea horse and we hovered nose to nose. My father and uncle fell out over the matter of my grandfather's will and that was the end of our visits as a family. It was many years before I went back. How easily I might have been the boat boy in Laura's story, though if I was I have no memory of it.

5

I advised Laura to hire contractors to fit the electric pump to the well and offered to oversee the work. I chose a company from out of town. The lining of the well needed some repairs and to be cleaned; the cracks and crevices were full of moss. Various tests for bacteria were conducted, even though most of us around here had been drinking water straight from the ground all our lives. When the men were gone I tested the turbidity of the water myself and in my own way: holding a glass to the light and drinking the contents.

How different the house looked already. I'd nearly finished painting the windows, the new tiles stared out from among the old ones on the roof. For some reason this pleased me, evidence of my labour, I suppose, a sign the house was being cared for again. Laura looked and shrugged and said no doubt no one would notice after a year or so and I didn't disagree, but the truth is the new tiles wear differently from the old ones, which were made by hand. There are houses in the town where most of the roof has been replaced and they still stand out among the rest after more than a decade.

I stood at the back of the house and viewed my

61

work. The glass of the windows reflected the sky, the hills, the branches of the nearby tree. I thought of the one dead tree on the roadside at the front and reminded myself it needed bringing down. So much to be done. It's true I'm happiest when I have a project, but all of this meant more to me than just the weekly rate Laura was giving me. Something that had been neglected and left to wither was being restored and if that bothered people, if it bothered Krešimir, then so be it. I raised my glass again, this time to the house, and I drank.

Later that evening, standing on the slopes of the lone hill, I saw the lights of the car as Laura arrived home. The family had left in the morning to spend the day at the national park, riding the boats up and down the rapids. The drive was two hours there and back. I watched the lights of the house go on one by one as they moved through its rooms, imagined Laura's pleasure at finding the water pressure doubled. Somewhere nearby a nightjar started up. Whirr. Pat, pat. Whirr. By my side Zeka and Kos sank to their haunches to wait for me, the minutes passed but I didn't move. Even in the dying light from where I stood I could see everything: the river and the town: in the forefront the grain stores on the riverbank, beyond them the coppered steeple of the church, the tiled roofs of the taller buildings, the roads and the cars upon them. I enjoyed the feeling of being there, able to watch over the family. But the dogs were hungry and became restless until Kos stood up and let go a long, low howl that reached out into the darkness and touched the blue house.

*　　　　*　　　　*

Laura's husband had to delay his plans to come out. She'd been hoping he would come this week, but now he'd called to say it wasn't possible. Laura picked up the message on her way to the national park yesterday. While she said this she ran her fingers across the surface of the table, backwards and forwards. Then she stopped, pushed her hair away from her face and sat up very straight.

I said, 'Grace and Matthew will be disappointed not to see their father.'

'He's not their father,' Laura replied very quickly. She'd been divorced from Grace and Matthew's father, married again eight years ago. Grace got along well with the husband, but the same couldn't be said of Matthew, at least not any longer. These days he answered back, there were rows, the rows ended with Matthew saying he didn't have to listen to this man who wasn't his father. 'The trouble is Matthew's right. I left their father and I feel very bad for them about that. It's my fault.' There were confrontations between Matthew and his stepfather so Laura made the decision to take all matters of discipline into her own hands, which hadn't pleased her husband, but Laura said that she was Matthew's mother and the responsibility belonged to her. This was how she explained it to me anyway. I didn't really understand but I said nothing. If it wasn't her husband's place to discipline a boy who lived under his roof and ate the food he paid for, then it wasn't my place to comment. Instead I raised the matter of the tree at the front of the house and we stepped outside into the sun to look at it.

'We'll have to bring in a tree surgeon,' said Laura. 'I expect that will cost a bit.'

'I can do it. Easy.'

'I don't know what I would do without you,' said Laura. 'I can't even think how to go about looking for a tree surgeon and even if I did I wouldn't understand what they were saying to me.'

'No,' I said. 'I don't mean I'll find a tree surgeon, I mean I'll bring the tree down myself.'

Laura and I stood on the road facing the house. A few metres away Grace was busy excavating the fountain. She looked just like an archaeologist with a red polka-dot scarf around her head. She'd finished work on the mosaic on the wall of the house, the giant bird taking to the wing behind her. At the bottom of the fountain a terracotta-coloured fish entwined in emerald weeds was being revealed.

'Duro?' said Grace.

'Yes?'

She stood up heavily and crossed to the mosaic and I followed and stood next to her. She smelled faintly of raw egg. Something about Grace prompted my pity and yet, though she was plain, much plainer than her mother and brother, she was a cheerful girl who'd at least found a way to occupy herself, whilst her pretty brother slept until noon and roamed the fields with wine stolen from his mother. 'You know some of the tiles are missing, well I've put back all the ones that fell off. And then there were some other gaps, but I've replaced most of them with the ones we found in the outbuilding . . . the green and blue ones. They're the same, you know. The problem is these ones.'

She pointed to the tail of the bird where several of the deep red glass tiles were gone and then to the body of the bird where the tiles, also red but a paler red, looked like they were made of quartz. 'And these ones too. I can't find any replacements about the house. There are others, the wing tips have a couple missing, but you don't really notice. I was wondering if you could help me, if you knew where I could get some.'

Before I could reply Laura interrupted. 'Don't bother Duro, Grace. He doesn't have time to help you look for tiles.'

'Oh, OK. Sorry.' Grace pressed her lips together and hummed her little tune.

Laura had already turned away. 'What kind of trees are these anyway? Do we need to plant another one?'

'Almond,' I said. 'They're almond trees. They'll fruit in another month or so.' I turned back to Grace who was once more bent over the fountain. 'Of course I can help,' I said. 'I know where we can find something like this. There is a town on the coast where you can buy crafts. We would have to take a trip, it's about two hours away, but I'd be happy to show you.'

'It's too much trouble,' said Laura.

'Not at all,' I insisted. 'I'd like to go myself, it's a long time since I went to the coast. Perhaps one Sunday when I have a little more time. They have excellent ice cream.'

Grace grinned. 'That would be so cool, Duro.'

I turned to Laura. 'OK, Laura?'

Laura shrugged and raised her eyebrows. 'It's OK with me.'

*   *   *

That evening I decided to go to town for a drink. I went to the Zodijak where Fabjan commented on my new sociability.

'Just looking for company,' I replied pleasantly. As I spoke I looked deliberately at the waitress. Fabjan grunted, took a long draught of his beer and set the heavy glass on the table in front of him; he stared over the top of it and cracked his knuckles.

I decided not to sit with Fabjan and chose a table near the railing which separated the Zodijak's terrace from the road. As far as I was aware nobody in Gost knew I was working at the blue house. Nobody had seen me there, and that included the drivers of the cars that had passed by (I had been up the ladder each time); Laura couldn't tell anyone even if she wanted to. Ever since he became the sole owner of the Zodijak, Fabjan has been busy getting his fingers into every pie in Gost; he rents out several properties and is part-owner of various other ventures: the hardware store, for instance, and a building company which also took care of wells: pumps, refits, that sort of thing. That's why I'd chosen an out-of-town company for Laura's well.

I drank my beer slowly. Fabjan's BMW was parked on the other side of the road. I decided that when the summer was over and I'd made my money I would buy a car, something to replace the old Volkswagen I was driving. Behind me the waitress stared at the road, switching her gaze back and forth between the phased movement of the cars like a sheepdog eyeing sheep. I signalled for another beer. When she brought it over I asked her name and how long she had been in Gost. In return she told me her grandparents lived here, she had come to visit and ended up getting a job at the Zodijak.

'What of your parents?' I asked.

'They left here when I was five.'

'And how old are you now?'

'I'll be twenty-one soon.'

'Congratulations,' I said.

She smiled and squirmed, tilting her head and rubbing her chin against her shoulder. I invited her to sit down and saw her eyes flick in the direction of Fabjan. I gestured at the chair. She shrugged and was about to pull it out, when Fabjan said, 'Go and wash the glasses at the back.'

'They're all done.'

'Then put more beer in the fridge.'

Fabjan spoke without once turning to look at her, or indeed moving his head at all. The girl disappeared. I took the exchange to mean Fabjan was sleeping with her, which was a shame. She was pretty and it would have been pleasant to spend some time with her, all the more so if she was one of Fabjan's. In the end it was all too much effort. It had been my pleasure just to irritate him.

I wandered home through the streets of Gost, the avenues of chestnut trees, the immaculate houses with their wooden balconies, window boxes full of geraniums and dark, gleaming windows. Front gardens full of roses: very popular this year, along with lilies. Lions on the gateposts; some people painted them yellow with brown manes. Green stone frogs crouched in the flower beds. Through the windows the blue flicker and drone of TV sets, from behind a pair of curtains: the sound of a man's voice raised. The hotel, which had a stuffed bear in the entrance hall and a new wing, was open for dinner in the evenings. The eight-page menu included: *Regional Specialities* and *International Dishes* as though the hotel was, at any moment, expecting a large delegation from the United Nations. Outside was parked a big tour bus. The tourists spend the night in Gost on their way to the coast from Zagreb, though never more than one night. And to my knowledge they never leave the hotel, but stay inside behind a wall of pink and white oleander. Other than the few businessmen who also pass through as quickly as they can, nobody has any reason to come to Gost.

Unlike the hotel and the houses, the municipal buildings in the centre of town were pockmarked and dirty. On an abandoned building at the corner of a road, an ardent football fan had scrawled *Volim Croatia Hajduk* and scrawled a heart with an arrow through it. I passed the bakery. The other bakery, long gone now, had been on this same street, just a hundred metres down. At lunchtime they sold soda bread and *devrek* through the window. They had a retarded daughter, a Mongol, whom the boys, Andro, Goran and Miro, used to tease, imitating her tottering walk, her slow, deep voice and stupid smile. The other daughter owned a white angora sweater and served in the shop. She'd something of a reputation, as though she was compensating for the shame of her sister by being an easy lay. I used to visit their house from time to time, usually on an errand for my father, and wait in the sitting room mortified by the presence of the Mongol. But their *burek* had been the very best, no doubt. Sometimes, on those days I was working in town, I would buy one of their potato or spinach pies for lunch. Ever since the bakery closed there had only ever been one bakery in Gost. Someone could have made money opening a new one, Laura was right. In all the years that passed since the family went away, nobody ever did. Not Fabjan: too much even for him.

The town was silent, save for the boys in the car park of the supermarket, playing with their motorbikes; moustaches of soft sparse hair, bitten fingernails and acne scars: boys in love with their cocks, who think themselves men. Boys who have been around for ever and exist in every town, in every place in the world. I was once like them, we all were: Andro, Goran, Miro, Krešimir and me. In the end you grow out of it, or you hope you do. We grew older and the lads who replaced us hung around the Zodijak where Fabjan had had the good business sense to install a pinball machine and make money out of them.

On the bridge I stopped and looked out over the river, upon which the last of the light played itself out. I followed the trail of the water back along itself where it wound through a route five times longer than the actual distance it covered, up towards Gudura Uspomena.

*　　　*　　　*

Some days Anka and I go up to the pine forest to shoot birds without Krešimir. How did we begin to hunt together? I have forgotten. Probably I arrived at the house one day to find Krešimir out and Anka there instead and so it seemed natural to invite her along after the way she shot the rabbit, plus hadn't her father bought her a shotgun with a design of a clover leaf on the stock? Soon enough I found I preferred hunting with Anka.

With Anka I shoot my first deer. I've taken my father's gun without his permission. To show off, no

69

doubt. It is an old bolt-action rifle with iron sights and we practise with it on a home-made target at fifty metres. As the gun belongs to me, or at least my father, I get most of the shots. On the way home we see a small bachelor herd feeding on the edge of the wood, drifting across the hillside towards us, and the wind coming straight up the hillside carries our scent away and into the pines. Anka and I begin to stalk them, not seriously, we're still playing at being hunters. Sure enough the herd soon becomes aware of us and begins to move away and we, because it is the end of the day and we have time on our hands, we lie back on the grass and watch a lone crow cross the sky.

A buck, separated from the herd, appears on the brow of the hill about forty metres downhill of us. He is young, concerned principally with reaching his companions and hasn't seen us lying in a shallow dip in the hillside between the two positions. He comes and keeps coming. Anka and I watch. Any minute I expect him to make a break for the safety of the herd, but he does no such thing. We are motionless, sharing a single thought. Slowly I train the sight on him. The breeze blows straight into my face. I aim fractionally ahead of him so that he walks straight into the bullet. The herd flees. We watch the buck: the moment of hesitation, the buckling of his back legs, the final lurch forward. Together we drag the carcass back to my house, where for the next week my father hugs me and brags to anyone who'll listen. He couldn't care that I took his gun, because that sin has been redeemed. And that I shot the buck out of season bothers nobody.

6

A yellow light. A surge of energy and the taste of electricity. The wind that day came from the south and arrived in the afternoon. A sudden rattling of the shutters and then the rain. I'd been watching the sky all morning as I prepared the outside walls for whitewashing. Grace was working on the fountain, Laura had gone to the supermarket and Matthew was sitting at the kitchen table eating a late breakfast, where Grace and I joined him.

Minutes passed, Grace said, 'Well this isn't much fun.'

'Tell me about it,' muttered Matthew.

'It will be over in fifteen minutes,' I said. 'Maybe if you go and look out of the window you'll see something.'

Grace stood up and crossed the room. For a few seconds she stood looking out of the window and then, 'How did you know that would happen?'

I only knew what everybody else around here knows, like when the rain is coming and when the wind will change, when to expect snow and which winter months are best for picking *rujnika* mushrooms in the pine forest. The western wind is carefree and light. The northern and southern winds are troublesome. The *bura* is the fastest wind in the world, so cold that at Karlobag the sea freezes: white horses are turned to ice, frozen in motion like characters in a fairy story; in the streets signposts snap like straws. This southerly summer wind arrives, as always, with all the fanfare of a Gypsy caravan driving into town with a new spectacle for

71

the townsfolk. First an empty stage. The wind dies, the sky is clear. Across the stage thunder gives chase to lightning. Up come the lights and the special effects: sunshine and transparent ribbons of rain. The Gypsy magician swirls his cloak.

'What is it?' asked Matthew.

'A double rainbow,' said Grace. 'Come and see.'

Matthew only grunted. At that moment Laura came back from the supermarket; her clothes and hair were wet, she'd run from the car. Grace pointed to the rainbows. Laura pushed her wet hair from her face and craned her neck. 'Mattie, have you seen this?'

'I'm good, thanks.'

Laura insisted. 'Come and look, before they disappear.'

'I said I was cool.'

Laura moved to behind Matthew's seat, she put her hand on his shoulder, bent and kissed the top of his head. Matthew pushed her hand away. 'What's the matter, darling?' she asked.

'Nothing, I'm fine.'

'Why don't you want to see the rainbows?'

'Because I don't, that's why. Just drop it, will you, I said I'm fine.'

'Come on, Mattie . . .'

'Oh for fuck's sake, I said drop it.'

Laura flinched, but persisted. 'Not until you tell me what the matter is.'

'Oh OK. Well where shall I begin? Um, no TV, the phones don't work, no Internet. Nothing to do all day, every day. It's fucking boring here, that's what.'

'You've scarcely given it a chance.'

'This was your idea, not ours, and just because

72

it's your fucking fantasy to live in the middle of nowhere doesn't mean it's everyone else's.'

The mood changes. The sky darkens, the rainbows are snatched away. The clouds close in, the temperature drops and down comes more rain, heavy and sullen this time. The caravan closes up, the locals drift away.

After Matthew had left the room Laura raised her head and gave a little sniff, which meant she was being brave. Grace, standing by the window, said, 'Wow, that was a mood killer.'

'I'm sure he didn't mean it.'

'I'll go and get him,' I said. 'Matthew shouldn't speak to you that way.'

'Leave him, Duro. It's just his age, he'll grow out of it.'

I was silent.

'You don't have children, Duro, otherwise you'd understand. I'll talk to him later.'

I breathed in, I said, 'There is no English television channel here, but you can get Internet at the library and there is a café in town called the Zodijak where you can get it too.' And because I needed to leave the room I went outside to bring the bags in from the car. Laura urged me to wait for the rain to finish, I pretended not to hear.

Soon afterwards I went to the outbuilding where the Fićo was parked. I pulled away the cover and began an inspection of the vehicle, something I'd been meaning to find time to do. The body was in reasonable condition, a few spots of rust here and there, along the edge of one window. Despite the day's rain this is a dry climate, as you know. The car was unlocked, I opened the driver's door. One of the seats was split and the foam bulged, but here again the car had survived the years and the rats well. I fetched a torch and crawled under the car to inspect the chassis; I assumed it would be sound and it was.

The rain had eased off. Back inside there was only Grace, eating biscuits from the packet along with a glass of milk; she looked up at me and smiled. I fetched the car battery and the engine oil I'd brought in a day before and returned to the outbuilding where I stowed them next to the car. I shook out and replaced the cover. Along the wall of the outbuilding was a shelf where the *rakija* had been stored. I ran my hand along the underside, snagging my finger on the splintered wood. I searched until I felt what I was looking for: a row of hooks and keys. I shone the torch on them, inspected each one until I found the key for the Fićo.

*   *   *

Laura complimented my hands. She sat opposite me while I worked the splinter out of my thumb with the pin she had given me; when she offered to help I held my hand out for her. After the splinter was gone she held onto my fingers, lifting my hand to the light the better to examine it. Piano player's hands, she said.

Piano player's hands. I liked the things Laura had said. True, I take care of my hands. I take care of them not despite my work but because of it. My nails are trimmed to a length of one millimetre, and by the side of my tub I keep a Lipari pumice stone. My sister Daniela gave me my first manicure; she was training as a beautician and had done my mother's hands and

74

those of my sister Danica. I begged her to do mine next and sat with my fingertips in a bowl of soapy water. Daniela massaged my hands and rubbed in my mother's rose hand cream, she painted my nails with a clear varnish and when it wore away I begged her to do it again, because I liked the way they looked so much. Daniela gave me a small piece of shammy leather wrapped around a matchbox and taught me how to buff my nails.

Laura's hands were slim and tapered, with polished, almond-shaped nails. On her left hand next to her wedding band she wore a gold ring, set round with diamonds, on the other hand a small silver ring in the shape of a heart.

*   *   *

Laura said, 'You don't talk much, do you?'

I said, 'What do you want me to say?'

She'd bought Pag cheese because she read about it in a book and wanted to try it. I told her where to go, because even though the cheese comes from the island, in fact you can buy it just about anywhere. Laura had been to the market in Gost and was disappointed. I know what she wanted: cheese and cured meats, olives soaked in oil and vine tomatoes, like in Italy. Instead she found imitation-leather jackets, mobile-phone covers and pickled vegetables. I explained that Gost market has always been like that. In years gone by the farmers sent their produce away to a central distribution point to be sold. What they didn't send they kept for themselves. Laura invited me to try the cheese and wanted to know what I thought about it and I said it was good, though the truth is, it was only OK. While

75

Laura enthused about the cheese Matthew rolled his eyes. Laura wanted everything to be special: the cheese the best cheese, the house she had found the best house in the best town. She was pleased there were no English people here.

We were alone in the house, the cheese between us on the table. She said, 'Tell me about your family.'

'I was raised here in Gost.'

Laura waited. 'And?'

'And what?'

'Well tell me more.'

'We were very happy.'

Laura laughed a great deal at that.

'What's funny?' I said.

'Sorry, Duro, but, well you're the only person I've ever met who said they came from a happy family.'

'Yes,' I repeated. 'We were happy.'

'What did your father do?'

'He worked in the post office.'

'A postman?'

'Not postman. In charge of the sorting office. My mother had different jobs. She helped in the school kitchens. I used to see her every day at lunchtime. When I was little I liked it a lot but when I was older I was embarrassed about it, I don't know why. Because my other friends saw her there too maybe, and I worried she would become the butt of their jokes like some of the other staff members. She found another job, went to work in the fertiliser factory. We were five: my father, mother, two sisters and me.'

'Do they all still live in Gost?'

'One of my sisters and my mother moved away. My father and my other sister died.'

Laura's smile disappeared, she said, 'Oh.' Her eyes slid away from me. 'I'm sorry.'

I saw that it was up to me to put the conversation right again, to steer it back to where Laura would feel comfortable, something bereaved people learn to do. I said, 'It was an accident. In any case they're gone. My other sister lives in the capital with her husband, work is easier to find there, not too much of it here. My mother wanted to be around for her grandchildren when they came. There it is.'

'Yes,' said Laura. 'There it is.' She still had the olive stone in her mouth, which she sucked and turned around with her tongue while she looked at me. This and the fact I had been made to talk about myself made me uncomfortable. I was about to make an excuse and go back to work when a car drove by. Laura's eyes followed it through the window as it passed. 'There must be a party.'

'Why do you say that?'

'Hardly anyone comes down this road usually.'

Word was getting around: someone in the blue house. I said, 'One of the roads is closed. Work on the water mains.'

'I hope that doesn't mean the water gets cut off.'

I reminded Laura she had a well.

*   *   *

I like to leave a job in a certain place, where I can pick it up easily. At the beginning of the day I set myself a goal and don't stop until I've reached it. It's just the way I am. I like to work hard and go to bed tired and begin again the next day, allocating tasks for myself in the right order and completing each one within the schedule I've set myself. I didn't like my work to be disrupted or disturbed, even the school projects I laid out on the kitchen table when I was a child. I grew mad if anyone touched them. My mother complained to my father that I was stubborn. Not stubborn but single-minded, my father insisted, like him. Two men marooned in a household of women: my father always talked as though we were outnumbered, two to twenty instead of two to three. Perhaps it was because I was the youngest, petted by my sisters and my father, so easy-going; somehow we'd failed to stamp our masculinity upon the household.

Shooting was one thing we alone shared. My first shooting lessons were given to me by my father, I was barely taller than the gun, still watching *Professor Balthazar* on television after school. My father came into the house holding a rifle, he said, 'Come on, chief.' The Professor was on holiday in Switzerland, skiing and riding in trains. I turned the set off, jumped down and followed my father.

Learning to shoot is a lot like learning to play an instrument. In time I got to know my rifle the way a violinist knows his violin, every curve and line of the stock and barrel, the slide of the bolt, the pull of the trigger. From all those hours with my father I brought a single lesson. Patience, focus, control: in all things and especially in shooting. Aged ten I lost a shooting contest. It was at the local fair; I was nervous. My father put his hand on my ribcage, he told me I needed to learn how to still my heart. By the time I was in my teens I was winning every competition and I understood what he had meant: to go to a place within, to feel my heart shudder, slow and pause, hovering in advance of the next beat. To begin to beat again only after the shot had been taken.

When I was satisfied with the outside walls, I went to the courtyard and washed my brushes one by one under the tap, laid them out on a sheet of newspaper and made sure the lid of the paint tin was firmly in place. I washed my hands and splashed water over my face. I opened my eyes to find Laura standing in front of me.

'Duro, Grace and I were wondering if you would like to stay and have supper with us.'

'Thank you, yes.' I dried my face on the sleeve of my T-shirt.

'Good, we hoped you'd say that.'

'First I need to wash and change my clothes.'

'It's just family.'

'I must also feed Kos and Zeka.'

'Bring them back with you, why don't you?'

'Thank you.'

It had been a while since I left the dogs alone for so many hours in the day; they were feeling sorry for themselves and let me know. I spent a few minutes raking their fur with my fingertips, searching for ticks, something they loved. On Zeka's haunch I found one, already gorged with blood. He held still while I burned it off, but the damned thing burst and left a mess. I'd have to take a pin to remove the head later, now time was short. I fed them and let them follow me into the house. After I had showered I wiped the mirror and decided to shave. While I lathered my face I inspected myself as I hadn't done in a long while. When you live on your own you forget how others see you. Overall I was not unhappy with what I saw. I had aged well, certainly compared to Fabjan and even Krešimir. I still weighed what I had at twenty and still had my

79

hair and teeth. Every morning I performed the same exercise routine. Squats, pull-ups, crunches, push-ups: twenty-five of each. I went to the door and hoisted myself up, raised and lowered myself five or six times, counted to one hundred and let go. I shaved, found a pair of kitchen scissors and snipped at some coiled hairs growing in my eyebrows.

In the bedroom I chose a clean shirt. I dressed quickly and left the house with Kos and Zeka at my heels. It was still warm, a crane flew overhead and we followed in its path towards the blue house. I tried to think of the last time I'd shared a meal with anyone. The last family dinner I remembered was when Danica left Gost. Danica's husband Luka worked for the railways and said the line through Gost was not so important any more, because the trains only came from one direction now. Osijek to Zagreb, Zagreb to Rijeka: that was going to become the most important. Wait and see. There were flats, he said, in Zagreb, vacated and going for cheap rents. Danica and Luka had their name down on a government list. Any tenant in social housing who left and didn't pay the rent for six months would lose the flat and the flat would go to someone on the list, end of story. There were hundreds going spare. You had to act fast for the good ones. Some people just moved in and claimed they'd been living there for years. Sometimes it worked.

'What if the tenants come back?'

'Too bad,' he shrugged.

Luka was confident. He roasted a lamb; there was walnut cake. Beer. My mother drank cola and red wine, her beloved *bambus*. A goodbye dinner, though no one said so. Luka went first, Danica followed, my mother the last. There must have been

80

suppers in-between, but I have forgotten them. I felt no particular sadness when they left: at that time I felt very little at all. Later I felt it. Later still, I got used to being alone.

Every year Danica calls to wish me Happy Christmas and New Year and passes the phone to my mother. Soon enough she tells me there are still flats vacant in the building. Theirs has a view of the Sava. They sent me a photograph taken from the opposite shore of the river: a row of six or seven high-rise blocks: their image reflected in the steel water. The riverbank is straight, of soft, black earth. On either side there is what looks like a strip of no man's land, though my mother insists it's a park. There was a running track, she told me, as though she was thinking of taking up the sport. The first years were difficult. Danica had trouble finding work. My mother disliked leaving the apartment. Once she witnessed the trees being felled in Tomislav Square, some were one hundred years old. People gathered in front of the railway station to watch, cheering as each one toppled, though they were perfectly healthy trees. Sapling planes were planted in their place. These days Danica works as a tour guide and has introduced my mother to the city the way she does her tourists. For Mother's birthday they visited the zoo, where my mother took a liking to the miniature hippopotamus. Then for a drink in Republica Square, I mean Jalačić Square, and then for supper on the terrace of the Hotel Dubrovnik. My mother liked the row of gift shops in the lobby, the restaurant with its red chairs and black-and-white-tiled floor, the buffet table covered in white cloths: my mother's idea of glamour. Now she is in awe of the city and in love with the city at the same time. She rides the trams. Everything in Gost is small and far away and there are no trams. She never asks about the people she once knew.

At the blue house Grace was setting the table, folding napkins. Laura came in with a bunch of sunflowers, their heads already lolling on the end of their narrow stalks. She set about searching for a vase, rejecting those too small for the giant flowers. In the end she took a pot from the windowsill and filled it with water. She picked up the flowers, exclaimed and dropped them. I picked them up. Hoards of glistening black beetles crawled through the stamens of the discs.

'Gross!' said Grace.

'Weevils,' I said. At the front door I shook the flowers and plunged the heads into a bucket of water that stood there until the remaining insects floated to the surface. I handed the flowers to Laura, who thanked me and told me (again) that she didn't know what she'd do without me. Of Matthew there was no sign.

'He's upstairs,' said Laura. 'He'll be down.'

'He's in his room. He's been there all day,' said Grace. 'He's sulking.'

'Grace!'

'I'm just saying.' Grace widened her eyes at her mother and turned to me. 'He's been in a bad mood ever since we got here. Just because it's not cool enough for him. And there's no Internet, of course.'

'Don't be silly. Matt's enjoying the holiday just fine.'

'Matt's too cool to enjoy anything,' said Grace. 'He thinks enjoying things is for idiots. We're all

82

idiots apparently.'

'That's enough, Grace!'

Grace flinched but said nothing, she twisted the dishcloth to wipe the inside of a glass, set it on the table and hummed a single note.

*   *   *

We ate: pasta, tomatoes, local cured ham, good red wine in fine glasses. Grace was sent up to call Matthew, but she came down and said he wasn't hungry. While her daughter was out of the room Laura had rearranged the settings, switching the position of the spoons. She undid and refolded two of the napkins. There was a carafe of water, not well water but fizzy, bottled water. New table mats and a tablecloth. Banished now to the windowsill: the sunflowers; candles in the middle of the table instead. The house had curtains, fastened with bows, even though I had yet to fix the patch of plaster on the wall. The order of things was wrong. Then Laura told me her husband was coming.

'I hope he'll be pleased.'

'I'm sure he will be. To tell you the truth when I first saw the house I was a bit worried it wasn't going to work out. Conor bought it without me, you see.' What Laura told me next surprised me a great deal. She said she'd found the house on the Internet and her husband had flown over from Italy where he was on business to look at it. Imagine Krešimir having the wit to use the Internet. He must have found somebody to do it for him. That young wife of his, maybe? No, Krešimir would never let anyone be privy to his finances, let alone something like

83

this.

To Laura I said, 'What made you want to buy this house?' For surely it could not have been Gost. I wondered how Laura saw the town, the churches and the school, the hills and the swimming hole, the people who lived here. I tried to imagine seeing it all for the first time, not knowing anything.

'Property here is cheap relative to the rest of Europe. Conor reckoned the coast had peaked or would soon and we should look inland, a little off the tourist track. It's got to be a good thing. People investing in the country again, getting the economy moving? I've been looking for something to do now the kids are more or less off my hands. If this works out, we'll keep going.'

'What do you mean keep going?'

'Buy another one and do it up.'

'You mean you plan to sell this house?'

'That's the idea. I've been scouting around. There's no shortage of empty houses, though some of them are in appalling condition and nobody seems very interested in repairing them.'

'The people around here are peasants,' I said. 'They don't see property the same way you do, they don't see the value and so take no care.'

'The odd thing is there don't seem to be any estate agents.'

'Most houses here belong to families. They stay in the family even after somebody dies.'

Laura thought about that. 'So how do you go about buying one?'

'By private sale. The way you bought this one.'

'They're almost grown-up.' Laura looked over at Grace petting Zeka, who stood with his head in her lap. Laura fell silent for a short time, drank more wine. She said, 'We bought the house five years ago, but it's only now I've really worked up the courage to come out and make it good. Mattie's off to university next year. Grace takes care of herself, she doesn't really need me.' Laura spoke as if Grace couldn't hear.

Five years? I stared at the table, I only came back to myself when Grace said, 'I think Zeka's hurt?'

I looked. The blood left by the exploding tick had matted in Zeka's fur. 'It's nothing,' I said. 'Just a tick.'

'Oh, OK. Can I take them out?'

'Yes.'

'Will they come with me?' She stood up and went to the door.

'Kos! Zeka!' I waved my hand and the dogs rose as one and went to Grace.

'They won't get lost, will they?'

'They're hunting dogs. They know the area and they'll do as you tell them.' I thanked Laura for the dinner, suddenly I wanted to go home, to be alone. To think. My head was bursting with this new knowledge. But Laura brought a salad bowl and plates to the table, heaped the remaining pasta on a clean plate and placed it on a tray along with cutlery and a glass of water.

'I'll just take this up to poor Matt,' she said. 'He's probably starving.'

The sight of Laura carrying supper upstairs to her son, taking the steps carefully. I climbed those stairs holding a tray once. It was the year before the family moved to the house in town after Krešimir's father was promoted to his new job in the administrative offices of the Town Hall. An important job, more so than my father's. It widened the space between me

85

and Krešimir even more. But all that was to come. Back then the Pavićs still lived in the blue house. I had run up and down those stairs a thousand times. In Krešimir's room we hung out of the window shooting wood pigeons with our first air rifles. One year Mr Pavić bought Krešimir a junior pool table and we played against each other for months. I owe it to Krešimir that I've never had to buy myself a drink in a bar where there's a pool table.

I've gone to the Pavić house, as I so often do. The door's open, though the parlour and kitchen are empty. It's after school so I expect to see Krešimir at least, and usually at this time of day Mrs Pavić is home. It is a clear autumn day; the house is without heating and cold inside. The kitchen bears all the appearance of a careful departure: sink wiped dry, dishcloths on their pegs, a pot at the back of the stove. The room smells of onions.

A sound from upstairs: a cough, the flush of the toilet, a faint shuffle and creak. There is Anka, standing at the top of the stairs, wearing a nylon nightdress. Her hair is damp and stuck to her forehead in sharp points; at the back it forms a tangled halo. The lower part of her face is massively swollen and she sways so alarmingly I hold out my arms because I'm afraid she might fall down the stairs. She turns and stumbles away. By the time I reach the door to her room she has crawled back into bed.

The air in the room is sweet and stale. I open the window. When I am ill my mother makes me rosehip tea, beef soup; but I've no idea where to begin, so I boil milk and pour into it some of the coffee from the pan on the stove, I fry an egg and carry it all upstairs on a tray. I straighten the

86

bedclothes around Anka, making noises like my mother does. Anka sips the milky coffee, the skin sticks to her lower lip. She says swallowing the egg hurts.

She has mumps. Where is everyone? I lie and say they have asked me to sit with her. I stay the whole afternoon and watch her sleep. I am too young to put my finger on the awfulness of it, but I feel it in my chest. Gone to town to buy new laces for Krešimir's football boots, such a small thing. To leave your sick daughter for such a small thing.

*   *   *

Sleepless in the dark later the same night I had dinner with Laura. The new knowledge that Krešimir had sold the house five years ago was like a rat gnawing at my gut. I clenched my fists beneath the sheets. All this time he'd been sitting smugly on his secret, making fools of us. The number of times I'd passed him on the street, he knew he had one over all of us. Fuck you, Krešimir, you cunt! The blue house was never yours to sell.

There are some things in life you don't set out to do. The arrival of Laura, Grace and Matthew was nothing to do with me. Krešimir sold the blue house to Laura's husband. Five years ago, I now knew. I went there because I needed work. I'd no choice but to do the things I did. I knew the house better than anyone and it made sense that if somebody was going to work on restoring it then that person should be me. I led Laura to the mosaic in order to divert her from doing the jobs she could be paying me to do.

So it irritated Krešimir to see the house looking

as it once had? Fine. What did he expect? I enjoyed rattling the bars of the cage that was Krešimir's heart. The truth is, I hated Krešimir, I loathed him, and the years of loathing far outnumbered those we'd ever been friends.

7

Krešimir waits for my approach, he slips out of the door and intercepts me halfway down the road, then he walks very fast until we are out of sight. I've told you how the pace would alter his gait: pitch his body forward and make his arse stick out. This time I laugh, which of course irritates him. He never explains what we are doing and at first I think the whole thing is a huge joke. It dawns on me only later that he was trying to leave Anka behind.

On the way back from our hunt, which has been successful this time, Krešimir has me in a headlock as we stagger towards home. We pass the Tomislav house, a modern bungalow painted a strong shade of pink. Outside, tied to the revolving clothes dryer, is the Tomislavs' dog, a shaggy black beast called Lujo, whom I made friends with when the Tomislavs first got him. When Lujo was little they let him run free, but now he's older they leave him tied all day, whatever the weather. On a hot July day I'd found the dog tied to the revolving clothes dryer with a rope so short he couldn't sit, or reach the shade or his water bowl. I untied him and took him home, and my father, when he returned the animal, had words with Tomislav. Our families hadn't been on speaking terms too much since.

'Hold on,' says Krešimir. He slings the rabbits at me. 'I need a piss.'

I do too. I leave the rabbits on the roadside, turn to the hedge and unzip. Before I finish I hear the sound of Krešimir's laughter. He has pissed all over the dog, which is shaking itself and wagging its tail at him. Krešimir still has his dick in his hand. I pick up the dog's water bowl and douse it in cold water. Lujo retreats from me, making the clothes dryer spin; he barks.

'He prefers piss,' says Krešimir.

I wonder if all this is because I laughed at him. He knows about me and the dog, Tomislav and my father.

That was maybe two months on from the day we returned empty-handed from our early morning shoot and were caught in the rain; Krešimir walked so fast he left us both behind. At the corner by the bakery I gave a backward glance and saw Anka running to catch up with Krešimir. He was angry at the failure of the shoot, angry at the rain and the absent birds, angry at me, but most of all angry at Anka who'd become somehow responsible.

That was a turning point, I saw it later, when I tried to remember the order of things. Even now it's hard. How do you trace your way back to the place where a feeling changed, the course of a friendship turned a corner and became something else?

– mumps
– their father's new job
– move to the house in town
– hunt birds in the rain
– K pisses on the dog

No, I have forgotten something. Their father died. Such a big thing. I don't mean I have forgotten it, only the order of events. Some months before the bird shoot in the rain, I don't remember, six, seven, eight months, their father had died: an aneurysm.

*   *   *

Anka cries; Krešimir's sorrow has a different texture. His relationship with his father had already changed and the change was sealed by old Pavić's fate. The shift went back to an argument between his parents in the year before a blood vessel bloomed and burst in Pavić's brain.

The argument was over a Licitar heart. I remember seeing it on the kitchen table a day I came to visit. In an earlier time Krešimir and I had seen it as our seasonal duty to steal and consume as many of these festive items as possible. We stole from shop windows, from the communal Christmas tree outside St Mary's Church, from school where every pupil was detailed to bring in a Licitar of their own making during the final week of the winter term. The hearts were used to decorate the school hall. They were never really meant to be eaten: the dough was rock hard and the icing was bitter with food dye. But for whatever reason we forced them down. So the sight of a heart there on the Pavićs' kitchen table came with both the lure and the ghosts of sins past.

That day the television in the room was showing an episode of *Ckalja*. Depending on how old you are, you might remember *Ckalja*, it was everybody's favourite show. Ckalja wearing a beret and a huge, patterned tie was sitting at a table with a man with

90

a Hitler moustache, a woman in a fur coat and another man with an accordion. He always wore funny hats, it was like a kind of trademark. Krešimir wanted to get out of the house. I wanted to watch the show. I took off my anorak. He told me his parents had argued over the Licitar heart, which sounded silly to me and not very serious. I went to turn the sound up, but Krešimir said we had to go and made me put my anorak back on.

Anyway, the sum of it amounted to this: the heart had been bought by Vinka Pavić as a Christmas gift for Krešimir's father's boss in his job, which he had been in for a year or two by then. There'd recently been some disagreement between the two (the boss and Krešimir's dad) and Mr Pavić thought the gift was overgenerous—amounting to an apology. The heart sat on the table for some days. I have no idea what became of it after that.

Then one day, many months after Christmas, we sat upstairs in Krešimir's room and listened to Krešimir's parents argue. This time they were arguing over another promotion in the father's office that had gone to someone else. A promotion Mrs Pavić was convinced belonged to her husband.

Mrs Pavić thought her husband had let the family down through his naivety. Not deliberately, but because of a flaw, a flaw in his way of seeing. Too much faith in the world, said Vinka Pavić to Krešimir after her husband's death. Mrs Pavić was a survivor, who survived by giving gifts of bright, brittle hearts to people in positions of influence. She kept up appearances on her widow's pension, even though common sense might have suggested she rent out the town house and move back to the blue house, but Vinka Pavić couldn't bring herself

91

to do it. Wild boar couldn't drag her back to the little blue house with all its rustic shame.

And time and death changed nothing, only hardened the judgement on poor Pavić.

So the order of events went like this:

- mumps
- their father's new job
- move to the house in town
- Licitar heart
- old P dead
- hunt birds in the rain
- K pisses on the dog

There was more to come, of course. I have thought about it a lot, and I am still thinking about it. There must be a great deal I have forgotten.

*　　*　　*

I was in the outbuilding looking over the Fićo when I saw Matthew pick his way across the courtyard: his hunched shoulders and loping gait. I watched him for a few seconds and then I said, 'Matthew!' quite loudly. It was perhaps the first time I had addressed him directly and he froze, then half turned as though in doubt that he had heard correctly. I said his name again. Cautiously he came to the door of the outbuilding and peered inside.

'Yes?'

'I need a hand. Do you mind helping me for a moment?'

'What is it?' He continued to peer into the half-light of the outbuilding as though I had something hidden there.

I indicated the car. 'The engine,' I said. 'Needs two people.'

'I don't know anything about cars.'

'Doesn't matter.'

'I can't drive, either.'

'No need to drive. Just do what I say.'

We stood and regarded each other. Matthew dropped his gaze first, he shrugged. 'Sure,' he said. 'In a minute, I just need to get something from the house.'

'You can put it on the shelf.' I turned back to the Fićo and opened the boot. Out of the corner of my eye I saw Matthew hesitate and then unwrap the bottle of wine from the shirt where he had it hidden and place it on the shelf, in as normal a way as he could manage. He turned round, looked at the car and said with some surprise, 'The engine's in the back?'

'Yes,' I said. 'That's how they made them in those days. Get into the driver's seat. Key's in the ignition.'

'I told you, I can't drive.'

'Just turn the key in the lock when I say so. One second only. Turn it back.'

I'd fitted the new battery. Now I attached the leads. 'OK,' I said.

'You want me to turn the key?'

'Yes, please.'

A click.

'One moment,' I told him. I tightened the battery connections. 'OK, again!'

Another click. I said, 'Put it into fourth gear.'

A short silence. I waited and then looked up. Matthew was fumbling with the gear knob. I moved to lean into the window and put my hand over his.

'Press the clutch down. OK, feel the gear, right and up. Good. Release the hand-brake. You know where that is?'

'Yes.'

I returned to the front of the car and rocked it back and forth. 'Now put it back into neutral and apply the hand-brake.' I cast around the outbuilding.

Matthew watched me and waited; after a minute he levered himself out of the driver's seat and asked, 'What are you looking for?'

'A hammer,' I said. 'Or a piece of wood will do.'

He went outside and came back. 'How about this?'

'Thank you. OK, let's have one more go.' I hit the starter motor with the piece of wood.

Matthew laughed. 'Is that all you wanted it for?'

'Yes,' I replied.

This time the engine whined. Matthew was twisted round in the driver's seat looking at me. I waved to give it another go. The engine coughed and turned over. I gave a thumbs-up. 'OK, let's leave it now.'

Matthew climbed out of the car, he came round to where I was standing at the engine. 'What was that all about?'

'To see if the engine was locked. Fortunately it's just the starter motor.'

He blinked. 'What does that mean?'

I explained as best I could. My English, some words were difficult—more technical words. I said, 'It means it will be quite easy to get the car going.'

'Cool,' said Matthew and nodded his head slowly several times while continuing to look at the engine as if he now understood something that he'd been pondering for a long time. He hung around for a while, watching me, not saying much. I'd finished what I planned for the day. I wanted to flush the fuel system before I took it much further and I needed to set the time aside for that. All I'd been doing was establishing how much work there was and I had the answer. I picked up a cloth and began to wipe my hands, which Matthew took as his cue. At the door he raised his hand.

'Thanks for your help.'

'Sure,' he said. He lingered a moment longer as though he still had something to say, then he turned and went, not quite able to summon the nerve to take his bottle of wine with him.

*   *   *

The house was empty, Laura and Grace had headed off after lunch, Laura said they planned to be back by early evening. I stood in the doorway, alone in the place for the first time. The house was much like all the older houses around here. The lower floor basically comprised one large room: kitchen area, dining table, fireplace and sitting area were all one. It meant that in winter the heat from the fire reached further; my house is exactly the same. The walls of the blue house had been washed down and cleared of cobwebs, though I'd yet to fix the patch of rotten plaster. I needed to get to a certain point with the outside jobs before I began on the inside. The walls around the kitchen area were cladded with pine and Laura wanted it removed. The wall around the fireplace alcove was stone, which Laura liked. She asked if all the walls were the same underneath the pine, or plaster and paint. I told her it was a stone house, and so the answer was yes. Could we remove the plaster and have all the walls stone? I said we could, only it would make the house very cold in the winter. Laura said it didn't matter. The house was a summer house and nobody would come here in the winter.

I remember this house in the winter. A couch and an old chair in front of the fire; there were lace cloths thrown over their backs and later, in another time, shawls and a crocheted blanket. A long, dark wood dresser covered the entire back wall. Gone along with the things that stood on it. Now I try to recover them one by one, like a game show contestant who's been given a glimpse of the goods he might win if he can remember them one by one. Invitations to christenings, weddings and funerals in the Church of Annunciation. A photograph of Krešimir and Anka's grandfather and grandmother when they married. She wears a long veil and a headdress, the points of which radiate outwards framing her head. Her dress is a good fifteen centimetres from the ground. On her feet a pair of large, flat lace-up shoes. All around is mud. A programme from the national theatre: a musical evening. A votive candle from the cathedral in Zagreb. A wooden Eiffel Tower and a model of a church also made in wood, complete with graves. A reproduction of a painting of a woman with naked shoulders and huge dark eyes. Vinka Pavić's collection of coloured glass animals with nubby little antlers. A boxed bottle of Stock 84 brandy, for which no occasion was special enough.

Laura had bought new furniture; she complained about the styles. No antique shops and yet there must be plenty of lovely old pieces, she said. What do people do with them? They burn them for

96

firewood, I replied. When they have finished with them, which takes a very long time. Laura had bought some large cushions to sit on, with a design of blue and green whorls. Only the old dining table remains.

The floor was tiled, the tiles were brown with a pattern of falling leaves. Marbles used to skitter across them and never halt. Laura didn't like the tiles either. I told her everyone had tiles; they were easy to clean. I said put rugs on top.

I stood in the middle of the room. From upstairs the sound of a tune. Three ascending notes, then down, up, down. Then the same three ascending notes. Then da, da, da-da. For a moment I thought Matthew had found his way back to the house without me noticing. I'd been listening to this song only the other day and before that I must have heard it a hundred or more times, here in this house. People said it was a song about drugs, but John Lennon said the name came from a picture his son painted of a girl at school. I waited for Lennon's voice but it never came. The notes simply repeated themselves and after a short while I realised I was listening to the ring tone of a mobile phone.

'Lucy In The Sky With Diamonds'.

I followed the sound.

'Lucy In The Sky With Diamonds'.

I put my hand on the banister and mounted the steps, automatically skipping the fourth, the one that creaked. I paused, went back and tested it. It still creaked. The same vinyl flooring made to look like wood.

The phone stopped ringing.

The door of the room at the top of the stairs where the parents had slept was solidly shut. At

97

the end of the corridor was Krešimir's old room, which Matthew now used. The door was open and I stepped inside. Empty except for a new pine chest of drawers and a pine bed. A suitcase lay open. Matthew's belongings scattered across every surface, the bed unmade, the window tight shut and a smell of unwashed clothing.

Krešimir had been exactly the opposite. Every object had its place, exact to the millimetre. If you moved anything, he grew mad. He even stored his records alphabetically. Like most of us he had a collection of porn, though his was ordered by date and hidden on top of the cupboard in a briefcase given to him by his father. Covers so pristine, hard to believe he used them for their intended purpose. The rest of us swapped magazines, but Krešimir would never lend his, just the way he never brought his Springsteen album to parties but only let you listen to it in his room. Do you know that in the top drawer of his dresser he kept a list of items he had loaned to his friends? A list of names written out in his crabbed, very neat and yet curiously almost illegible writing. If you ever broke something of his he'd make you pay for it.

I had forgotten these things about Krešimir. For some reason we all put up with it, I more than anyone, because back then I was his friend. We became friends, I suppose, because we lived close to each other and it suited us and because when you are young friendships go unquestioned.

The Pavićs' old bedroom smelt of Laura's perfume and the skin cream she used. A vase of wild flowers sat on the dressing table. Laura liked flowers. So many fields and fields, she said one day, left for the wild flowers to grow. 'I've never seen anything like it.'

Nor, in fact, had I. All the time I grew up here those same fields were planted with crops. The flowers were recent, a matter of years. These were some of the things I didn't tell Laura. Instead I showed her which fields she might walk in and which she should not, I hinted at difficult owners. She thanked me and I knew I'd been right. For somebody who spends as much time alone as I do, sometimes I can tell a lot about people. I guessed that Laura was one of those people who preferred the music of a lie to the discordance of truth.

A chair with some clothes draped on the back. A small heap of unwashed clothes and a screwed-up tissue on the floor. On the bedside table: a tube of Vitamin C, the effervescent kind, hand cream (I unscrewed the top and tried a little), two design magazines, a spiral-bound notepad. I picked it up: shopping lists for the house as well as the kitchen, a list of the names of towns and villages in the area. Some had ticks against them. A hairband.

Anyway I never lied to Laura. I simply let Laura believe what she wanted to believe. I told you I can't imagine coming to Gost and seeing the town and the people for the first time and it's true, I can't. But I knew Laura had a story about us, this place, the house she'd just bought. It was her story, one she told herself long before she came here. And if her story brought me work, then I'd help her hold onto it.

Never ask a question you don't need to, my father told me. To which he may as well have added: and never answer a question that hasn't been asked.

'Lucy In The Sky With Diamonds'. Once.

From the side table next to the bed Laura's mobile phone flashed. I pressed the button. *Are you*

99

getting my messages? Laura's husband. It's ironic the network reception around Gost is so bad. The man who invented radio waves and three-phase electricity was born right near here. There's a big centre with wooden huts containing reproductions of all his equipment and showing the experiments he conducted, although all that's a bit of a lie. Most of his work was done in New York, where he died penniless while Thomas Edison walked away with all the credit.

They say it's the mountains; sometimes the clouds clear and messages arrive, arrows out of the blue.

Scrolled back through the other messages. *Conor. Conor. Conor. Sorry, darling. Doesn't look like it's going to happen any time soon. Know more Friday. Sorry again. Going to have to hold off travelling. More later.* I scrolled forward. *Sounds like you're doing a wonderful job. Can't wait to see it. Once I wrap this up. Miss you.* The most recent said: *Looking at flights*.

Laura's messages to Conor. *Missing you. More to do on house than we thought. Try to get here soon.* Several saying more or less the same thing. *All swam in the river. Cold.* She didn't mention me. Only one text contained my name. *Hired man. Duro. Wonderful find. Absolutely all local info.*

From the window I saw Matthew walking down the road towards the house. I replaced the phone and went back down the stairs, picking up my tools from where they stood by the door. I waved to him from my ladder as he entered the courtyard.

*   *   *

Seventeen years old.

A wall, near the railway; from there you can watch the trains pass by on their way from Bihać to Split and from Split to Bihać. Six trains an hour. They carry grain and people. Now there are far fewer trains, Luka was right. And borders where there didn't use to be borders, so now the trains only carry grain. They travel through fields that used to be ploughed, but are now full of wild flowers because nobody dares to walk in them in case they put their foot on a mine and are blown to pieces.

We sit on the wall: Krešimir and I, Andro, Goran and Miro. We hold cigarette stubs pinched between freezing fingers, blow smoke rings without ever inhaling. Sometimes we share a beer between us. We have no trouble getting served in the bars, because around here nobody cares if you're underage, our trouble is we have no money. Girls walking alone cross the street rather than pass us by. Sometimes we throw comments, timed to coincide with the exact moment of passing, so that if she's to answer a girl has to turn round and confront us, which hardly any of them dare.

Because we are all virgins we talk about sex all the time, covering our ignorance with stories about other people caught doing it. We swap magazines and trophies.

A photograph of a blonde sprawled across an unmade bed. Pubic hair on her thighs. In the corner of the frame is a drying rack covered in kids' clothes. A pink bath mat on the floor by the bed, an overturned shoe. Miro says the woman is his aunt who lives in Split. We are appalled by the stretch marks across her stomach and joke about having sex with her. Someone makes a crack. What do you call a woman's twat after she's had kids? A manhole.

Andro asks if he can borrow the picture, promises Miro he'll bring it back tomorrow.

Another day Miro's brother holds his right hand under the nose of each of us in turn. Faint, sweet, briny. Pussy juice, he says. He laughs and walks away, waving his right hand in the air like a politician.

Miro's brother is older than us. He has his own car, a Fićo of course, like everyone else, except his is painted with stripes down the sides. Another day Miro's brother produces, with a flourish, a pair of panties he claims to have removed the night before. In front of us he sniffs them deeply. Andro grabs the panties, rubs them in Goran's face. Goran lunges at him and misses, grabs the waistband of Andro's jeans and slaps him on the back of the head, too hard. Goran gets angry and tells Andro to go fuck his mother. Then Andro gets angry and walks away. At the corner he turns round and rushes towards Goran with his head lowered, straight into Goran's gut. Goran is winded; bent double he sucks the air and dry-heaves. A passing car blows its horn; a couple walking towards us cross over.

Andro brings a stolen love letter, from one of the girls in our class to a boy we hate, and he reads parts of it out in a high-pitched voice. We see her in the street and run behind her calling out phrases from the letter.

A pack of three rubbers.

A bra, once. Stolen from somebody's washing line or perhaps from an older sister.

Dumb stuff. Until the day Krešimir brings Anka's diary.

Red leatherette, brassy little lock, easily picked. Small, round letters, crabbed to fit into the space for each day. Some are left blank and some are full. *Dear Sonja, Sorry I missed you yesterday.* Sonja had been the name of her best friend from primary school, who left to live in Sarajevo. Anka named her favourite doll Sonja, then a kitten. In her diary she wrote to Sonja.

Dear Sonja, Sorry I missed you yesterday.

We wear faded blue jeans and anoraks and our hair as long as we can get away with. Miro has a feather-cut he is proud of. Krešimir a leather jacket that once belonged to his father. Makes him look older. Everyone crowds around to listen.

Dear Sonja, Sorry I missed you yesterday. I was too tired by the time I got to bed to write to you. I had to go shopping with my mother and then do my homework. In school I read about something called astral flight, which is when your spirit leaves your body and flies to another country. Two people can meet like that. I am going to try it tonight and see how far I get. Then I'll write you a letter and you can practise, and then maybe we can meet.

The lads hoot. Andro drains the last of his bottle of beer, drop-kicks the bottle over the wall. Encouraged, Krešimir continues, works us like a street performer works a crowd, but I see that only later.

Dear Sonja, Dear Sonja, Dear Sonja.

Dear Sonja, Horrible day. All my friends at school have bras, but when I went to Vinka (my mother) and tried to talk to her she laughed and told me I didn't need one yet. But my chest really hurts. Do you wear a bra?

Here was the genuine thing, a beam of light shone through the darkness of female thought, like looking up the skirt of a sleeping woman. Someone makes to snatch the diary out of Krešimir's hand, but he holds it up out of reach. Someone else, Andro, I think, climbs up on the wall and grabs it from behind. For ten minutes they pass it around, reading sections out loud. Andro throws the diary to Goran, who throws it to Miro, who misses. Goran snatches it up again. A page flutters free.

Krešimir stands and watches, watches and smiles.

At the end of it, the diary lies in the road, on the edge of a puddle, face down like a fallen bird. I pick it up. 'What are you going to do with it?' I ask Krešimir. I am angry, too late. He knows it. I am ashamed and he knows that too.

'Put it back, of course.'

'Promise?'

'Yes. Don't be stupid. Give it to me. Before anyone gets back to the house.'

And I do. I have to collect a set of jump leads from my uncle's house.

It doesn't occur to me, not until late into the night: Anka would have found her diary and wondered how it came to be ruined. Somehow the not knowing, the imagining, seemed the very worst possible. Better I had destroyed it.

– mumps
– their father's new job
– move to the house in town
– Licitar heart

104

- old P dead
- hunt birds in the rain
- K pisses on the dog
- diary

Where did the hatred come from? For years I sifted the possibilities, the things that had happened, the sequence of events, examining each one for clues and then the characters of Krešimir and of Vinka, for some other answer. Was Krešimir looking for an outlet for his own frustration? What of Vinka? Somehow none of it seemed enough. Maybe hatred like that is bred in the bone, or maybe it belongs to some darker and more distant place.

In a long-ago past, wolves lived in the mountains to the north-east, now some say they are back. Acid rain has stripped the leaves and killed the trees in the forests to the north and this has forced the wolves south, if you believe it. The deer have moved south and the wolves with them.

Once we went on a school trip to a wolf sanctuary. It was the height of summer and the wolves were moulting: hanks of matted fur hung from their haunches. I was disappointed: these gaunt, furtive animals were far from the majestic hunters of my imagination, the creatures I'd read about in my stories of hunters and trappers. At the sight of us they rose and began to move away, except one, which ran in the opposite direction, towards rather than away from us. On its way it passed a large female who twisted her neck and lunged, you heard the snap of teeth in the air. The lone wolf feinted but carried on. One. Two. Three. Four. A raised hackle, a lazy lunge: every wolf did the same. Go away, they seemed to be saying, I don't want you.

The omega, who bore the brunt of the pack's aggression and frustration. The omega wasn't allowed to eat until the rest of the pack were finished, so this one begged for food from visitors.

Because she was the youngest, because she was a girl, because her brother had always been her mother's favourite. Or because she shared her father's easy temperament and now her father was gone. Or simply because she was there and there was nobody else, Anka became the last to eat at her mother's table.

8

Anka. By the swimming hole, in the shadow of Gudura Uspomena. For both of us, the first time. In the moment Anka tenses beneath me and afterwards squats at the edge of the swimming hole to wash the blood from her thighs. I watch, angry at my own clumsiness. Anka stands and turns. It is early summer, the water is freezing. Anka's skin is luminous, her breasts small, nipples turned to the sky. She shakes her hair and hugs herself, rubs the goose pimples on her arms. Then she comes back to me, tucks herself under my arm and kisses the underside of my chin.

In the pine plantation I make a home for us, like the dens Krešimir and I once built. I drag an old quilt and some cushions up there. Anka picks wild flowers and weaves them into the roof thatch. We lie on the quilt on our bed of pine needles, imagine a life in which we are alone in the world. I watch Anka sleeping in my arms and see how she laughs as she sleeps; when she wakes up I ask her why she was laughing and she tells me that sometimes her dreams are funny. That summer it never rains, never rains, not once, as though Perun saw us and took pity on our makeshift home. Times I take my gun, so my family doesn't ask too many questions. We meet after school and, when the school term is finished, we meet whenever we can. That summer I take a part-time job at the mechanics' yard. I have two more years of technical school. Some of my teachers were disappointed I didn't go to the *gimnazija*. They say I could have gone to college or even university, but I don't want that. Everything I know, everything I want, is here in Gost.

For Anka shooting rabbits no longer holds much interest, but sometimes I take a rabbit or a pigeon. At home they think I've lost my touch. In the late afternoon Anka gathers her clothes, dresses and leaves before me. This is not something we talk about, we know these afternoons are secret, our whole relationship is a secret, from one person, in particular—though we never say his name.

I lie back, close my eyes and listen to Anka's soft tread as she makes her way to the edge of the woods. I wait. Then in the blue of dusk I follow the path she has taken with my eyes closed, following her scent.

* * *

Friday, four o'clock, the Zodijak: empty except for Fabjan, watching television at the end of the bar. He grunted when he saw me and returned to the television. I ordered a coffee and leaned against the bar. On the screen an African woman dressed in a long black gown sat on a chair upon a raised plinth. She wore a judge's wig and a pair of headphones.

Now the camera focused on three men sitting side by side; each of them also wore a set of headphones. One sat with his back hunched and his elbows resting on his knees, staring straight ahead. The second leant back in his chair, his arms folded behind his head. The third appeared to be trying to catch the eye of someone in the room: he was smiling and flicking his eyebrows up and down. Behind them stood two men in blue uniforms. The picture changed again to show rows of men dressed in black gowns seated behind computer monitors. All of them were wearing headphones. The camera returned to the black woman in the judge's chair who began to read aloud from the piece of paper.

'Cunt.' Fabjan pointed the remote at the television, changed the channel then stalked off to the back room.

Let me tell you about Fabjan. Fabjan was not born in Gost. He arrived twenty-two years ago and brought with him a wife and a son. He had an uncle here, who lived alone. Fabjan and his wife moved in with him and when the old man died they had the house. People said he'd made money working in Australia, in the opal mines; the truth is nobody knew. I didn't live in Gost at that time and when I came back Fabjan was already somebody in town, part-owner of the Zodijak. His partner at the Zodijak was Javor Barac, who I'd known for years. Javor's father was head of the post office, my father's boss. Every year I'd see Javor at the post office Christmas party, both of us pressed into wearing our smartest clothes, in both our cases a pair of black trousers and a ruffled shirt. Different kinds of men: I'm talking now about Javor and Fabjan. Javor was as easy-going as Fabjan was flash, but they made a good team. By the time I arrived back in Gost Fabjan was driving the only BMW in town. His teeth were a whole lot better back then.

Javor looked up to Fabjan, because in that time of shortages Fabjan always seemed to be able to get hold of whatever he wanted: coffee, sugar, even a pinball machine. Later, a video, a Betamax unfortunately. All the same, no other bar had one. You needed to know somebody, or know how to work the system to do anything in those days, whether that was to become the owner of a private business, or buy a pinball machine or get hold of black market videos. I used to wonder why Fabjan needed Javor at all, but maybe he saw Javor as the quickest way to be accepted in Gost, because Javor's father was head of the post office and an important man in the town. The pinball machine made sure the bar was full every night. Full of lads in denim jackets and flared jeans, out of fashion everywhere but Gost. They played Turbo-folk day and night, drank beer and played pinball.

Fabjan's wife wears a fur-collared coat and heavy jewellery. She draws the shape of her mouth with pencil and smokes skinny menthol cigarettes. You could say she's good-looking, though she's grown heavy around the jaw and if she knows about the women Fabjan takes into the back room at the Zodijak, she doesn't let on. She has two grown sons and a hair-dressing salon. Last year when Fabjan arranged a party for her birthday he took over the whole banqueting suite of the hotel and hired a tribute band from the city.

People often wonder why Fabjan, with all his money, doesn't leave Gost and try his luck somewhere else: one of the cities on the coast where he could own a bigger bar, maybe a hotel even, and then he could really be somebody. Gost is such a small place for a man of his talents. Nobody has ever asked me, but if they did I would say to them: maybe Fabjan just likes it here too much.

*　　　*　　　*

I asked Laura, Grace and Matthew to come and have dinner at my house, a return invitation. Too few chairs: I spent time in the morning fixing one with a broken leg. I took a haunch of venison from the outside freezer, potatoes from the store and helped myself to some more of the chard at the back of the blue house. In my store I had some *ajvar* I'd made with aubergines and peppers from my own beds the year before. Later I went into town for bread and wine. In the bakery, the woman behind the counter—I told you she'd been married to a cousin of mine—as she wrapped my loaf, asked, 'Where's your friend?'

'Who?'

'*Engleskinja.*'

I shrugged. I said, 'I don't know her, I was just helping out.'

She stood with her hands on her hips and regarded me through narrowed eyes, shrugged to show me she didn't care and shifted her flat gaze to the next customer.

At home I made a caramel pudding and put it in the fridge. After I prepared everything for the rest of the meal I went upstairs to wash and change

110

into my other good shirt. Back downstairs I put on a Johnny Cash cassette and laid the table. I have a lot of crockery. My sister didn't want to take all this stuff to Zagreb, but my mother wouldn't give away the serving plates, vegetable dishes and gravy jugs which had been her wedding presents, so she left them with me, to bring when I followed, which is how she gave herself permission to leave. They also left me a pair of goats, which I slaughtered in the yard three days later and froze. The meat lasted me two winters.

I remembered Laura liked flowers and was outside picking cornflowers from the verge when she appeared beside me. She wore a shirt knotted at her waist, a long tiered skirt and a pair of espadrilles. Her hair was tied back and a pale blue shawl draped across her shoulders. She handed me a posy. 'Look, I've brought you some.'

'Thank you,' I said. I looked around. 'Are you alone?'

'You could say I'm the advance party.'

Inside Laura stood in the middle of the room and turned on the spot. 'Very compact, isn't it?'

'It was used for pigs,' I explained. 'Until I made it my house. Pigs, they don't like too much space, they like to stay warm. And I don't need much either.'

'I love that,' she said, pointing to where I had set rows of bottles into the plaster of a wall, their ends out. 'Clever. Do you think you could do that for me? Is that your family?' Now she was looking at the photograph on the windowsill. I crossed the room, picked up the photograph and handed it to Laura. In the picture I am about ten years old and I wear an enormous pair of heavy-framed glasses. They belonged to my father and I loved to borrow them, to play the clown. My father stands behind me, his hand on my shoulder.

'Daniela, Danica.' I pointed to my sisters.

'And Duro!'

'Exactly.'

'All your names begin with D?'

'Family tradition. My father—Dejan.'

'Didn't you worry about running out of names?'

'Why worry? Begin again. Same names, new generation.'

'Any special reason it's D?'

I said I didn't know. These are the things you don't think about until somebody else points them out. And even then, often there is no good reason, just the way it's always been, that's all. Laura said my family looked like nice people, handed me back the picture and carried on looking about the room. As I mentioned, it's much the same as the blue house, only smaller: stone walls, tiled floor, wood-burning stove. There's my armchair in front of the television. Next to the chair, a table where my father's glasses lie (because now I have to wear them every day to read) along with whichever book I'm reading—most recently one I'd borrowed from the library about the Galápagos Islands. Like many people, I knew about Charles Darwin and the different variety of animal species he'd found on the islands, but did you know people lived there, too? Slaves, convicts, stranded sailors, pirates. Once you were on the islands it was very difficult to leave, you understand, and life there was brutal with any number of crimes committed between such violent inhabitants. There was a man called Patrick Watkins, a marooned Irish sailor, who hunted and farmed on the Galápagos and whose

112

story was included in the book. I became very interested in Patrick Watkins. He stole a longboat and got out. There were other escapees with him in the boat, but when they arrived at Guayaquil, only one man remained on the longboat: Watkins. What happened to the others? Nobody knows. I spent some time imagining what could have taken place during that voyage. Had the other men been somehow swept overboard? Had one turned murderous, crazed by lack of water, the endless horizon, or the inescapable company of the others? Had Watkins killed them with his bare hands, one by one? What passed between them when they were down to the last three men?

Next to the table is a wooden chest where I keep my papers and where, when I have finished, I shall put this manuscript. On the other side of the room: the table where I eat my meals, laid for the first time with four plates. In the corner a gas stove, porcelain sink, wooden counter. A wooden plate rack hangs on the wall. Small pantry. Beyond that the wood store and outbuildings. On the windowsill, forgotten, the tiles I'd brought with me from the blue house. As I went to replace the picture, I covered them with my hand and slipped them into my pocket. I wiped the glass of the frame before putting it back and took a last look at my father. I remembered the smell of him—the hair oil he combed through his hair on special occasions, scented with limes, as now is Danica's wedding and those of all my cousins, baptisms and feast days and every Christmas I can remember. Gost is beautiful at Christmas. Glowing lights around the buildings. Blazing floats on the river. Drifts of deep snow, sculpted into dunes by the wind. I told Laura this.

113

'A proper winter.'

'I suppose so, yes, but very cold. So cold the rats go mad with it. They try to come inside to where it's warm. You have to stop them chewing their way in.'

'How awful.'

I continued. 'Not so much in town, but out here, yes. They cannot survive even in their nests. At night you hear them scrabbling against the walls, their claws.' I realised Laura was staring at me, her cheeks were pale, she was no longer smiling. I stopped talking. Matt and Grace were at the door.

'Gross!' said Matt. 'What do you do?'

'Trap them.'

'What do you use to trap a rat, like a giant mousetrap or what? How big would they have to be?'

'Not those kind of traps. You would need too many and besides, with the dogs around it's not safe. We use cage traps. Then you can catch a lot at the same time.'

'Don't you have to kill them afterwards?'

'By morning they are frozen.'

'That is totally gross.' Matthew grimaced.

'How do they die?' asked Grace. 'I mean slowly or quickly? What's it like to freeze to death?'

'Don't be ghoulish, Grace,' said Laura. 'Let's talk about something more pleasant.'

'Of course,' I said. 'Let me get some drinks.' I went to the kitchen and came back with a glass of wine for Laura. To Matthew I handed a Karlovačko.

'Matt?' Laura looked at him pointedly and with raised eyebrows.

'I'm seventeen.'

I said, 'One beer. This way a boy learns to hold his drink. How my father taught me. One beer for

114

my birthday. One beer at Christmas. Plus one plum brandy.'

Laura let it go. I went to the kitchen to fetch a Coke for Grace and she followed me in. 'Duro,' she said. 'How do they die?'

'You really want to know?'

She nodded.

'It's very cold, maybe minus ten or more degrees centigrade. Their metabolism slows down and they go to sleep, they die in their sleep.'

Grace looked at me. 'That's not true, is it?' Normally she could barely look me in the eye, now she gazed at me steadily. It was that look more than anything that made me tell her the truth. Because Grace was not a child. And because Grace was not her mother's daughter. Standing in the kitchen with her that evening I caught a glimpse of part of her nature I would grow to understand. Grace liked to examine every inch of her surroundings in a way that went beyond childish curiosity. Grace wanted to understand what the world was made of, the way that I had wanted to as a child. She watched and she listened. Grace asked questions. 'How do they die?' she said for the second time.

At first the rats huddle together. As the cold goes to their brains they become confused, stumble around the confines of the cage and into each other. The cold makes them aggressive. They fight, viciously, with what little strength remains. They try to burrow through the wire bottom of the cage. When their strength is all gone they lose consciousness, sometimes the ice melds their bodies into one grey mass. In the morning when I empty the cages, I pick them up by their tails and toss them in the river.

115

'Is that what you wanted to know?'
Grace nodded slowly.

*   *   *

'Does Gost mean anything? We were talking about it today.' We'd eaten the venison and were leaning back in our seats. Grace, thinking no one was watching, slipped pieces of food to Kos and Zeka under the table.

'It means visitor,' I told Laura. 'No, let me be more precise. In English you would say guest. Is that right?'

'Guest and visitor mean more or less the same thing. Although guest is somehow more special. Anyone can be a visitor. A stranger can be a visitor, somebody uninvited can be a visitor. A guest is somebody who is being treated in a certain way, the way you'd treat somebody you had asked to your home. Hopefully you'd treat a visitor that way too, but not necessarily. But what's the reason for the name, do you know?'

'Gost was once an important place, if you can believe it. This was the provincial capital for the district, when we were part of the Austro-Hungarian Empire. So people from many different areas visited or settled here. Also we are close to the mountains and they are the highest in these parts, so the crossing is hazardous, especially in the winter. Mountain people have a very strong tradition of hospitality. In such a place a traveller's survival often depends on it. Also, in those days of wars and bandits, I suppose people thought if they treated a stranger as their guest, then he wouldn't do them harm. Even today if you go from north to south or east to west you must

116

pass through Gost. That has also brought a lot of strangers here.'

'My husband said it was easy to get here from the city and the airport or from the coast, and that was one of the advantages.'

'And as you see, you are my guests.'

'Thank you. Gost in English sounds like a cross between guest and host.'

'Or ghost,' said Grace.

'In Cro that would be *duh*.'

Grace repeated the word several times.

'Correct. Or *prikaza*, well that would be more like a kind of vision. The last thing you would see before you died, something like that.'

'Like angels, or somebody who's already dead and who's been waiting for you.'

'That's how it is in the movies. Who knows what people really see.'

'I want to learn to speak Croatian. I'm already learning French and German. My teachers say I have a good ear,' said Grace. 'Could you teach me?'

I was about to say I would when Matthew, who'd left the room to go to the toilet, reappeared. 'Are those your guns?' he asked.

'Of course. You want to see one?' I went to the rack at the back door and came back with a .243 rifle I'd owned about ten years.

'What are they for?'

'Hunting.' I slid the bolt to check the carriage and handed it to Matthew.

'Hunting? No kidding!' He raised it to his shoulder and swung the barrel around, pointing in different directions. I reached out, took hold of the barrel and pushed it down. 'Never do that.' I showed him how to hold it, to press the butt into

117

his shoulder, rest his cheek against the wood and cradle the stock in his left hand. Matthew held the rifle and peered through the sights. 'Will you take me next time you go hunting?'

'It's not the season to hunt. But if you want I will teach you to shoot, hunting we leave for another time.' I removed the rifle from him.

'Maybe we should talk about it first, Matthew,' said Laura.

'What's there to talk about?' said Matthew.

'This is the country, not the city,' I told Laura. 'Here it's different. You don't have to worry. Besides Matthew is nearly a man.'

'It's not like there's anything else to do around here. What about this one?' Matthew had my old 7.62 in his hands and started to raise it, but I stopped him.

'Not that one,' I said. 'That one's not the right gun for you.' I took it from him.

'Then I guess it's up to you, Matt,' Laura said.

'Duro?' Matthew turned to me.

'Of course.'

I looked from Matthew to Laura and back—the two were so much alike. Light gold skin and hair, they actually seemed to shimmer in the evening light. The slanting eyes, which in Laura looked feline but made Matthew look sleepy, careless. High forehead, long eyebrows. Matthew wore his hair almost as long as his mother did and his face had a feminine delicacy about it. By contrast Grace's skin was paler, her hair darker and overall she carried more weight. Her nose was longer and rather sharp, she'd none of Laura's poise. I don't think I'd ever met a daughter so different from her mother. At that moment she was bent over kissing Zeka on the nose. She looked up at me, as though she'd felt the touch of my gaze. 'Can I take them out for a run?'

*   *   *

Laura and I were left alone at the table. Grace was with the dogs, Matthew, outside with an old telescope of mine he'd found, was looking at stars. I fetched more wine, filled both our glasses and took my place opposite. Laura had her elbow on the table and was cradling her chin in her palm, her head angled away from me. For a while neither of us spoke and I was glad that Laura was so relaxed in my company. She sat up straight and sipped her wine.

'I do worry about Matthew,' she said. 'He hasn't really grown into himself, if you know what I mean. Quite the opposite from Grace who is very easily amused.' The way she said it, stressing the word easily, made Grace sound defective. 'What was it like for you growing up here?'

I shrugged. 'No problem. We had the outdoors. So, freedom.'

'I grew up in cities. We moved a lot. I changed school four times so I was always the new girl and on the outside of things. By the time I had a group of friends we'd move on.'

'Your father's job was the reason you moved?'

'Yes and no. My father worked overseas, he was an engineer. Before that he had been in the Army, we lived in Germany. After he left the Army we went back to England. He worked for private contractors, he used to go away to consult on projects: Nigeria, Abu Dhabi, those kinds of places. Then he took an overseas posting. We only

119

went out once, to Thailand. My mother didn't like it and we came back. I was fourteen, I thought it was great and would have stayed but it wasn't up to me. The idea, I think, was that he would go back and forth, but I think the marriage was on its last legs and so he ended up hardly coming back at all. By all accounts it's pretty easy for men in Thailand. At first my mother did up houses to keep herself occupied while my father was away, it was more of a hobby. Later, after the divorce, she did it for the money. She'd buy a house, we'd live in it for a couple of years while she got it sorted, and then sell. I always lived in unfinished houses. As soon as the house was ready and I finally had my bedroom the way I wanted it, my mother would put the house on the market and we'd start again. Then we moved to Wales where she started doing up cottages to sell to people as holiday homes, but when the locals started burning English people's houses the bottom fell out of that market and she had trouble selling the place we were living in. Back to square one. That was the only time I ever lived in the country. Out there it was just the two of us, we never had guests that I can remember, and I never had the sense I could bring my friends home. She refused to eat out, even when we could afford it. So by the time I was in my teens I was off with my friends as much as possible. I dyed my hair and hung out in the town centre. It was hard on her, I guess. I went away to tech in Bristol and while I was away she changed. She had an offer on the house and decided she didn't want to move after all. She was happy. She's still there . . . huge vegetable garden. I envy you. I'd love to have grown up in the countryside, you know, properly . . . Did you live here all your life?'

'For some years I lived on the coast.'

Laura sighed. Her eyes were bright, she was quite drunk. 'Growing up in the same place, where everyone knows you and you know everyone. In and out of each other's houses with no locked doors. That's how it was, I bet.' She drained her glass.

'Something like that.'

Grace burst through the door; she was panting and out of breath.

'What is it?' asked Laura.

'It's Conor!'

'Has he called?'

'Conor's *here*.'

'What?'

'He's here! Honest!' said Grace. 'I saw the car parked outside the house when I was on my way back. He'd been off and come back.'

'Good heavens!' Laura was on her feet. 'I'm so sorry, Duro. We have to go. It's been a lovely evening.'

I didn't know what to say, so I said, 'No problem.'

At the door Laura said to Grace, 'But why didn't he wait inside?'

'He didn't realise the door wasn't locked.'

And they were gone.

For a few minutes I sat surrounded by the wreckage of the meal. Less than two hours had passed since they'd arrived. I stood up and cleared the table, scraping the leftover food into the dogs' bowls. On the back of a chair I found Laura's shawl, forgotten in her hurry. I folded it and put it on the windowsill.

When I'd finished with the table I went to the fridge and opened the door. There was the caramel

121

pudding. It had come out well, perfectly in fact. I upended the dish straight into the bin.

*   *   *

I woke from dreaming of a wooden boat and a crew of men. Salt-dried skin, a vaporous heat, the terrible stillness of the ocean. We were becalmed. Six men marooned in a boat, water all around and lawlessness, the seventh man, huddled together with us in that small space. For a few minutes I lay on my back watching the images and colours of the dream drain away. In the dream, as only in dreams, I was both Patrick Watkins and myself, at times looking at the other men, knowing only what he knew and at other times I was one of them, watching Watkins for his next move. But what was it Watkins knew? What had seemed absolute in the dream had gone. I was left with the taste of salt in my mouth.

A memory creeps into the space vacated by the dream.

Waking to the scent of burning pine needles: Anka and I. We have been dozing in our makeshift home in the pine forest. Up above us a breeze steals over the trees and slips down the valley towards Gost, where it is late afternoon: shops all shut, main road silent. Earlier I'd shown her how to roll a coin across her fingers and sometime later on she'd taken that same hand and put it between her legs, showing me how to do something she already knows. When her back arches and she cries, I take my hand away thinking I've done something wrong, but she pushes it back. Then we fall asleep and the coin, a cold spot, lies somewhere beneath our bodies and the quilt. We sleep and something

122

causes us to wake. A crescent of fire perhaps five or six metres long, as though somebody had been drawing a ring of fire around us. Not close enough to be a threat, and the pine needles are damp beneath so the fire burns slowly, only the drama of a cone as it spits and pops. I seize the quilt, run naked towards the flames and beat them out. Back in our shelter, Anka shivers. The quilt is scorched and useless. Above the trees, a blue sky, a sun full of fire: that same furious summer sun which burned now outside my house, slowly reaching through the space between the shutters.

9

Saturday morning after my exercises I walked directly to the blue house. There were the family, sitting at the table at the front of the house over a late breakfast. Grace saw me first. 'Hi, Duro.'

Laura, who had her back turned to me, looked round, cleared a frown from her face with a smile. 'Duro. I wasn't expecting you today. I thought we'd see you on Monday.'

'There's a lot to do,' I said. 'You left your shawl.' I handed it to her.

'Duro, this is Conor, my husband. Conor—Duro. Duro's the one I've been telling you about. He's come to our rescue. Haven't you, Duro?'

Laura's husband extended his hand and we shook. He was taller than me, which isn't hard, still he wasn't exactly tall. He was dressed in a T-shirt and a pair of khaki shorts. He looked odd with his white legs. He wore his grey hair short.

Pale blue eyes. Ten or more years older than Laura. A heavy-set man, the handshake he gave me was strong. Perhaps it was his natural grip, all the same I tightened my own in response, so that for a few seconds we stood locked together. Conor released his fingers first and let his hand fall to his side. 'Good to meet you, Truro.'

'Duro.'

'Du-ro,' he repeated. He sat down.

'Coffee?' asked Laura.

'Thank you.'

'Sit here. I'm finished anyway.' Grace cleared some plates and went into the house.

Conor said, 'Thanks for all your work.'

I nodded. Laura poured a coffee for me. We drank in silence, broken by Conor. 'So, Duro, how much more work is there to be done, d'you reckon?'

'Still more,' I replied. 'The roof is done, the paintwork and outside walls I'm doing now. This dead tree here must come down, before it causes damage. Also depends on what you want inside. One thing, the wall needs repairing. I have fixed the leak in the roof which caused the damage.'

'But the structure is pretty sound, is it?'

'The house is good. Built the old way. Will be here one hundred years from today.'

'Fabulous. Told you, Laura, didn't I?' Conor smacked his lips, leaned back and crossed his arms as though he had built the house with his own two hands and just eaten a piece of it.

Laura smiled and laid her hand on his knee. She turned to me. 'Take today off, Duro. Come on Monday. You've worked so hard and we'll probably stay at home today, so Conor can get a feel of the place.'

124

'No problem.' I finished my coffee, said my thanks and pushed my chair in. As I walked away I heard Matthew's voice. 'Hey, Duro, if you're not too busy today, do you think maybe we could go shooting?'

I thought for a moment. I had plenty I could be doing, nothing urgent. 'Sure,' I said.

'Brilliant!'

'What do you mean shooting? Shooting what?' That was Conor.

'Guns. What do you think?' replied Matthew.

'Are you really all right with this, Laura?'

'Mattie says he wants to.'

'OK, well, if Matt wants to then it's certainly none of my business.' Conor shrugged.

'It will be perfectly safe,' I said.

'I'm sure. Used to shoot myself, actually. Just didn't think it was your kind of thing, Laura. Or yours, Matt.'

'How do you know what my kind of thing is?' Matt looked dangerously at his stepfather who raised his hands in mock surrender.

'Hey, go ahead. Enjoy. I've no doubt you will.'

I needed some time to prepare the guns. Less than an hour later I returned carrying two rifles: my old .22, I'd had it since I was a child, and the .243. The door of the house was open and inside were Laura and Conor, he standing behind her in the middle of the room, arms around her waist, his face in her neck. He raised his head and kissed the top of her head. 'Man of few words,' I heard him say as I got closer.

'Who, Duro?' replied Laura. 'He is that. He likes to get on with the job. He's normally a tiny bit more talkative. Maybe you make him nervous.'

Conor laughed. 'Nice of him to bring your shawl

this morning.'

'Yes.'

'I think he's sweet on you.'

Laura laughed but said nothing.

'No really,' Conor went on. 'And the perfect pocket Romeo. At that size you could take him anywhere.'

'Oh shut up, twit!' Laura smiled and pretended to elbow him, pulled herself free and swung round to face him. He reasserted his hold around her waist and she looked up at him; as she did she caught sight of me. 'Ah, Duro.' She didn't miss a beat but widened her smile, as though the smile had been meant for me all along. 'I think Matthew's waiting for you at the back.'

I walked away. Behind me I heard a muffled giggle.

I carried the guns, Matthew walked by my side, issuing explosive sounds and shooting at the sky with the fingers of his right hand. He watched me as I set up at the far end of the long field that stretched out from the back of the house. I stapled the target to a board and leant it against the thick base of an oak tree. Next I dismantled the gun and showed Matthew the component parts, had him repeat each one. 'Keep the barrel pointed down. With many guns a bullet can travel more than a mile. You miss, you kill somebody in Gost. Understand?'

Matthew nodded.

'Understand?' I repeated.

'I understand.'

'Face the target always. Don't swing around. If you have a live round and it goes off maybe it's me you kill.' I looked at him. 'Understand?'

'I understand.'

126

Once he was holding the .22 correctly and had taken a few dry shots I loaded the magazine and allowed him to shoot. It's a light gun, no recoil to speak of. He placed the shots in a good group upon the target, which was all of twenty-five metres away.

'Nice shooting.'

He grinned, pleased with himself. 'Yeah, I think I got the hang of that.'

I let him take a few more shots. By the time the magazine was empty he was placing them all pretty much dead centre. He punched the air.

'Good. Now try this one.' I passed him the .243, stood back and folded my arms. 'Make sure you have the butt well into your shoulder.'

Matthew fired. The recoil jerked the barrel upwards and his shot missed the target, the bullet entered the trunk of the tree. 'Fucking hell!'

I laughed.

Matthew rolled onto his side, shielded his eyes from the sun. 'You knew that would happen.'

I smiled. Matthew laughed. 'Duro, you are one ace bastard!'

Matthew took five more shots and began to hit the target. I gave him another five. A tendency to tug at the trigger, otherwise he was pretty good. I moved him back another twenty-five metres, returned him to the .22 for five more rounds. I showed him how to change the magazine. If I hadn't already heard Conor's tread behind me I would have guessed who it was by Matthew's changed expression: his features slackened, except for a faint tightening of the jaw, his eyes hardened and glazed over.

'How's it going up here?'

'Fine,' I replied when Matthew didn't answer.

'What have you got there?'

I handed Conor the .243.

Conor weighed the rifle in his hand. He stepped forward and raised the barrel and set his eye to the sight. 'Mind if I give it a go?'

I passed him the full magazine.

'Safety catch?'

I showed him and he pressed the butt into his shoulder, moved around, making himself comfortable with the gun. Finally he squeezed the trigger. The shot was wide, but not far off. He squeezed off three more rounds, then flicked the safety catch back on. 'Let's see what you can do then, Duro?'

'Matthew was about to shoot,' I said, passing the gun to the boy.

But Matthew had heard the base note of a challenge in Conor's voice. 'I don't mind,' he said. 'Go on, Duro.'

'What do you say? Best of three?' said Conor.

'Then you must go first.' I handed the gun back to him. 'As my guest.' I turned and strode away from the target, putting another seventy-five metres between it and me. 'We shoot from here.'

Conor followed and took up a position beside me. Two shots were slightly wide: a four pretty much on the inside line and a three. The last one he placed in the centre. He shrugged as he handed the rifle to me, but he looked pretty satisfied all the same. 'Bit rusty still,' he said.

I placed three shots in the centre. Behind me Matthew clapped. I could feel the heat of his excitement. Conor ignored him, instead he said, 'What do you say, Duro? Three more?'

'If you like.'

The first of Conor's shots was a five, it lay

128

towards the outside of the centre ring. A four at eleven o'clock. Another four at five o'clock. He remained with his eye to the sight, assessing his score. Matthew snorted. Conor passed me the gun. Behind me Matthew willed his stepfather's defeat, it was almost audible, vibrating through the air. I aimed, fired three times and lowered the rifle. Matthew ran forward to fetch the target.

Six shots. Conor's three: one in the centre, the two fours at eleven and five. My score was the same: a five and two fours. One o'clock and seven o'clock. Even my five sat at exactly the same distance from the centre point as Conor's, though on the opposite side of the small ring. All my three shots were the perfect mirror image of Conor's. He peered disbelievingly at the target. He pushed his hair back off his forehead. 'Would you look at that? Never seen the like. Some kind of fluke. Guess we call it a tie.' Conor extended his hand.

*   *   *

I've had enough of Krešimir. When it comes, the end is a small thing, as endings often are. You have to look back to spot them, to see where things changed for good, the before and the after. I challenge him to a shooting match.

He makes jokes about my size, something he has never done before, the crossing of a line which has lain invisible and undeclared. During those years we ribbed each other about many things and not others, which surely is the nature of friendship. Now he does it in front of Andro, Miro and Goran. He enjoys it all, especially the way I have

129

to endure it, suck it up, the only possible way to make them stop. When they give up trying to get a rise out of me, there is Krešimir with another joke, to set them off again.

Another day he brings up the wild boar from so long ago I have forgotten. He tells them I once pretended to have shot a boar, when all I'd shot was a tree. I feel myself get mad. I tell him to fuck off, I tell him I can outshoot him with my eyes closed.

Between Krešimir and me: dark channels of resentment. We are awkward around each other and act like we're not; Krešimir watches me and I avoid his gaze. I spend as little time with him as possible, wonder if he knows about me and Anka and, if he does, how much. Surely it is no coincidence he has chosen to resurrect that particular incident from so long ago. I shot at the boar. Anka, practising ballet upon a rock, had jumped off and into my arms.

On the grass slope below the pine forest, the place where I shot my first deer. Alone because no one else is interested. I bring a home-made target. Five shots. If Krešimir's nervous it doesn't show, a pitying smile rests on his lips. What had seemed noble to me when I challenged him now seems pathetic. But condescension is an old trick of his.

I lose the toss. Krešimir shoots first and takes his time over it, repositioning himself between shots, deliberately making me wait. The five shots are good. Krešimir lays down his gun, folds his arms across his chest, pleased with himself. Mine is an old bolt-action rifle without a magazine. Four beats to expel the cartridge, insert and slide the bolt on a new bullet. The fifth to fire. I count each beat, a habit of mine. I reach twenty-five in as many

130

seconds.

We walk towards the target and the nearer we get the greater Krešimir's puzzlement grows: there should be ten bullet holes but there are only five.

In a moment he realises what I have done, which is to place every one of my five shots on each of his. A moment of stillness and then rage consumes Krešimir. He has a temper, it can break—just like that. He hides it well, so most people don't see it coming, but over the years I've developed a sense for it, learned the triggers—so to speak. He hates to lose, to be made a fool of even more. I knew what I was doing.

Krešimir, being Krešimir, goes for the softest target: Anka's old primary-school friend Sonja, come back to Gost on a visit with her family. Frizzy hair, a small waist and breasts, heavy thighs. She has the lips of an angel and thick-lashed hazel eyes, which contain the hint of something knowing. On the cusp of becoming a beauty and she knows it. Krešimir hangs around the house during her visits.

There was a time I suspected Krešimir was a closet queer. When we were younger it was his favourite taunt: fag, poof, gay. Now I think he simply despises women, as he despises all living creatures. Hard to imagine Krešimir tolerating the soiling nature of sex, the need to pleasure a woman. It's true though that Krešimir enjoyed a certain success with women, or rather success with a certain kind of woman, the ones who were impressed by his air of superiority and scornful smile, even when he belittled them. Sonja is that kind. Krešimir makes an assignation with her. Imagine the girl's delight, the edge it gives her over her friend Anka. He takes her to a café, buys her hot chocolate and reaches out his hand

131

to play with her golden curls. When Anka and her mother are out one afternoon, he brings Sonja to their house and fucks her on Anka's bed. Anka notices the smear of blood on the bedspread and puzzles over it, because she doesn't have her period. She washes the cover when nobody is looking and hangs it out to dry. Afterwards, whenever Sonja comes to visit, Krešimir leaves the house; he ignores her in the street.

Sonja leaves without saying goodbye; she never writes again.

*   *   *

Gost cemetery: row upon row of the dead, asleep under the cypress trees. It's the size of a football pitch, nearly full: the town authorities are searching for another site and trying to persuade people to be cremated. But we are the kind of people who love to mourn and anyway, who wants to prostrate themselves before an urn or throw themselves upon a vase? What we like is to build colossal black granite tombs, adorn them with votive candles and statues of the Virgin, plant them with carnations. The stone engraver in town advertises himself with an outsize gravestone in his front garden, that reaches up to the height of the first-floor windows. He's done all right for himself. In Gost cemetery the old heroes have golden stars carved on their graves, though these days a great many stars have been scratched away or else are hidden behind a vase, strategically placed by the visiting widows. There are new heroes now. Some relatives have paid a vast sum to have the likeness engraved on the black granite itself, but mostly there are photographs of the young men, in their uniforms and caps, mounted on the gravestones. The photos are all retouched in exactly the same way, most likely in the same photographic studio, so the heroes all have very rosy cheeks and lips and light hair.

To the east of the cemetery, the Orthodox end, there are a few stars, but no other heroes, pink-lipped or otherwise. The graves here are untended. The grass is cut by the men who take care of the graveyard, probably the same ones who removed the old vases and faded flowers years back. The graveyard is just like Gost, with rows of tombs instead of houses and paths in the place of streets. There are different neighbourhoods for the rich and the poor and for people who worship in one church and people who worship in another. Everything you need to know about Gost is here in the cemetery.

That Sunday in August women were in the graveyard scrubbing the headstones and arranging flowers. I filled the vase I'd brought and went straight to Daniela and my father. Some mould had grown in the crevices of the lettering and I pulled a cloth from my pocket and worked on it until the inscription was as new. *Dejan Kolak. 1.2.35—5.7.91. Daniela Kolak. 6.4.59—5.7.91.* My mother wanted more. Danica and I resisted. Now I don't really remember why, but it had something to do with the excess, the excess of funerals and weeping, the excess of loss. Also my father, unlike almost everyone else in Gost, hated funerals: the deliberateness of the mourners and the prurience of the onlookers, the piety of the widows. Whenever he was asked what somebody had died of he'd reply (with immense gravity), 'Lack of breath.' But his favourite joke was this: 'A woman goes to a fortune teller who tells her she will become a widow within the year. Her husband will die a violent death. The woman is shaken. She puts her hand on her heart, takes a deep breath and asks, "Will I be acquitted?" '

We posted death notices on electricity poles and lamp posts throughout Gost and after we buried them went home and drank a bottle of Chivas Regal, brought by my father's boss at the post office. In the corner of the room the television silently relayed a live football match from the other side of the world; mourners slid sideways glances at it. A near miss made one person shout out loud and stop to watch and soon he was joined by another man and then another: a silent vigil, not to death but to sport.

Nobody asked what my father had died of, denying Danica and me the opportunity to answer, 'Lack of breath.' People kept dying. In the year that followed funerals grew less and less lavish. My father would have approved.

On my way out I passed other graves of people I had known: a boy in my class who'd died of meningitis in 1970. The class accepted the fact of it with dry eyes; he'd not been especially popular: a habit of showing off his boils. The school janitor who electrocuted himself trying to fix the generator during a blackout. A friend of my father's who drowned in a freezing pond (dead drunk, said my father). Old Pavić's grave, where once a month many years ago Vinka Pavić, Krešimir and Anka would be seen laying flowers. Yellow carnations, orange stargazer lilies. Vinka Pavić's choice: bright, practical and plastic. A pair of lolling sunflowers in a glass jar, daisy chains looped over the headstone, a bunch of wilted cornflowers—that meant that Anka had visited alone. She took to reading there, sitting on the grass with her back against her father's tomb, sucking the end of her thumb, her nose in a book.

That year, the first and last year of my happiness, the summer months slid over us. Anka and I met often. No repeat of the fire in the woods, but sometimes I felt we were being watched. I did not speak of it to Anka. Whenever I passed Krešimir in the street he would stare at me hard but say nothing. In front of other people he behaved as though nothing had happened and sometimes I managed to persuade myself that we were all right with each other, then a day later we'd pass in the street and he'd give me the same unsmiling stare. After a while it ceased to matter: I told myself Krešimir couldn't hurt me.

That year a drought visited Gost as I told you; if you're old enough you might even remember it for yourself as all of us do; it began in April and stretched the summer by weeks at either end. The sky was a brilliant blue, the heat weighed heavily upon the town and people moved slowly. The deer came down from the hills in search of water. Anka and I claimed the swimming hole as our own. There the dry air of the ravine came scented with rosemary and fennel. On the riverbed trout and dace moved slowly around each other in an ever-shrinking space from which I took fish after fish with my bare hands. We'd cook them and eat with our fingers, pulling apart the charred skin and seared flesh, the crumbling bones. An afternoon as we sat by the swimming hole a snake, desperate to escape the heat of the scorching rocks on its underside, came down the hill and slithered up Anka's back and down over her breast, at such a speed neither of us had time to react. We watched it enter the water and swim away, head held high above the surface: a small, dark question mark.

Anka likes to model things in clay, things she gives away or arranges on her dressing table: small coloured hearts, discs imprinted with the pattern left by a walnut shell, a button, or scored with the whorl of a snail's shell, an open flower. Later she glues fittings on the back and makes them into brooches. One of the hearts she gives to me and I carry it in my pocket.

Anka's hair smells of vinegar. She says it makes her hair shine. Anka's hair is deep brown, the colour of good earth. I lift a hank of it and let it fall from my fingers, like dark water. She wears it in a pageboy and has a habit of blowing her fringe upwards when she's too hot. She's lying on her back with her arm raised writing my name upon the sky. That day she showed me a picture of her father when he was a young man, found in the dresser drawer. Old Pavić—who was at least fifteen years older than his wife—standing on a grassy lakeside wearing black swimming trunks, the remains of a picnic laid out on the grass just behind him. I know this place well, near Šibenik, where lakes rise, linked by rapids and waterfalls. Syndicates of workers from the city holiday there in lake-shore cabins, sit on deckchairs submerged in the water and fish, drink beer and gorge on liver sausage.

In the centre of one of the lakes, behind a screen of cypresses, lies an island monastery. The monks there keep an ancient copy of Aesop's fables, which they show to visitors. Some years ago I went on a

136

pilgrimage to see the monks' book. I rowed myself over and wandered across the lawns. The monks were still there, they'd been protected from the madness by their circle of water, and, I suppose, by their vocation. I waited for a challenge; when none came I found the main door of the building. All was quiet: the time for prayer. A monk detailed to welcome visitors guided me to the library where the manuscript was stored. He put on a pair of white cotton gloves and one by one he turned the pages to reveal each illustration. The avaricious man and the envious man, each of whom prays to Jupiter for his heart's desire. To punish them Jupiter agrees, only if the other receives double the gift. The avaricious man, dwarf-like and dressed in dark robes, asks for a room filled with gold, is grief-stricken when his enemy receives twice the amount. But the envious man, thin and long-nosed, has already been overcome by the sight of the first man gazing at his room of gold. So he asks to be made blind in one eye, that the other may be blinded in both. 'There are people like that,' I said to the monk. 'God doesn't punish them.' He walked me down to where I had tied my hired boat and threw the line to me. As I rowed away, counting the oar strokes, I watched him disappear back through the cypress trees.

In the photograph old Pavić leans against a wooden drinks kiosk, flexing his muscles for the camera. His dark hair is oiled and parted in the middle, you can see the tracks of the comb. A handsome man. There's something uncomfortable about looking at pictures of your parents at a time when they made each other happy. This is a photograph Anka and I should never have seen, because it tells of what Vinka had once seen in her husband and of which she doesn't want to be reminded. No wonder she hid it away in a drawer. Theirs was an ordinarily unhappy marriage. Pavić had done well enough, but Vinka blamed him for her unhappiness. Once a beauty, she could have married any man she wanted, but she squandered her worth (as she saw it) on Pavić and then he died, leaving her a young widow in a town where widows are shuffling shadows. And because now money is short Vinka takes a job doing the books at the fertiliser factory. She has a diploma in accounting, talks of leaving for the city, to Split or Sarajevo, and she drinks. I have known drinkers, some of my father's friends are drinkers. It is there in the carefulness of her movements, the sudden rages, the bruises on Anka's upper arm.

Vinka Pavić is an angry woman and her anger shows in the set of her teeth, the lines around her mouth into which her lipstick bleeds, the way she folds her arms. When she laughs it is to mock and in this she finds an ally in her son. But Anka, Anka was born with joy in her soul, to which they feel she has no right. Behind it all, as with so many things in life and in death, lies envy. In the end it gets the better of them.

Vinka in one of her rages: a letter sent to her place of work, a letter about me and Anka. Anka pleads, 'But nobody knows.'

Vinka twists her mouth and holds the letter in front of Anka's face. 'Somebody knows! Somebody knows! Everybody knows!' With her free hand she reaches out, but instead of slapping Anka she scratches, scoring the skin of Anka's neck. And Krešimir, watching silently from the top of the

138

stairs, turns away.

My mother works at the fertiliser factory, not in the management offices but on the shop floor. Vinka rarely speaks to her, but on this day, when my mother's shift is over, there is Vinka waiting. Vinka has brought Krešimir. My mother doesn't know what it can be about, but dares not ask and walks them home to see my father. All the way her varicose veins hurt. In the hills high above the house Anka shows me the scratches on her neck.

My father is not angry, still something must be done. When the talking is over he says, 'Go to the coast. Find work until the end of the summer.' He even offers to call his estranged brother. Danica has married Luka and moved out. Daniela's tears leave dark streaks of mascara down her cheeks. My mother's nature is to accept what she sees in front of her. Some things have consequences. Danica and Luka come over. Luka agrees with my father. 'The girl is underage. If they want they can make it bad for you.' The living on the coast is good, Luka knows many things. 'Forget her, for two years at least, my friend.' He winks. 'Come back and marry her if you still care.'

*   *   *

Next to old Pavić is a place for Vinka, and next to it is Krešimir's grave. The date of his birth is carved into the granite. September 1961 to 20–. Two blank places waiting to announce the year of his death. The graves are in one of the better parts of the graveyard, though perhaps not the best. Still, a long way from the eastern wall where the explosion took place three years back. The police said it was

139

an abandoned grenade and dropped the case. The blast wrecked a number of headstones, but they were only headstones belonging to the dead of those families who'd already left Gost.

10

Conor stepped out of the house. He was carrying a holdall, which he placed on the back seat of his rental car. This was now Monday, I'd been at work no more than two hours. He came and stood at the bottom of the ladder. 'Good job you're doing, Duro. Can't thank you enough,' he said and extended his hand. I climbed down the ladder, laid the saw I was using on the windowsill and we shook hands. Conor shaded his eyes as he looked up at the dead tree. 'Good luck with that. I wish I could stay to help. Maybe Matthew could give you a hand. You could ask him. Never know. You did teach him to shoot, after all.'

I nodded.

Conor half shook his head and seemed about to say something more, changed his mind and went inside. I climbed back up the ladder and continued what I'd been doing: removing the dead tree's limbs, ready to bring the whole lot down. Ten minutes later the family came out. Grace and Laura kissed Conor, Matthew shook his hand and muttered goodbye. As soon as the car moved off Matthew turned away and went back inside. Laura and Grace stood waving until the car was gone from view. That was the first and last I saw of Conor the whole summer.

An hour later when I went to the field at the back of the house, easier to piss there than in the family's bathroom upstairs, I found Laura sitting against the walnut tree; she was smoking a cigarette, jabbing with the forefinger of her other hand at the root of the tree. She started when she saw me and then said, 'Oh Duro, thank God it's only you. I thought it might be one of the kids.'

I said nothing. Laura stood up, took a last puff of the cigarette, threw it to the ground and dusted off her hands. I walked over and ground it out. I glanced at the place on the tree she'd been jabbing with her finger; there was a line of ants coming from the loose earth around the base up the trunk of the tree, now a line of dead ants, their living companions racing around them in panic. I said, 'I didn't know you smoked.'

'I don't. Well obviously I do. Occasionally. It's no big deal. I just don't need Grace on my back about it. Frankly I'm a bit out of sorts right now.'

'Out of sorts?'

'You know: annoyed. Well no,' and she continued, 'more like—disappointed, fed up even. I just didn't imagine when we bought this house that it would be me and the kids out here on our own.'

'Your husband had to go back for work?'

'I just wanted a family holiday for once. So Conor and Matt might have a chance to work things through. I thought if they had some time together . . . oh well,' she said. 'Fuck that.'

I didn't reply, I felt sad for Laura, but then I thought I understood why Conor found so much in his work to occupy him. Laura allowed him a place by her side as her husband, but not as father to her children. Matthew was a teenage boy and needed

141

a firm hand. What was Conor to do? But I didn't say any of that, instead I said, 'Let me show you something.' I stepped forward, opened the double doors to the outbuilding and pushed them both back, positioning a couple of bricks to stop them closing again. Light filled the space. I went forward and lifted the cover of the Fićo. I'd managed to put in a good few hours here and there and so far I was pleased with my progress. The car's mechanics were simple and because it had been stored inside had survived the sixteen years remarkably. I'd given the bodywork a polish even though I still had plenty of work to do on the engine. I did it because I liked to see the car looking as it once had and because I knew Laura would be impressed. I've worked on enough houses to know that it's the first coat of paint or plaster that makes the difference.

I said, 'Not ready yet, but soon. First I must change the cables and hoses and then we test it. Maybe you can drive.'

Laura turned to me and smiled.

*   *   *

Kos lies on the floor by a cold stove. Her eyes are open, though she is fast asleep. Eighteen years ago she was a pup of five months tied to a tree, waiting for her owner's return. That was how she came to me. I'd already brought her home when I realised why someone had left her to die: she was blind. They thought a blind dog would never be any good for hunting, but they were wrong. At the top of her game Kos was the best tracker I ever knew. Now take Zeka, her son, he's a great hunting companion but differently so. He loves the chase and races through the woods with his nose high. He's best at the start, at locating the herd. But Kos could track a single animal, hunt it down all night, long after Zeka grew bored with the whole game. It's the difference between the sexes, some say: the sensory system of the male designed to catch the scent of a bitch in the wind, and the female who can follow the trail of a lost puppy. And Kos's useless eyes made her sense of smell doubly good.

This is as I told Grace. She'd seen us coming up the road for our evening exercise and walked with us part of the way. A farmer's trailer had been left at the side of the lane; I called a warning to Kos who slowed down, swinging her head from left to right in the way she did, until she located the obstacle. When I told her, Grace couldn't believe Kos was blind, so I called Kos to me, held up my index finger and moved it in front of her eyes. Kos never blinked and nor did her eyes move.

'But how does she find her way around?'

'She knows the roads, the fields and the hills. She has lived here since before you were born.' At that moment Kos jumped a ditch and ducked the wire into a field. I explained to Grace, 'For instance, she knows that there, right after the bend in the road, there is a good place to cross into the field where she might pick up the scent of a rabbit. She'd never catch one, but it makes life more interesting. And further ahead where there's loose gravel on the road, that means we're nearly home. She relies on what she feels and smells. Sometimes on Zeka, who she follows. Sometimes on me.'

At the next bend Grace said, 'I'd better go home. Mum's made lasagne.'

'See you tomorrow,' I said.

Grace turned to go and then turned back. 'Why don't you come and have supper with us? I bet Mum won't mind.'

'Another day,' I told her. 'Kos and Zeka want their run.'

'You can come on the way back.' Despite her insistence, I shook my head. The last few days, Conor's visit, had changed things. I wanted my own company again.

'I'll see you tomorrow.'

'Yeah, sure . . .' She rubbed the toe of her shoe on the surface of the road, her head bent.

'Are you OK, Grace?'

She looked up, shrugged. 'Yes,' she said and made the strange little humming sound which meant she was unhappy. I watched her go, I called her name. She stopped and turned.

'Maybe we go to the coast soon to find tiles for your fountain, yes?'

She nodded, smiled briefly and ran on.

Kos came to me after I returned home from the islands. I'd been gone ten years by then. I'd missed my last two years of technical school and my chance for college, if I'd ever wanted it. A year working on my uncle's boat and then military service. The first year I was based in Vojvodina. Flat fields of corn and wheat, where the snow covered the ground many months of the year. We trained shirtless and the barracks had little heating. For R&R we went to Novi Sad, where there was a theatre that played entirely in Hungarian, and where I once spent an evening escaping the cold and my drunken comrades. That's what I remember most. When that was over I reapplied to stay in the Army three years more. I exchanged the plains of the north for

144

the fruit groves of the south. After that I didn't go back to live in Gost, instead I went to the islands, of which I had heard so much. People had told me there was a good life to be had there and besides I no longer felt any desire for Gost, I'd changed that much.

The Army changed me.

In that place strength was everything: if you lacked backbone you faked it, and if you couldn't do that you made sure never to catch anyone's eye in case they chose to make something of it. I'd always had some degree of self-control, but now I gained a new command of myself. Restraint was the way. There were bullies and their victims, and then there were the rest of us. In the Army there was nothing you could do to help the ones who were picked on. Some of them even seemed to enjoy the humiliation. A few learned to stand up for themselves. That worked if it happened soon enough, before the pack had its claws into you. Or you could go your own way. One guy spent the entire time playing a little tin flute. When it was stolen he produced another one. When someone took that one, he came up with another, like a magician (he had a box full of them somewhere). He never said a word, never commented that they kept disappearing and in the end whoever had it in for him decided to leave him alone. One or two guys managed to pull on whatever strings they had on the outside. The rest of us waited it out. You did what you had to to survive.

I wrote to Anka through Danica, but Krešimir rifled Anka's belongings and showed my letters to Vinka. There was trouble. Danica wrote saying things were impossible. For Danica's sake, for

Anka's sake, for my own sake, I stopped writing. The last letter from Anka came several months later, a bundle of letters in her round schoolgirl hand, written over the weeks. I kept them the whole year I was in Vojvodina and then when the time came to move on, I burned them. That's how much I had changed.

I changed in order to survive. You could even say I did well. I stayed on in the Army. And yet, even in those years, Krešimir infected things. The one part of me I failed to suppress was still at war with Krešimir. I couldn't stand to give him the satisfaction of knowing I grieved and I went on this way for years: joining the Army, staying away. I did it to spite Krešimir; he retained his grip on my imagination and in that way I'd become his creation.

Sage and rosemary, boat diesel, decayed fish, cooking oil, a salt breeze: the coast smelled of these. Work was easy to find. For a while I waited tables where I learned English, also Italian and French. I discovered a talent for languages. I made extra money translating menus, advertisements and brochures. I could have made more money doing that kind of work, but I enjoyed café life, the foreigners, the comings and the goings. The boss asked me to give his son English lessons and I did. We read English books together, books left on tables by the tourists. Most were trash, some were good. After a while I grew bored. I moved islands and went back to the boats.

Anka no longer wrote, or if she did the letters went to an address from which I'd long gone. Nothing was forwarded.

Life on the boats suited me. I liked the early mornings, the silence, the days that passed in a blaze of light, the purity of the blue skies and of the darkness that followed, summer storms, the sound of rain on the sea. At one point I worked an old ketch—I told you—in Hvar; we used to take the tourists on a tour of the smaller islands and stop for swimming and snorkelling. Mornings I rose ahead of the others to ready the boat, hose down the decks, prepare the ropes and the rig although the skipper rarely bothered with anything but the motor. After one season I'd had enough of that life, too. I craved my own company. I spent my savings on a small boat and joined the water taxis ferrying passengers to the various beaches. This way of being suited me. If I didn't want to talk I pretended I didn't understand what my passengers were saying. The tourists forgot their books, suntan oil and sunglasses just as they did in the restaurants and in my lunch hour I read. I motored up and down the same stretch of water and dreamed of a life: a shepherd's hut, cliffs. I sold the boat, hitched to Zadar and took a ferry over to the island of Pag. Pag was everything I had been searching for. I found a cottage surrounded by sandy, salt-soaked, barren earth with no road leading to it, only a small slipway and a boat. Salt corroded everything, even the rocks. I planted basins of tomatoes, made a pair of beehives and kept bees; they feasted on the sage, which grew everywhere.

*   *   *

Tuesday I raised my fist to knock on the door of the blue house: inside I heard Grace and Laura.

'Nowhere near here, darling.'

'Where then?'

147

'Much further away. Where there were Muslims. It's not even the same country any more. None of those sorts of things happened here, or we would never have bought this house. Think about it. Anyway, it was for ever ago. You were only just born, it's all long forgotten now.'

I knocked. Laura turned round. 'Here's Duro. Ask him if you don't believe me.'

'What do you want to know?'

'Grace has been filling her head with all sorts of things. I'm just saying there was never any fighting here, it was all far, far away. In another country. These are decent, good people, you've met them yourself.'

Grace didn't reply. She looked at me. I said without hesitation, 'Gost is a safe place. You have nothing to worry about.'

'There you go, darling. Straight from the horse's mouth. Now you can stop worrying. Good heavens, this isn't Africa.'

'I never said I was *worried*,' Grace replied. Then to me, 'Where then?'

'East,' I said. 'A long way away, as your mother says.'

Grace nodded, she trusted my answer.

'Sorry, Duro, did you want something?' asked Laura.

'The tree.'

Laura stood up. 'Come on, Grace, let's go and watch.'

The dead tree came down without so much as a groan, the earth beneath us shook with the impact. I'd secured it with a guide rope and, having done most of the work with a chainsaw, gave Matthew the final strike of the axe. He pushed his baseball

148

cap back from his forehead and grinned. The tree lay across the verge, its crown in the road. I hadn't wanted it to come down too near the house, but now it was blocking the road. 'Come on,' I said to Matthew.

'What will you do with all that wood?' asked Laura.

'Firewood,' I replied. 'We can store it in the outbuilding.'

'You take it, or at least as much as you need.'

I nodded. I turned to the boy. 'Shall we deal with it?' As well as workman's gloves I gave him a pair of goggles and ear muffs, though in fact I was the one who'd be working the saw. I put another pair of muffs on my own head, erasing the sound of birdsong, of Laura and Grace's voices. I pulled the cord on the chainsaw and the motor started up; the howl of the saw filled the air and the space inside my head. I ordered Matthew to stand back while I worked, bending, twisting, moving all the time, holding the dangerous chain well away from my body. The possibilities of what a chainsaw can do are never far from the mind. But I enjoy the bite of the teeth into wood, the flying yellow sawdust and the antiseptic smell of wood resin, the satisfying pace of work. First I cut the branches away near the trunk and then cut them into lengths, those of a size I could use for firewood, the rest, the smaller branches, twigs and leaves to be turned into a bonfire sometime in the winter when the family was gone. After the first branches were off I waved Matthew forward to haul them away into the field behind the house. He was enjoying himself, you could see. Then I cut the trunk itself into sections. After a while I turned the chainsaw off and the peace of the day resumed around us: pale blue sky and the hum of insects, the flap of a woodpigeon's wings, the laughter of a magpie mocking our hard work. Finally we rolled and heaved the giant logs to the side of the road, where we sat on them and drank a glass of water, after which I patted Matthew on the shoulder.

'Shall we finish?' I said.

And the boy replied, 'Let's go for it.'

*   *   *

Early next morning we drove to Zadar. The thought of Zadar had made me want to see the city again. I used to travel to and from Zadar when I lived on Pag, sometimes when I needed nothing but a break from my own company, to sit outside a café and be served a coffee. The inside of the car smelled of leather. We took the road west out of Gost, which leads directly to the coast and then follows the water's edge down to Zadar. Laura handled the wheel confidently through the twists and turns of the road, past the saw mill where I once worked, up to the summit of the mountain. There you pass through a short tunnel beyond which comes the first view of the sea, and of Pag: smooth, pale and elongated, half submerged in the turquoise water. There is a place where you can park and look at the scenery, which is what we did. Laura read aloud from the signboard there, about the Karrens and sinter-pools, the sink holes, caves and pits which lay below us. I took myself off a small distance and gazed at Pag. So many years since I had laid eyes on her, I had wondered what I would feel when this moment came, but it was not as I imagined. The feelings did not come.

We climbed back into the car and drove on to Zadar. The green of the mountains turned to rock and wild rosemary. Villages clung to the base of the cliffs like swallows' nests. At the side of the road people sold jars of honey and lavender oil.

At Zadar harbour we stopped for coffee and ate *burek* walking along the front looking at the boats. The smell of diesel, salt and fish was the same as it had always been and my stomach tightened with the odour of the memories it brought with it. There was a pressure in my bowels. I wondered if I would see anyone I knew, and if I did if they would be the same or changed: missing an arm, a leg, or maybe just some part of their soul.

Lumbering, steep-sided ferries headed for the islands. The old Italianate buildings on the harbour front had been painted and restored; the trees were trimmed, flowers bloomed beneath them. The old town was another story: football slogans defaced the old stone of the entrance. From somewhere came the wail of a car alarm. From an open window music: the voice of an American crooner from the 1950s. Inside the city walls the streets were littered, building façades chalky and chipped, the fountains ran dry. Strings of washing fluttered like banners from high windows. Some shops had their windows papered over, a few gift shops were open. Cats. Bony and scarred, they slunk and stared dangerously up from beneath the cars, watched us from high windowsills. I threw the paper from my *burek* into a skip and found it full of strays picking over the rotting garbage. One leapt out right past my shoulder. I have always had a faint unease around cats, especially numbers of them: something

151

in their sliding movements, voices like a baby's cry.

Once, for a while, Gost was overrun with stray cats and dogs. People abandoned their pets; the animals turned feral. The cats fucked, bred, survived. The dogs mourned their masters, begged from strangers, grew thin. Then after a while the dogs found each other and joined to form packs: they turned on the cats.

I saw a cat once, cornered by a pair of dogs, a German shepherd and another dog, a spaniel whose golden hair was matted with filth. A cat, when it is angry or frightened, simply looks ridiculous. The ears of the cat were flattened against its scalp, its eyes were narrowed and its teeth bared; it warned the dogs with a throaty, high-pitched whine that rose and fell like a piece of faulty machinery. The dogs were growing bolder, taking turns to run at it. One had a bleeding muzzle.

Laura was relaxed, enjoying the day. She stopped to admire a courtyard, painted a deep red. Columns and stone stairs, in the centre stood a monument like an urn. Someone had drawn a penis on the red wall. I stopped to ask a waiter who was serving tables in a square where we might find a shop selling tiles and he issued directions in a grave manner which encouraged my confidence. In a street behind one of the smaller squares, between two shops selling ceramics and souvenirs, we found a tile shop. From her pocket Grace brought the red quartz and the glass tiles, but we couldn't find a match on any of the shelves. I spoke to the young attendant. She told me to give her a minute, made a telephone call during which she nodded a lot. *Da. Da.* She replaced the receiver and led us out to the storerooms at the back where she tapped on the boxes of discontinued lines. Beneath layers of dust, we found what we were looking for.

On the harbour front Laura found an upmarket pizzeria she liked: chairs and tables set out under a yellow-striped awning and with a view of the harbour. I had waited tables in a place like this, though not in Zadar. On the table Grace arranged and rearranged tiles upon the tablecloth. Matthew read the menu through a pair of dark glasses.

'Do you know Zadar well, Duro?' Laura asked after we'd ordered.

'I used to come here.'

'It's a long drive from Gost.'

'I didn't live in Gost, I lived over there.' I pointed out to sea.

'On one of the islands? What took you there?'

'Nothing, an idea.' I shrugged. 'I had a cottage close to the water.'

'Sounds wonderful. And you came here on the ferry?'

'Yes, there isn't much to do on the islands, in winter even less. And some things you need to come here to buy. In fact there is a bridge. The time I lived here it was in a bad way, but it has been renovated recently. So once you could drive there and now the same again. Takes about a half an hour.'

'We should go.'

'Another day.' To change the subject I began to talk about the bridge, how salt and wind ate the concrete and steel until the whole edifice nearly collapsed into the straits. On the table Grace had arranged the tiles into the shape of a bird, while Matthew, whose mood had generally improved since Conor's departure, seemed sulky and had

153

barely spoken. On our walk through town he'd spent most of the time hunched over his mobile phone and now during the meal he brought it out again and carried on playing with it. He ignored Laura's suggestion to put it down while we ate and I saw her hesitate, afraid to ask him for a second time. Matthew's mood was faintly dangerous, as if he was spoiling for an argument. After a while Matthew stood up and walked to the harbour edge where he threw pieces of a bread roll to the fish.

Three giant pizzas were placed in the middle of the table. We helped ourselves. Grace ate with gusto, keeping an eye on the food, ready to pounce in case it scuttled away. In between mouthfuls she sucked her drink noisily through the straw. Otherwise she was silent, totally absorbed in the act of eating, she never looked up from her plate. When we were all full she helped herself to the last slice of pizza.

After coffee we took a walk around to the other side of the harbour. Sheets from a magazine floated on the surface of the water: a naked woman, open-legged. Out of a cloudless sky the sun beat down and the blood in the veins of my scalp throbbed. The air was dry and filled with colourless fumes, and I felt a little nauseous after the meal and the coffee, which had been too strong. At a stand outside a shop Laura and Grace tried on hats while I sat on a bollard to wait. They switched and swapped hats, looked at their reflections in the small mirror on top of the stand. Grace picked a red straw hat with a brim that dipped down at the front and gave it to her mother to try on. Laura, who was standing with her back to me, put the hat on her head and at that moment chose to turn round. Maybe she was looking for Matthew, but it was me she found watching her. She smiled and opened her arms and tilted her head to one side, as if to ask, 'What do you think?'

I couldn't speak: something about the gesture, the cast of the sunlight, most of all the red hat. I drew a sharp breath and then breathed out again, hard. My mouth was dry and, for several seconds or so it seemed, my heart stopped. Then both my heart and breathing started up again violently. I could hear everything: the cry of a gull overhead, the grinding of gravel under the feet of passers-by, the whine of a winch somewhere and the sound of the blood rushing to my brain. I stood up and walked towards Laura, my legs were practically shaking. I said without thinking, 'Please let me buy it for you.'

'Don't be silly.'

'Yes,' I insisted, maybe too firmly because Laura blinked with surprise, so I added, 'To say thank you for lunch and this very nice day. It's only 50 kunas. If you like you can buy the ice cream.'

Laura smiled and shrugged. 'Well in that case, what can I say?'

'You can say yes.'

'OK, then yes and thank you.'

It's interesting what you remember and what you forget and what gets hauled up from the past when you aren't expecting it. How does it work? I don't know. So many years and I'd never once thought of Anka's red hat, the one she owned in the last year she lived in the blue house. She'd worn it through two summers, it had been her favourite thing. When Laura turned, for a moment, for just one moment— it might have been Anka standing there.

After I'd paid for the hat we walked on along

155

the harbour front. A scattering of clouds appeared from nowhere and the sun disappeared, so instead of wearing the hat Laura carried it in her basket for which I was suddenly grateful. Matthew walked behind us kicking a plastic bottle along in front of him; it rattled on the cobblestones and lay still, he kicked it again. Another car alarm screamed, this time from the car park on the opposite side of the harbour, and the noise carried and magnified across the water. We walked with no particular idea where we were going.

We'd stopped for ice cream and walked on, each holding a cone, except Laura who said she was still full from lunch, she spotted something she liked and went into a shop, we waited outside. Something happened between Grace and Matthew. Grace was enjoying her ice cream, swaying slightly, licking steadily at the head of it, oblivious to everything around her. A man in a black jacket tried to pass Grace to go into a shop. 'Excuse me,' he said, but Grace, so absorbed in the act of eating her ice cream, didn't hear him. The man repeated himself. Grace didn't move. Matthew said, 'For fuck's sake, fatso, get out of the way.' Grace's head snapped up as if she'd been hit, her eyes widened with hurt, automatically she stepped aside to let the man pass. Before I even had time to think I was behind Matthew, holding him by his arm and neck. Somewhere on the periphery of my narrowed vision I saw the man glance at us and then away as he stepped into the shop.

'Apologise to your sister!'

'Christ, man! You're hurting me. Let me go.'

'I said apologise.' I tightened my grip, felt the pulse of his veins beneath my fingers. I shook him.

'Sorry,' Matthew said to Grace, who stood watching with her mouth open.

I let him go and pushed him away. It was over in an instant. Laura stepped out of the shop. We walked on. I was breathing hard and my heart was still racing. I clenched and unclenched my fists and forced myself to calm down. Matthew flung his ice cream into a dustbin. He rubbed his neck, but kept his eyes on the ground. Grace followed slowly, I could feel her staring at me, then at Matthew and back. Laura walked ahead of us, looking into the windows of the gift shops.

We drove back on the motorway, towards the ridge of the mountains and through the sequence of tunnels, into which the cars disappeared like boats into an enchanted grotto. Beyond the first two tunnels lies another ridge and then another; after the third you are in the mountains proper, you leave the heat of the coast behind, skirt a single peak of rock and then come the wheat fields, the bridge over the river and the first neat pink and blue houses on the outskirts of Gost. The journey home took place more or less in silence though Laura talked some of the time, I can't remember now about what, but I made the effort of answering her. She appeared to think nothing of the silence; I suppose she was used to teenagers and their behaviour. At one point she asked me to take over the driving, which gave me an excuse not to talk. I was angry with myself for the loss of control, though it's hard to say I was sorry. Matthew was a brat who'd been begging for a slap for a long time. Plus, I had a feeling he wasn't going to tell his mother.

*   *   *

157

Carefully Grace fitted tiles to the mosaic of the bird. She held her breath as she pressed each tile into place, the tip of her tongue pushed at her top lip. Her face was moist with sweat and her hair stuck to her forehead, her cheeks and shoulders were pink. When enough time had passed for the glue to take, she carefully released the pressure. I sat at the table shaping tiles for her with a knife. With each success Grace looked triumphantly over at me.

Within the hour the restoration of the mosaic was complete. Then we began on the fountain, where the damage was much worse. Grace had already cleared the grass and weeds, but a great many of the tiles were loose and quite a few were damaged. Some days ago we'd lifted them all up so I could resurface the cement bed. Before we moved the tiles Grace fetched her camera and took several photographs. Afterwards she fitted the pieces back one by one, working from the digital image on the back of her camera to recreate the fish and the ribbons of weed exactly as they'd been. It had taken her hours. Now, once we fitted the tiles we'd bought in Zadar all that remained was the grouting.

*   *   *

Something else I should mention. The way it all fitted together, as I have said, that summer, with the sale of the blue house and the arrival of Laura who brought with her Matthew and Grace. I went to work for Laura: I needed the money and I knew the house. Small things happened, things that didn't surprise me. Krešimir seeing the mosaics

158

uncovered, for example. His rage. I didn't care, in fact if anything it encouraged me, pleased to get his goat. The red hat, though, that was quite by chance; I bought it for Laura on an impulse, because I couldn't do anything else.

The evening of the day I helped Grace with the repairs to the mosaics I saw Laura in town; she was carrying a basket, out shopping for groceries. The sun was at its lowest and struck over the rooftops and between the buildings. Laura wore a pair of sunglasses and, brim pulled down low over her forehead, the red hat. She walked alone, in a leisurely way, not at all self-conscious. I don't know why I mention it, she'd nothing to be self-conscious about, except that she was a foreigner in a small town and other people in the same position might have been, I suppose. Laura never seemed to be able to see herself from the outside, to have an idea of what other people might think of her, or even that they might be thinking at all. She didn't notice what happened next.

A woman walked towards her, an older woman, the kind who wore a housecoat to do her cleaning and sometimes her shopping, the same kind of woman as my mother. Head bent, trotting from one chore to the next. She looked up, saw Laura and almost stopped in her tracks. She looked down, up again, down again, nodding madly for a few moments. She slowed her pace and turned her head, following Laura's progress; she shook her head, raised a hand and sort of tapped herself on the chest, then she bowed her head and walked quickly on.

I walked home. I relived the moment Laura turned to face me on the harbour front in Zadar:

159

the stop it put to my heart. And just now, the woman in the street.

I thought: I am not the only one who sees it.

11

I want to tell you about Pag. Not that I want to dwell on it, but simply because it needs telling. Pag is part of my story, because in the end what happened on Pag brought me back to Gost. So today I'll tell you all about Pag. I went to Pag looking for something. I was a young man, I had a dream of how life might be. I found an island surrounded by still water, an island of salt beds, upon which practically nothing grew except sage, of white churches standing alone in an empty landscape and slim, black snakes. I found the house I had been looking for, facing the sea with a stone wall around a patch of land and a slipway for a boat. The first few weeks I spent repairing the stone wall, fitting the rocks against each other, building my new life piece by piece. Inside the stone walls I built the hives that would house my bees. Each day brought something new: a pair of juvenile seagulls waiting for their mother under the broken hull of an upturned boat; she never came, I fed them and in less than a week they treated me as their step-parent and began to shriek at the sound of my tread. Another day, picking my way along the rocks on the shore, I found a pair of women's shoes. They must have been there for a very long time: the soles were curled and the leather cracked and broken. That there were two was strange. They couldn't have been washed up, but must have been left there, as though the owner had removed them and set them there, walked into the sea.

Then after six months of solitude, sleeping and waking with the light and darkness, with only an occasional candle, the only female in my life my queen, I met a woman and she became everything to me.

The way I met her was quite comic. In the tourist season, in Zadar, I sat in a café with my back to the wall and drank a beer. The room was full of men, it was that time of the day. A woman appeared. She wore white sandals with high cork soles and walked on strong legs and with deliberate strides across the room where she pulled out a chair, smoothed her skirt and joined me at my table. She sat with her handbag on her lap and her fingers on the clasp and nodded briskly in my direction as if she was now ready for me to say something. Because I was confused, I offered her a beer. When it came, she drank some of it and continued to look at me in the same expectant manner and so I asked her name and she told me; in return I told her mine and I made some conversation, I forget about what. I wondered if she was a very well-mannered hooker. Something I said flustered her and she gathered up her belongings, apologised, said she'd made a mistake and was gone. Her beer sat unfinished on the table. A case of mistaken identity. When I saw her in the same bar a fortnight later I introduced myself. She remembered me and blushed, but accepted another beer. In the time we were together she never did tell me who the man was she was supposed to meet, only that it had something to

161

do with work.

She was older than me and separated from her husband. That's why she'd been looking for work. Her ex-husband was deputy manager of a shoe factory. Her family came from Pag, and it was to Pag she returned at the end of her marriage. Her parents didn't approve of me because there was a child who now lived with his father. They wanted their daughter to go back to the shoe factory deputy manager and the child. But she didn't, instead she moved into my cottage. By then I'd begun to cure skins: sheep's, goats', rabbits'. Some I used to cover the floor of the house, some I sold and used the money to buy things, things I hadn't given much thought to before, but came to want because she wanted them and I wanted to give them to her: patterned dishes, new chairs, aluminium pots.

She loved me, she said so. At times she was as playful as a child and at other times she would withdraw her affection for days. I didn't ask why. It was my first adult relationship. You'd think I might know better, being raised with women, but sisters are different to lovers. Because I loved her, I let her be. But her melancholy grew. I didn't understand, because the life I thought we had was good. And because I didn't understand, I thought it must be sadness for her child, who lived with his father in a distant town.

The smell of the cured leather reminded her of the shoe factory, she said. So I took away the skins and bought wool rugs instead. Another day she asked me where the skins were, and wanted them put back.

One day, after we had been together for three months and the good weather had gone, I went

162

to Zadar with a bundle of freshly cured skins. We motored in our small boat to the village near by where I could catch a lift across the small stretch of water to Karlobag, and from there hitch to Zadar. I turned to wave as she motored away from me (I had taught her to manage the boat, so she wouldn't be stranded on days when I wasn't there), saw her lift her hand and wave to me. The next day I stood in the same place, the money from the sale of the skins in my pocket. I found the boat moored by the jetty, but no sign of her. I knocked on the doors of the houses and learned she had gone away, on the ferry. I went home to an empty house. I wondered whether she had left straight away, or whether we had passed somewhere upon the straits. I wondered whether she stood out on the deck in the wind, with Pag behind her, whether she followed the progress of every oncoming boat and wondered if I was on it, or whether she hid below deck.

After a week I went to see her parents, but they knew nothing, or would tell me nothing and did not invite me inside but stood together on one side of the stone wall that surrounded their house and their front garden planted with cabbages, shrugged and shook their heads, regarding me through black eyes, like a pair of trolls.

I waited for a whole winter for her to come back. The winter was a cold one. When it was over I went out to check the hives and found the bees were dead. I went for a long walk around the island. Once I stopped and looked up at the mountains on the mainland, the white rock and dark trees. I realised that for ten years there'd been a pebble in my shoe, and the word engraved on it was Gost.

'She went back to her husband,' I said to Laura. 'Then I couldn't believe it. Now I know this kind of thing happens all the time.'

'She went back for the child,' said Laura. She smiled sadly and that irritated me; I wished I'd never spoken. She poured more wine into her glass and mine. We were sitting at the kitchen table at the end of the day. My hands were white, chalky cement dust filled the creases; I'd just finished grouting the fountain mosaic. I had never told anybody except Anka about Pag, even now I'm not sure what made me tell Laura. I suppose because Laura asked me questions. She could be very persistent and anyway, Pag had been on my mind since our trip to Zadar. My mind had been running along all sorts of lines it hadn't run on for years. Most of these memories I'd put safely away, as we all had, then something or someone comes along, like a plough through a fallow field in which all kinds of things lie buried under the crust of earth.

'Maybe,' I said. Laura wanted to spare my feelings, but she probably wanted to believe it, too. The truth is the woman I loved went back to the life that suited her better, as the wife of the deputy manager of a shoe factory, a man who also smelled of leather, but of a more expensive kind. I went once to the town where she lived and found her house. It wasn't difficult. I followed her to work and then, in the afternoon, I followed her from her place of work to the school. She wore make-up and heels and a suit made of a synthetic fabric, she smoked as she walked along the street. The kid had a crew cut and a bit of a belly. When he jumped in a

164

puddle she smacked him over the back of the head with the hand that held the cigarette. I wondered some years later what became of her, whether she survived or died, whether she was widowed. It never occurred to me to look for her.

Laura patted my hand, which lay on the table. Her fingers were cool and soft. Somewhere inside me, a nerve twitched.

*   *   *

In the space of nearly ten years everything and nothing has changed in Gost. My parents and sisters give a party to welcome me. My mother drinks *bambus*, lines like sun-rays spread from the corners of her eyes. My father has been occupied for several years building sheds so that the back yard has begun to resemble a small shanty town, as though a family of refugees have toiled across the continent and moved in. Talk of the sheds makes my mother puff and roll her eyes. The house is full so I sleep in one of them, wrapped in an old quilt with the smell of cut pine in my nostrils; it reminds me of the den I shared with Anka in the pine plantation. In the morning I draw water from the well to shave. At the party I am introduced to children I hadn't even known existed, who blink, squirm and are pressed to kiss me. One boy refuses, breaks free of his mother and hides. In ten years I had been back perhaps two or three times, never staying for more than a night or leaving my parents' house. My father had come to visit me several times, once when I first moved to Pag. He had loved the island almost as much as I did; he brought me a motor for my boat, understood why I was there.

165

The next morning, in the glare of our hangovers, Daniela and I walk to Gudura Uspomena. Anka is married, Daniela tells me, to Javor the son of my father's boss at the post office. Javor runs a bar in town called the Zodijak, it's very popular. Daniela and I are walking side by side, she puts her hand on my arm, stops and turns to face me, trying to find my gaze while I try to avoid hers. Later, I return to Gudura Uspomena without Daniela but with my old rifle, kept good by my father, who beams when he hands it over. It had belonged to him for three decades, before that to his father, who had been issued it on his first day as an infantryman in the war and had held onto it after he came down from months of fighting and hiding in the hills to be demobilised.

Just as they've been doing every evening of the last decade the deer drift out of the woods, camouflaged by the play of a pale green light. A long time since I've been out hunting. I wonder about my aim, whether to risk a head shot. I have no dog. The does are cautious as ever, holding their heads high and flicking their ears back as if they've already scented me. A young buck, maybe four seasons old, suddenly trots forward ahead of the herd. Old enough to know better, and so I fell him with a shot to the temple. My father claps me on the back and laughs until he has a coughing fit. He hangs the carcass in one of the sheds.

The next day I go looking for Anka. She'd moved into the blue house, left to her by her father. All over the country people lived together, generations in the same house. Life in the cities had become unbearable: apartments cross-hatched, divided and subdivided, with flimsy walls and curtains each time a baby came. Not so bad in the country, but even where there was space, building a house wasn't easy: materials were expensive. So there was Anka, with a house of her own, a small house of her own. Perhaps old Pavić had decided to give his daughter a way out of her mother's and brother's reach. Who knows? Or maybe he just thought it was fair: after all Krešimir would one day inherit the town house. Pavić never counted on dying. On the other hand, he had the foresight to make a will. That said something about Pavić. He'd died when Anka was a child, so Vinka Pavić must have known for years that Anka would inherit the blue house and yet kept it from her daughter until Anka was more than twenty. That said something about Vinka. I wondered too how long Krešimir had known.

The knowledge must have simmered.

But when I round the corner whatever words I have in mind to say to Anka when we meet disappear. On the wall of the house a great bird rises, wings outspread, beak pointed to the sky. Glorious. Alive. A bird with blue wings, tipped with azure. A red-bodied bird, golden-plumed, dragging a golden tail. The bird's head is turned to the left, as though it's looking at me with a haughty stare. Its breath is exhaled in curls. Green hands outstretched below, trying to catch the bird or having just released it, who knows? I stand in the road and stare for a long time. I know nothing about these things, but I know Anka made it, this beautiful bird, because she is there in every detail of it, her joy. There is a fountain in the courtyard too, with brilliantly coloured fish swimming in the water. The house looks like something from a children's

167

story. It looks like no other house in Gost.

When she opens the door Anka is wearing a cotton dress and has her hair tied up in a scarf. I stand with my back to the fountain and to the sun. At first she doesn't recognise me (though later she denies this). She blinks and pushes her hair back, finally says, 'Duro? Duro! *Duro!*' more loudly each time, she throws her arms around me, presses the length of her body to mine and her nose into my neck. Her hair smells of vinegar. She kisses me hard and loud on each cheek.

Afterwards she steps back, puts her hands on her hips, cocks her head and looks at me, grins. She blows her fringe up from her forehead; to see her do so, the way I had seen her do so so many times, goes straight to my heart.

She doesn't blame me, has never forgotten me. And she has forgiven me. Why? Because now she is ten years older, just as I am, and now the contours of her face are made up of hollows as well as curves, just as there are new straight lines and shadows in mine.

Because now she is ten years older.

Because now she loves another man.

There's nothing new about this story of ours, such things happen. Love misses its mark, arrives too early or too late. Nobody dies, except in novels.

Most people in Gost never knew why I left; those who did have forgotten, even my parents seem to have forgotten, because neither my mother nor my father makes any mention of Anka. My father is only occupied with his sheds, and my mother is occupied with my father and his sheds. But this is a small town and so Anka and I reconfigure our love into a friendship, broad enough to include Anka's husband Javor. I remember him. He's a decent sort. I pretend to be more pleased than I am for them both. I don't think Anka has told Javor about us, but then why would she? Ours was a calf love from a time long gone, from the days when we were children.

Of this I persuade myself.

*   *   *

With Javor and Anka, the summer following my return, back at the house from an evening at the Zodijak where we have celebrated the third anniversary of the bar's opening. We are all drunk, but some are drunker than others. Javor, for instance. Times are lean for everyone, except Fabjan and Javor. The Zodijak thrives: misery likes company and beer. Javor has bought Anka a kiln and a car. He has installed the kiln in one of the outbuildings and Anka has been working hard these last weeks: the tiny back seat of her new red Fićo is crammed full of boxes of brightly painted ceramic ashtrays, bowls and plates, brooches, wrapped in newspaper. She wears one of her brooches, the imprint of a walnut in blue ceramic. I still have the little heart she gave me years ago, found again among those belongings of mine my father had stored in one of his sheds. I put it in my pocket. Every Wednesday or Thursday Anka takes the road down to the coast, to Zadar, where she sells the things she makes to the owners of tourist shops. Sometimes Javor goes with her to buy supplies for the bar and they drive the Fićo back rattling with bottles.

With the start of winter it became too cold to

169

carry on sleeping in the shed. My father had a solution, which was to fix up the old pig house in the lower field. The field belonged to our family, it was used for grazing from time to time. The house had been abandoned years ago, but when I pushed open the broken door I saw my father wasn't wrong.

For two days I shovelled shit and stinking, rotten hay, washed down the floors. While I worked I thought of nothing except hosing walls, scrubbing stains from the stone floors and spraying the whole place three times with diluted disinfectant. I ripped the rotten door from its hinges and threw it on a bonfire. Hard work took my mind far away from Pag. I was building myself a future in Gost. After his work at the post office my father came to lend a hand; having a project made him happy and it made my mother happy because he'd stopped building sheds in the yard. Working side by side, within a week we had the place weather-proofed and in another week we'd installed a new floor where the bedroom would be. Within a month I'd moved in and I added improvements all winter. My new home was even closer to the blue house than my parents' place.

Then in November I found Kos tied to a tree and left to die and I took her home with me.

Anka puts plates on the table, Javor wants to help, but he is too drunk, he stumbles and catches his hip on the edge of the table. The plate flies from his hand and Javor tries to catch it, grasps it fleetingly. The plate breaks on the floor. Javor himself overtopples. He has removed his trousers and is wearing a T-shirt over a pair of blue Y-fronts. On his knees on the floor he begins to collect pieces of the plate, holding each one close to his face and

170

examining it as if it is evidence of some immense crime. Anka pulls him to his feet. He sways and puts his arms around her. 'I'm sorry, baby.' Anka pushes him into a chair and returns to laying the table.

Once, they had an argument and Anka came over to my place and stayed a few hours. I cooked, she talked but not about Javor. While we were eating Javor telephoned, but Anka refused to speak to him. 'OK,' said Javor. 'Tell her I'm sorry.' I told Anka he sounded miserable and then Anka changed her mind and called him back, but Javor had accidentally left the receiver off the hook, she could hear him humming to himself and the sound of him biting into an apple, she shouted into the receiver but he didn't hear her and then he must have stubbed his toe, she began to laugh and passed me the phone so I could listen to Javor stumble and curse. Javor never knew why she showed up at the house minutes later, her face stained with tears of laughter.

The door is open to the tepid night air. Fabjan arrives, accompanied by his wife, then a taut, blonde Venus with plastic hoops in her ears, her gaze permanently narrowed against the smoke of her own cigarettes. Javor levers himself to his feet and goes out of the back door, returns with a bottle of *rakija*. He puts a tape into the player on the windowsill, picks out a tune on an air guitar and makes a twanging sound to imitate the sound of the instrument. Three ascending notes, then down, up, down. Then the same three ascending notes. Da, da, da-da. He spins with surprising grace, as drunks sometimes do.

'What the fuck is this crap?'

'The greatest song ever written.'

171

'By a coke head.'

'Acid head. Anyway Lucy was a girl his son had a crush on so he made a painting of her. It was a kid's painting, that's all it was. "Lucy In The Sky With Diamonds".'

Fabjan moves over to the recorder and jabs a stubby forefinger at the row of buttons. The music stops, leaving a ringing in the air. Javor puts an arm around Fabjan's neck and kisses him, waves at Fabjan's wife. 'Fabjan, Fabjan! My good friend,' he slurs, locates the *rakija* bottle and pours drinks all round. Javor is an excellent drunk. Fabjan has brought beer and a bottle of Stock 84. He refuses Javor's *rakija* and pours himself a brandy which he knocks back in one and pours another. In between brandies he takes long draughts from the beer bottle. He lights a cigarette of a local brand, Morava, which smell strongly. In between draughts of beer and puffs on his cigarette his eyes follow Anka: his gaze slides down her back and comes to rest on her buttocks as she reaches for plates. The way Fabjan looks at every woman, but especially the way he looks at Anka, pisses me off. I move to insert myself in-between Fabjan's gaze and Anka's body.

'I'll help you,' I say, and take the plates from her hand.

We eat: grilled pork and cabbage salad. A piece of food flies down Javor's gullet and lodges there. Anka bangs him on the back; he reddens and coughs it up. Afterwards she kisses him on the back of the head. I see her do these things and know how she loves him. And I love Javor too, everyone does except maybe Fabjan, but then Fabjan only loves himself.

As for me, I have taken a few women out since I came to Gost, but somehow nothing lasts. I've come to depend on Javor and Anka, the door to their house is always open to me. I've been given the privileges couples in love bestow upon hopeless bachelors. Namely: the right to eat at their table without an invitation, the right to get drunk, the right to spend the night on the couch when I am too drunk to go home. In return I bring venison to their table, sometimes a partridge or a quail. And I make them a table, a belated wedding present. I use wood from my father's stash in the sheds. I work on it in secret and my father helps me carry it to the blue house one day when the house is empty. Tricky getting it inside with just the two of us.

Among my privileges as a frequent guest, bachelor, supplier of fresh game, is the right to be alone with Anka. It's something I am careful not to do too often. I am bruised by Pag and a year after my return I am haunted by the ghost of an emotion for which I have no name. It rises to the surface in odd moments, sometimes when I am alone with Anka, is submerged by Javor's dogged goodwill, his neck-locks and jokes, his *rakija*.

Anka is the only person I tell about Pag. Not my mother, who is unsentimental, and not my father, because he is far too sentimental. Daniela would have been upset for me. Anka listens without interrupting; when I am finished she stretches out her hand and holds my wrist lightly with her fingers, like a doctor taking a patient's pulse. We are quiet for some time. Then she lets go of my wrist and leans across the table to take my head into her hands and shakes it, the way a child does a piggy bank. Eventually she says, 'Silly bitch. She'll never be happy with that attitude.'

When anything happens to me, good or bad, Anka becomes the first person I tell. I love her, but it's a chaste love, bleached by time and familiarity, like a long marriage. In my love for Anka, even when we were teenagers and lay on a quilt under the pine trees, there was none of the hurt of Pag. If Javor ever left her, I would look after her, perhaps even ask her to marry me. But more than that, more than anything, I want to protect Anka, can't bear the idea of her ever being hurt. I would sleep all night across the doorstep of the house if she asked me. In some strange way I fear for her. Because she has forgiven Krešimir and Vinka, you see. Something I cannot bring myself to do, but Anka has reworked the whole episode in her mind, rubbed away the stains, the malice and jealousy, painting on new, less wounding reasons.

Fabjan tips brandy down his throat and begins to outline his new plans for the Zodijak: folk night, karaoke, girls. Why not? Once a month. Javor slaps him on the back, grins. 'Fabjan's plans for world domination.' Fabjan ignores him and carries on. The two men are so unalike, it is hard to think how they can be friends. Fabjan has thick hair on his forearms and his head. Javor looks like a fledgling fallen from the nest: his neck is long, his nose is prominent, his pale brown hair stands up to form a soft fuzz around his head.

Javor starts to sing, quietly at first and then louder. One by one the rest of us join in and Fabjan gives up. The song has been played on the radio all year. '*Hajde Da Ludujemo.*' That was 1990, the year we hosted the Eurovision Song Contest in Zagreb. Fabjan organised a Eurovision evening in the bar.

174

His wife kind of looks like the singer, at least she dressed the same in a pink dress with a short skirt. I've forgotten the singer's name. Anyway, now it has become a standing joke between us, to begin to sing the song and for the rest of us to join in. What Javor likes best is to start this at the worst possible time, under his breath: last week during his cousin's wedding vows.

'Fuck head,' says Fabjan.

So that's Javor for you.

*　　　*　　　*

You're wondering about Krešimir.

According to Anka her brother was doing fine, living in the town house with their mother, decent job and all the rest. At first I raised the subject of Krešimir carefully, but Anka talked like everything that happened in the past had been left there. She'd forgiven him, as she forgave everybody. You must remember, Krešimir and her mother were family, the only family she had, and we always say blood and water aren't the same.

At Christmas the first year of my return there was a reunion party, in the old school hall where the Licitar hearts still hung. The old gang were there: Andro, Goran, Miro. I'd seen them about in the last few months, of course. All married, to wives who fell pregnant as soon as they were up the aisle. Still cracking terrible jokes. Miro had brought a stash of porn videos and was trying to sell them for a few thousand dinara each. That was before the currency was revalued. The only person I hadn't seen was Krešimir, though I'd seen Vinka Pavić. She'd finally given in to widow's black, dyed her hair red, walking down the street with the careful, erratic gait of the habitual drunk. She greeted me as though the alcohol had rubbed her mind clean.

A billow of air through the double doors carried the smell of wood polish, rubber and feet. Tables covered in paper cloths, plates of food brought by the women, cups of cheap wine and home-made streamers. A band: some of the guys from school, not bad. Later, a DJ. Not much had changed, except that it was no longer the 1970s, instead it was the last year of the 1980s. We wore our hair shorter: Goran's cut close to reveal the great swell of his head; he'd become a warehouse foreman. Andro had put on weight, he'd joined his father's business as an electrician. Nobody had left Gost for the simple reason nobody wanted to. They were afraid if they did they'd lose their place in the ranking of second-hand cars and motorbikes, drinking bouts and blowjobs. A few of the guys gave me a slap on the back and they seemed really pleased to see me, but interest in what I'd been doing didn't last long because people were only really interested in what happened in Gost: even the coast was another country.

Krešimir leant apart from the others, his back to the wall. I saw he was still wearing his father's leather jacket. It gave me a jolt to see him, but I was relaxed, coming home had been good, I'd found my place again. The one time we talked about any of it, helping my father move things around his shed while we looked for wood to make a table for Anka and Javor, my father stopped and placed his hand on my shoulder. 'The past is the past,' he'd said to me, and I'd caught his meaning straight away, he was telling me, warning me to let it go. I thought:

176

Yes, my father is right. Hadn't Mrs Pavić greeted me in the street, hadn't Anka found happiness with Javor? 'Things happen. Forget about it.' He touched my cheek, he looked tired. Time had passed. Now my father preferred to build sheds in his yard rather than drink with his old friends. My mother said he was becoming tender-hearted. So I walked towards Krešimir and extended my hand. And Krešimir looked at me and then looked away. He pushed off the wall and walked past me, as if I were never there.

The next day I told my father he was wrong: the past is never passed.

*   *   *

In the bakery, a man and a woman ahead of me in a short line.

'After all this time. Now he comes back. The neighbours thought they were seeing a ghost.'

The man behind her gave a snort.

'Everyone knew it was him,' she continued. 'He had a harelip. And they say the daughter was with him, a grown woman.'

'They've moved back into the old place?'

'Yes. And a row with the neighbours, over their tractor.'

The man grunted.

Every few months a newspaper article or something else kicked something off, put people on edge, set them talking. The same could happen anywhere. The knowledge was a shivering child locked in an upstairs room. The dark child haunted our dreams, invaded the places in our minds even we didn't dare go. The couple in front of me

177

stopped talking, having gone as far as they dared. They collected their loaves and left. I asked my cousin's ex-wife. 'Where?'

'K–' She gave the name of a town forty kilometres to the east, larger than Gost. Nothing more was said. People were becoming mindful of what could happen here. Another plough had broken the crust of the fallow field of memories.

I left the bakery and I thought I might go by the Zodijak for a beer. It was still early, the sky a pale blue and heat left in the sun. I reached the road and was about to cross, when I got a shock. There was Laura. Sitting at an outside table with Fabjan. Laura laughing—as though Fabjan had just said something really funny.

*   *   *

Yes, Tatjana something. The papers called her Tajči—she sang the Eurovision song the year we hosted the contest. I remembered it later that night as I got ready for bed. I cut my nails: they grow fast in the summer. I had a callus on my thumb. I picked up a jar of rose hand cream; just as the smell of lime hair oil reminds me of my father, the scent of rose hand cream reminds me of my mother. She made it herself, as people did in those days, out of rose water and glycerine which she bought from the chemist's, or better still beeswax, when she could get hold of it. Simmering pans of petals. An aunt swore by olive oil and sugar. Every so often my father bought her a pot of Atrixo from the men in the market. I like to use the cream from time to time, never obviously when I am going hunting, for then it would give me away. The smell of the cream

178

brought back the past, as it always did, and with it the name of the singer. Tajči. We didn't win. And anyway the memory is a useless one, but it was part of a time.

Out of curiosity I went a few days ago to Gost library and looked on the Internet. Tatjana Matejaš is her full name. She lives in Cincinnati and sings in churches.

I went to bed. I thought about Laura sitting with Fabjan. Later that night I dreamt of Laura and woke suddenly in the dark with a warm, wet belly. I lay and thought about her for a while. I'd never been able to imagine her any other way than the way she was, never imagined her angry or aroused, or even sweaty for that matter. And in the dream too nothing had happened, except that she'd lain on her back and let me fuck her.

12

Laura asked if I could recommend a hairdresser. I rubbed my hand over my cropped hair and gave her the address of the salon belonging to Fabjan's wife. I said, 'Her husband owns the Zodijak.'

Laura frowned.

'On the same street as the bakery.' I couldn't help it. I asked, 'What were you doing in there?'

Laura laughed. 'Is there a law against it?'

'No, of course there isn't. I just wondered. I mean, not many women go to the Zodijak.'

'Oh I see, and you were worried I'd fallen into bad company. It was you who told us about it, don't you remember? Matthew wanted to use the Internet.

We stopped by there yesterday. I met the owner. Wouldn't think of letting me pay. He was absurdly charming.'

I'd forgotten and now I remembered—the day Matthew had let his exasperation with the holiday show, the day I'd shown them the double rainbow. Yes, the Zodijak had Internet access, one of the first places in town to do so. 'That's Fabjan for you,' I said. Matthew must have been sitting at the back where the computer was, while Fabjan flirted with Laura.

'Do you think she'd be able to do highlights?'

Laura's fair hair, when you looked closely, was composed of strands of hair each a slightly different shade from gold, through red to brown. It looked complicated. I remembered my sister Daniela, who trained to be a beautician. She might have known where to go. 'Maybe Zadar is better,' I said. 'The salon here is small. They only know one or two styles.'

'Oh well.' Laura picked up a strand of her hair and examined it; she shrugged lightly. 'I don't think I want to go all the way back to Zadar for a hair appointment. Maybe I'll leave it.'

'Or maybe something simple. I think they could do that.'

'Do you know what I've always wanted? A bob. Neat, short, dark. Chic.' She flicked the back of her hair and let it fall. 'My real hair colour is actually much darker than this. I've often thought about going back to it.'

'I believe dark hair would suit you, Laura,' I said deliberately. 'It would make you look younger.'

*　　　*　　　*

180

The fountain was almost completely restored. Grace planned some kind of grand opening when we would turn on the water and asked me to help. I ripped out and replaced the pump and added a centrepiece to the fountain: a stone ball resting on a plain dais, which I paid for myself as a gift. In-between I worked on the house and occasionally on the Fićo. I should mention that what happened between Matthew and me in Zadar seemed to have passed: he was respectful, you could even say pleasant. From time to time he offered to help; once he asked if we could go shooting again.

'Sure,' I said. 'Any time.'

'When can we go hunting?'

I still hadn't decided if I liked him, but I said, 'The season starts a few weeks from now. If you're still here we can go.'

'Awesome,' said Matthew.

The day was Saturday, the grand opening of the fountain planned for the evening. I'd guessed Grace wanted it to be a surprise so I didn't say anything to Laura. Mid-morning I found Grace at work in the kitchen baking a cake.

'For tonight,' she said. 'Do you like cake?'

'Yes,' I said. 'Coffee cake especially.'

For some reason this statement made Grace blush and return with a furious vigour to beating her cake mixture into submission.

In town to take coffee earlier that morning I sat outside the Zodijak where I was served by the girl who worked there. Afterwards she went back and sat at the bar, her chin low, her hair hiding her face. She was certainly a great deal less cheerful than she'd been two or three weeks ago. I doubted she would last. Not many people come to Gost and want to stay.

The bar was busy as always at that time on a Saturday. Fabjan's folk music played. Men drank coffee and *rakija*. Fabjan was there; the girl sent him looks through her hair. Fabjan ignored her. When he saw me he nodded and redirected his stare to the street. I passed him and had a waft of his odour, which no amount of cologne will disguise: sweat and cooked meats. Fabjan's fingers are swollen and red. A wedding ring cuts into the flesh of his third finger, like a corset on an obese woman. His lips are virgin pink and shine with saliva. A family of hairs peeps from his nostrils and his ears, while a crowd of hairs seems to strain upwards, out of his open collar, as if they're trying to catch a glimpse of their upstairs cousins.

If you listen you can hear him breathing.

That day he sat with crossed arms, his mouth set into a down-turned line, his brow dark and low. Fabjan has the ability to sit like that for hours. Watch him and you'll see that every now and again he frowns, as though bothered by some fly of a thought risen from the swamp of his subconscious. Seeing him like that, I had an impulse to goad him. I said, 'Did you hear of this thing in K–?'

On the surface of Fabjan's face nothing stirred, his grunt was non-committal. I left it a few minutes and sipped my coffee. Of course Fabjan would have heard the talk, so would the whole of Gost; they would discuss it just like the pair in the bakery, stopping before they took a step too far and betrayed themselves. I pressed on. 'They thought he was dead. And then he turns up. They say his daughter was with him. Maybe it was the first time she had been there. I wonder how much he told her.'

Fabjan licked his lips, a slow sweep of the thick tip of his tongue across the top lip in one direction and back the other way across the bottom. He sniffed deeply.

I said, 'I wonder if they'll stay.'

Fabjan turned his head slowly in my direction. 'Do you want something?' he snapped. 'Can't you see I'm busy?'

*   *   *

Back at the blue house I satisfied myself the fountain would do all that was required of it in the evening. Late afternoon I walked the hills with the dogs, counted roe buck and some deer. I thought about Matthew and my promise to take him hunting. I used to take businessmen hunting from time to time, to make a bit of extra money. Some people, when they come to it, can't bring themselves to pull the trigger. Nothing wrong with that, the hunt teaches you about yourself. They never come again. Others come only wanting to kill; they don't have any patience for the work of tracking, the long waits and the cold. When the chance comes, they'll shoot anything, even a doe with a fawn. I've seen it happen. Over the years I've learned to recognise the type. Now I prefer to hunt alone. But Matthew—I couldn't imagine a boy like him waiting motionless as dusk fell, not making a sound. And though he had done well enough out with the targets, I still couldn't see him holding his nerve steady enough to take the final shot.

By eight o'clock I was back at the blue house

183

wearing a fresh shirt. To make more of the occasion I'd strung up some lights which made Grace very happy. There was something strange about her appearance and after a minute or two I put my finger on it. She had pasted a heavy layer of blue eyeshadow onto her eyelids, otherwise her face was bare: no mascara or lipstick. It gave her face a clownish look.

Matthew came down. 'Hey, man, Grace says there's going to be a surprise. Do you know what it is?' He fetched two beers and handed me one. Laura appeared with a glass of wine in her hand; she wore a touch of pale pink lipstick and her lashes were dark with mascara. It seemed strange that she didn't take her daughter aside and show her how to fix herself properly. When I was young I sometimes watched my sisters transform themselves. Once I'd even sat alone at the dressing table in the room they shared—lair of scents and secrets, where I loved to spy and eavesdrop—and brushed rouge onto my cheeks, found a stub of lipstick and applied it to my lips. I must have been eight or nine. Later I forgot this and when my mother called me for my tea I ran downstairs. 'Eh, Duro!' My mother clapped a hand over her mouth. My father looked up from the newspaper and began to laugh. Daniela—she had left school at sixteen and was already training to become a beautician—turned me around in my chair. With her thumb she blended the edges of my eyeshadow, pinched my cheeks and said, 'There, you look beautiful. Eat your food.'

'Grace said you were coming,' said Laura. She came up to me and, for the first time, kissed me on each cheek. She turned those slanted eyes of hers on me and narrowed them so they wrinkled at the corners. The overall effect was extremely attractive. 'I wonder what it is. But I bet you can keep a secret, Duro. Don't worry, I shan't bully you. I love surprises.'

Salad and pizza, made by Grace during her kitchen frenzy. Laura opened a bottle of red wine. In the quiet you could hear the sound of cars on the main road.

'Something must be going on,' said Laura.

'Wedding reception,' I said. 'The season has begun. From now every Saturday there will be a big party at the hotel. It will go on late and everyone will be drunk. Then they'll fight.'

We ate and drank. Coffee cake for dessert. When it was nearly dark I nodded to Grace and she slipped into the house and put on a CD. There was music. 'Ah,' smiled Laura. 'Handel. Now I wonder what that could possibly mean.' I stood up and threw the switch on the fountain. Water bubbled up and rippled down the sides of the sphere of stone. This part of the display lasted about a minute. Then from the sides of the pool frothy plumes of water shot up into the air, dropped down and rose again. Next I turned on the lights to reveal the mosaic. Underneath the water the fish appeared to move, the weeds ripple. What a spectacle! Cheering and clapping. More drink, we popped a cork and toasted the fountain. Laura allowed Grace a glass and Matthew helped himself freely. Grace sneezed and hiccuped. We sang 'Jailhouse Rock', which was being played on the radio a lot for some reason. Our singing subsided into chatter. Grace and Matthew began some kind of guessing game I had no hope of entering, as it seemed to rely on knowing a great deal about famous people. Laura joined in and then withdrew. Grace complained the game couldn't be played with two people, but somehow she and Matthew carried on. Matthew changed the music. In this way it grew late.

Around midnight a car cruised by. It drove neither fast nor slowly. I watched it pass. Laura sat, her head tilted back, looking at the stars. At the end of the road the beam of headlights swept the field opposite as the driver turned, the fractious whine of the engine, tyres slipping on the gravel, whorls of dust rose in the cones of light. After a pause the car began heading back. Laura noticed nothing, sighed and drew her shawl round her shoulders. The headlights of the car switched to full beam. Now I rose from my chair. The vehicle picked up speed and as it drew parallel to the house slowed. The sound of a woman's coarse laughter. The driver gunned the engine. A gobbet of spit caught the light as it flew through the air, an obscenity hurled in English was left echoing in the darkness and something else—a glowing arc which landed in the grass in front of the table and exploded with a sharp crack. Laura jumped and screamed. The car drove on.

At first nobody moved. Laura stood, her hands across her mouth. All of us stared in the direction of the car: the tail lights could just be seen dipping in and out of view as the car rounded the bends of the road.

Matthew said, 'Fucking hell!'

'Matthew!' said Laura automatically.

'Drunks,' I said. 'From town, probably looking for somewhere to smoke weed. Nothing to worry about. They're not coming back.'

'Why did they shout at us?' asked Matthew.

186

'They saw us sitting out in the evening having a nice time, so they tried to spoil it. Ignore them. It was just a firework. They think they're being funny.'

'They told us to go home, in as many words,' said Matthew.

'Because they guessed you're foreigners. Some of the kids, they call themselves nationalists. They have no idea what it means.'

'They didn't seem that young,' said Grace.

'But still idiots, yes?'

Laura said, 'I'm sure Duro's right. We mustn't take it to heart. Are you two OK?'

Matthew shrugged. 'I guess.' Grace nodded, her face pale.

'Then let's clear these things up. Come on, everybody carry one thing inside.'

We cleared the table together, after which Matthew said, 'I'm going to hit the sack, I think.'

'Me too.' Grace followed her elder brother.

I said, 'Goodnight, both of you. Hey, Grace, the fountain is great.' I gave her a thumbs-up. She gave me a thin smile.

'Thanks, Duro.' And she headed up the stairs.

Laura turned off the music, whose beat had accompanied the incident and its aftermath. 'That's better. Now, there's a bit left in the bottle. What do you say to a nightcap? Shall we have a last glass?'

We carried the remainder of a bottle outside, where the air was cool and soft. Laura went back inside and came out with a packet of Malboro Lights. She smoked one, drawing deep lungfuls of smoke. We drank without speaking.

In the silence you could hear, carried across the field from Gost, music.

'I told you,' I said. 'Drunks from a wedding.'

'Yes, I am sure you're right.'

'If you are worried I can sleep here—on the couch.'

'Now that would be asking too much.'

'It's OK.'

'I'd feel much more relaxed if there was a man in the house. I know I have Matthew but—'

I interrupted her. 'Laura, it's no problem.'

*   *   *

I sat on the edge of the couch and wound my father's watch just as I did every night. Counted the revolutions of the winder between finger and thumb, stopped at ten, same as always. When I was eight my father bought me a watch and that first night he showed me how to wind it. He told me to remember to do so every night and be careful not to overwind it. The best way to do this was by winding the watch at the same time every night and counting the number of turns I gave the winder. Of course, left alone, I wound the watch as far as it would go and broke the spring.

My father looked at the stopped watch. 'What's the difference between apes and humans? Apes learn by experience.' He had the watch fixed and gave it back to me. 'See if you can make it last longer this time, chief.'

My father's watch had a black face, a large 6 and 12. The chrome was pitted, the face water-stained. I should have it cleaned, but that would mean opening it up and, since the day I took it from his wrist, I'd never let the watch stop. I held it to my ear, and then in my palm, watched the staccato sweep of the second hand. I laid it on the floor and placed

188

my head on the pillow Laura had brought down for me. I lay still and let the rhythm of my heart join the rhythm of the watch's ticking. I thought of the three other hearts beating on the floor above me, three different rhythms, the walls of the blue house pulsating with them.

In the night I woke once and listened to the sound of the breeze through the tree tops, the whispers and murmurs of the house: the roof, walls and floors, windows, shifting with the wind, keening with the myriad, minute movements of the earth beneath the foundations. The low hum of the fountain pump. Above it all the water, like a descant sung by a choir. I rolled over on the narrow couch, stood up and went to the window. A waxing moon in an empty sky cast an unwavering light, creating shadows of the deepest blue. The wedding party had finally worn itself out. For a moment I thought I saw the silhouette of a man standing beyond the hedge across the road. I watched, but it was nothing, a sign on a post and a trick of the light.

The next morning was Sunday. The family slept late. I walked to my house to let Kos and Zeka out and returned bringing yoghurt and honey. I picked some wild flowers and put them in a jar of water. Laura was up, sleepy-eyed, she apologised for putting me to trouble. Matthew and Grace appeared and Laura started making breakfast, scrambling eggs and cutting bread for toast. Once she stood behind Matthew's chair and pressed her nose and lips to the crown of his head. Matthew, who took no notice of these shows of affection, carried on chewing his food. As I watched them casually touching, leaning over or against, nudging and bumping, they reminded me of animals in their

189

lair, treading on each other on their way in and out, or in search of a better position, at night pressing themselves against each other in search of warmth.

I thought how fine it would be to have a son, though perhaps one with a bit more spine than Matthew. A daughter like Grace would be a fine thing. Fabjan had sons, God only knew if he had other children with his girlfriends. Maybe the new girl was already pregnant, maybe that's why she looked so depressed. Fabjan was the kind who'd press a girl into an abortion. Even Krešimir was married and had a child. As for me, I had my sister and my mother. No one else.

Suddenly I felt like being on my own. I stood up. Thanks and goodbyes. Nobody was asking me to go but on the other hand nor did they beg me to stay. Once home I exercised hard, heaving myself up to the cross bar above the door. Afterwards my muscles ached, but I still felt tense; in the pit of my stomach lay a queasy anticipation, like when I was challenged to a fight at school. I'd wake up after a night of dreaming, I'd have forgotten and then the memory would come back, and my stomach would collapse into my bowels with fear but also a fluttering excitement, knowing there could be no turning back, no choice but to see it through.

I picked up a fork and went to work in the garden turning over the soil in one of the beds. The ground was parched and rock hard, each strike set the fork quivering and shock waves travelled through my arms, my shoulder blades and back down into my guts. Forty minutes passed. When I stood up to wipe the sweat from my eyes I saw Grace coming down the road. She was alone, wearing a dress and the hat she'd bought in Zadar, a plain straw hat with a narrow brim. She smiled, waved. I said, 'You look smart. Where are you going?'

She smiled shyly. 'To church. I just came to ask which one is the nicest.'

'St Mary's or Annunciation. Both. You need to hurry though.'

'What about the other one?'

'Those are the only two.'

'No, there's a third. We drive past it all the time.'

'That's the Orthodox church,' I said. 'There are no longer services held there.'

'Oh,' said Grace. 'Why?'

'It's closed down. Come on. I'll walk you to St Mary's. My mother's favourite. Smaller than Annunciation and much more beautiful. They have a big tree outside at Christmas. We can walk along the river.' The Orthodox church had been beautiful too, with paintings instead of statues, of the saints doing what saints did, painted on the wooden panels of the walls, deep dense colours.

I pulled a shirt on, called the dogs and met Grace at the front of the house. I said, 'Your mother and brother don't go to church?'

'No. Matt thinks it's dumb. Mum says she doesn't see why anyone should have to go to church to worship.'

'And you do?'

'Not really. I just like it. I like the music and the singing, you know, and the quiet. I don't know yet if I believe in God. I'm sort of waiting to find out. If I do I'm going to be confirmed. Some of my friends were confirmed last year, but I didn't do it. Actually, I think they just wanted the presents.' She marched heavily up the hill. Ahead of us a magpie bounced from tree to road. Zeka lunged sloppily. The bird bounced back up. We reached the bridge.

'Careful, it's steep,' I warned. I ducked under the railing at the near end of the bridge where a rough path led down to the riverside and joined a gravelled path on a high bank. The gravel path was overhung by birch and willow trees and followed the course of the river towards the centre of Gost. The surface of the water shivered beneath a light wind, the clusters of water lilies shook, in the middle of the river were two pontoons used as floats at Christmas and by swimmers in the summer.

Grace followed unsteadily, panting, still talking as though she'd waited all her life in silence for the opportunity. 'Laura married in church twice. First to my dad and then Conor. That time I was bridesmaid; I wore a yellow dress. The kids at school teased me about her wearing white. I thought it was kind of odd too, actually. Because you're supposed to be, well you know, a virgin. Anyway. When I was little she used to call herself Aura. She hates anyone mentioning it.' Grace giggled and bit her bottom lip as though to stop her mouth from opening; her eyes widened in shock at herself, she frowned and said, 'I shouldn't have told you that. Don't say anything, will you?'

I shook my head. 'Your father, where is he? Is he alive?'

'Yes, of course he's alive. He lives on a boat and sails around the world.'

'Is that true?'

'No, I made it up. I wish he did. He lives in Edinburgh.'

'Do you see him?'

'Not very often.' She shrugged. 'I think Matt has an idea about going to live with him, but Conor's

192

richer and so we live with Mum and Conor. I'm not sure Dad really cares much, though he doesn't actually say so. Anyway, I like Conor, he's been around a lot more than our real dad has. It's just that him and Matt don't get on. But then Matt doesn't get on with lots of people.'

'What about you and your father?'

'I don't think he knows I exist.'

I said, 'That's sad.'

'It's OK. I never really knew him anyway.'

The path swung away from the riverside, behind one of the old grain stores. 'There's the church. Up there. One hundred metres.'

'Thank you,' said Grace. She kissed me on the cheek. I stood in the shadow of the trees with Kos and Zeka and watched her go.

I remembered the last time I was in St Mary's Church. How many years ago was it? I'd taken this same path to town without knowing why, I changed my course, walked to St Mary's and went inside. The church was empty, it was that time of day. I sat in a pew. I didn't know why I was there, I hadn't been to church in many years, not since Daniela and my father were buried, except for the funerals that followed, I attended one or two of those, I remember how the services became shorter and shorter as demand on the priest's time grew. After a while I stood up to leave, and decided at the last moment to light a candle for Daniela and my father. I placed it among the huddle of dead and fluttering flames at the plaster feet of the statue of the Virgin in the small chapel. Of the several statues of her in the church, this had always been my favourite, ever since I was a small boy: her open hands, the slight downward and sideways turn of the head, which on that day made her appear to have noticed me and be listening. I knelt down and pressed my head against the low wooden altar. I thought to say a prayer for the souls of my family members, but I couldn't bring myself to it. If there was a God, I wouldn't be lighting candles and praying for them.

Instead I prayed for the one thing I wanted more than anything else. I didn't care if it was blasphemy and if it was, then God could strike me down. I prayed for the death of Krešimir.

13

The restoration of the mosaic and the fountain caused a great deal of excitement in Gost. If you're new to Gost you might not know that we are people of muted emotions, unless we're drunk. Then of course, anything might happen. But that's as true everywhere. Monday, midday, in the queue at the post office where I waited to pay my electricity bill, a man in a blue boiler suit turned and asked me if I'd seen it for myself. He was a builder's foreman I had worked for occasionally and stank of cigarettes. He didn't wait for me to answer but went on, 'I drove past this morning and I saw it with my own eyes. That great big bird is back on the wall. It was gone and now it's back.' He shrugged.

Nobody in the bakery except the woman who had been married to my cousin behind the counter, who on this day looked unusually pleased to see me. As she served me she said, 'So, Duro, tell me about the house.'

I replied that I had nothing to tell. For this my

cousin's ex-wife withheld my loaf, passing it from hand to hand like a thug wielding a baseball bat. She tilted her head to one side and gave me a malevolent little smile. 'I thought she was your friend.'

'I helped her.' I shrugged. 'If that makes us friends.'

'You're the nearest neighbour.'

'OK, so I lied. We're the best of friends. What do you want me to tell you?'

'What's she doing?'

'Nothing. They're English. They like old houses.'

My cousin's ex-wife raised her eyebrows. Then she repeated her chilly little smile and passed over my loaf. I left the bakery. I felt sorry for my cousin: no wonder he'd divorced her.

More talk in the Zodijak an hour later where I stopped for a coffee. Two guys, one I had seen there before, the one who worked in the municipal offices: the guy with the jug ears who'd been the one to confirm the sale of the house here in the Zodijak only weeks ago, a pen pusher who enjoyed the authority it gave him. He said, 'No planning permission would be necessary, you see. Now, if they wanted to build an extension, but even then . . . a lot of people don't bother. That's when the problems start.'

His companion interrupted him. 'Where did you say they are from?'

'England.'

'They say there are a lot of our people in England,' said the other man, more or less to himself because his companion was still talking permissions.

I looked for Fabjan's reaction, but there was none. You had to give it to him. He must have felt like somebody was walking on his grave. A few weeks ago Fabjan had been suffering from toothache. He has terrible teeth, I told you that already, I think. I'd kept forgetting to ask how he was feeling. Now I said, 'How's your tooth? Been to the dentist?'

'Piss off,' said Fabjan. He cracked his knuckles. Bad habit. Carry on like that and he'd end up with arthritis. Briefly I imagined Fabjan old, failing, being pushed around by his sons whom he had raised to be men as merciless as himself. The thought gave me a tiny twang of glee.

*   *   *

Laura and I were in the old courtyard of the house. She stood with one hand on her hip, the other shielding the sun from her eyes. She had been to the hairdresser's and now she looked different. Her hair was much shorter and curled under her ears and it was several shades darker too, something like the colour of good earth. The biggest change was that she had a fringe, which made her look a great deal younger. I'd helped her carry things from the car. Laura checked her reflection in the car window. Grace, who was sitting at the kitchen table examining the detached wing of a dragonfly, looked up. 'Wow, Mum!'

'Is it all right?'

I said, 'I think it suits you very well.'

Matthew came down the stairs, he raised a thumb. 'Duro's right. Looking good, Ma. What do you call that?'

'A bob,' said Grace.

Laura smoothed hair down on either side of her face and tugged lightly at the fringe. 'You don't

196

think it's too young?'

'You look lovely, Mum,' said Grace.

'Well thank you all!' Laura gave a small curtsey.

That was two hours ago. Now we were discussing the future of the outbuildings. Laura had had some ideas while she was under the dryer at the hairdresser's. She said it was a good place to think. 'One could be a place for guests to stay. Or we could put Matt in there. He'd love his own space. He's old enough,' she said. 'We could have a den, or a studio of some kind. Turn this space into a courtyard garden.' She showed me a magazine, full of pictures. Tall windows. Brick-laid floors and wooden beams. The kind of cushions on the floor Laura liked. 'There's a lot to think about. Obviously we can't get it all done straight away. I wanted to ask—I was thinking, say we set up some sort of system of payments—would you manage the work for us? I mean you'll do as much as you can yourself, but some of this is going to need extra labour.'

'I thought you had planned to sell it.' As I spoke I looked at Laura. The afternoon was still new and in the bright sun her hair looked even darker than it had in the house. Strange how a change of hairstyle can make such a difference to some people and none at all to others. An uncle of mine once shaved off his moustache after many years and nobody noticed, not even his wife, or so it was said anyway. With Laura it was more than just the hair. She looked completely different; in the light and with the blue sky reflected in them, her eyes glittered and she seemed to shine. With her tanned skin she could pass for a local.

Laura carried on. 'I've been thinking . . . we use

197

this as a base and choose the projects we do. There are plenty around here. So many houses, so many gorgeous villages, and of course, so many summers. People are looking for just this kind of thing. I was going to wait to talk to you about it, but since we're on the subject, I was wondering what you thought about the idea of working together. We'd have to sit down and talk about it properly, thrash out the details, but I thought I'd raise it in principle.'

This came as a complete surprise. I'd no idea what to say, of what it meant. To take over houses in other villages and change them, sell them to people from outside to come here for their holidays. People with money they were so anxious to spend they scoured the whole of Europe looking for houses, who would come here and be overwhelmed by the beauty of our mountains and rivers, who would drive into a town like Gost and think the fields around had always been full of wild flowers. People like Laura. I liked Laura, yet I couldn't stomach the idea.

Laura was waiting for an answer. I looked up but the sun struck my eyes, I couldn't meet her gaze. Blood pounded in my temples. The conversation bothered me. The heat bothered me. Laura's new hairstyle. Everything bothered me. Something said in the Zodijak, it had bothered me too, ever since I got back from town. The jug-eared man—I don't mean him—the man he was talking to, his words whirled around the back of my brain, like a tune half remembered that you can't quite catch. It happened every time I looked at Laura. And now, in that moment I remembered what it was he'd said. He said something like, 'There are lots of our people living there.' He'd been talking about England.

'Even after last night? You still like it here? You still like Gost?' I asked Laura.

'I'm certain you're right. They were just drunks.'

I didn't know what else to say. What I really wanted to do was go away and think. Maybe I shouldn't have, but I said, 'Okay.'

Laura put out her hand. I shook it.

*   *   *

Time spent working on the blue house meant I was behind with my tasks at home. In the afternoon, after my conversation with Laura, I went home and freed Kos and Zeka from their pen. After greeting me they ran into the road and began their routine of sniffing around the hedgerow and pissing on parts of it. Normally I am very clear-thinking, but that day I felt very far away from my usual self. Hard to describe it. I think I was unused to so much company, so much talking. I often went days without speaking to anyone. I'd gone on the same way for years. So had Gost. There had been few changes. People went about their lives, did up their houses and planted their window boxes; this was how we had learnt to live, you understand, had kept on living. We made sure we were left alone.

If I could go hunting it would clear my mind, as it always had done. I could take a problem out hunting and by the time I came home it would have been resolved. But it was still too early in the day, so I unravelled the hose and watered the vegetable bed. I'd taken some of the young chard from the blue house and replanted it here. I thought about the plant, how it had self-seeded year after year; this plant was the offspring of the plants that grew

199

there sixteen years ago. Next I cleared out the dogs' pen and after that I finished turning over the soil in the last bed. Later as I stood in the kitchen peeling onions for my supper, parts of the conversation with Laura replayed in my mind. Looked at in another way, of course, her suggestion presented opportunities anyone else would have been grateful for. I could make money, become as rich as the people who came to buy houses. How did people make money anyway? The only person I knew who'd done so was Fabjan. Laura and Conor had money obviously, and this was their plan to make more. I tried to think what I was feeling, became confused, struggled and gave up.

*   *   *

The edge of the woods up by the ravine. A silver light cast doubt on the shape of things. All was quiet. No wind. No sign of the roe buck, which at this time of the day were usually to be seen grazing beyond the tree line. Even the birds were still, silence except the smoker's cough of a single woodpigeon. Zeka stood a few metres ahead, his nose in the air. Kos, by my side, stared sightlessly into the trees. None of us moved. We were waiting, though I cannot say what it was we were waiting for. Without warning an owl flew overhead, pursued by a flock of pigeons. The owl swooped and dived, turning its great head to one side and then to the other, mobbed by the pigeons, who took turns at it, but lacked the courage to strike, like dogs baiting an oxen. They were driving it away from their nests. Kos trailed the arc of sound with her nose.

We moved into the woods. Neither Kos nor Zeka had yet picked up a scent. Every thirty paces I stopped and looked around. In time we reached a small clearing where I expected to see the herd, but it was empty. No flash of movement between the trees. There were still one or two places where they liked to gather: the opposite side of the trees, where the ground dipped and where there was a small pond. I kept the dogs close. Zeka moved forward at a steady pace, Kos kept her nose close to the ground, practically touching the leaf bed. At a certain moment she sniffed rapidly several times, darted forward only to turn back on herself. Then she moved forward in tight zigzags over the same ground. Zeka ran towards her excitedly, practically prancing. Kos ignored him. Now she had the scent she started to trot and Zeka and I fell in behind her. The herd must have been in the trees, where they went if they felt threatened. Possibly another hunter had been this way. I kept close watch for any sign of movement. Now Zeka had caught the scent too and he rushed ahead of Kos, only to lose it and circle back behind her. Kos trudged on, never raising her muzzle from the ground. She stumbled on a tree root, kept going. We were moving faster, both dogs had the scent again. All at once Kos stopped dead. She raised her head and scented the air, then she stood quiet and still. Ahead Zeka braced his legs and barked. He began kicking up a fuss, bouncing on his paws, tail stiff, barking warnings. By now it was nearly dark. I quieted him, I searched through the darkness. I hadn't yet raised my rifle. My eyes are good, I told you. If they weren't I doubt I would have seen him, because he stood without moving, his head held low, he didn't stamp or huff, as though

201

he had no intention of dignifying our presence with a charge or even the threat of one. Great pale tusks grew from his bottom jaw. Zeka whinnied and retreated by several steps. Kos stood her ground. Then came the gleam of an eye as the great beast turned.

Together we walked back through the trees, towards the ravine, down the valley to the road. In the years since I returned to Gost I had scarcely seen a boar. Once they were quite common, but then the animals had been hunted to near extinction. Men from Zagreb. Men from overseas. Men with pale hands and expensive rifles. Then came the chaos, when men turned to hunting each other.

Now, like the wild flowers, the boar had returned.

* * *

The boar's flight had carried with it the mood to hunt and besides too much of the light had gone. As we rounded the last bend towards the blue house I saw Krešimir's car, a black Saab a few years old, parked with two wheels on the grass verge. As we passed it Krešimir himself came walking back towards his vehicle, keys in hand. He had come to look at the fountain for himself, no doubt. I remembered him coming by here when the mosaic was first uncovered, waving his arms at Laura, and Laura, oblivious to his outrage, imagining he'd come to exchange pleasantries. The thought brought a smile to my face. And now here he was again. He didn't acknowledge me, but lowered his head and with his next step placed his foot forcefully on the ground as though bracing himself

to knock me down. I said, 'Good evening, Krešimir.'
He raised his chin as if surprised to be addressed,
pretending he hadn't noticed me there.

'Good evening,' he muttered. He glanced at the
rifle in my hand. Kos, having scented him, arced
around him, a low rumble deep in her throat. Zeka,
missing the point as ever, excited after the sighting
of the boar, bounded towards Krešimir. Krešimir
took a step back.

I could have called Zeka off, but I didn't feel like
it. Under his breath Krešimir cursed. 'He likes you,'
I said.

Krešimir sucked his teeth.

'How are your new people settling in?'

'What do you know about it?'

I replied, 'I pass from time to time, much as I see
you do.'

If I haven't told you, I should mention Zeka has
a habit, like others of his species, of taking the
hands of certain people into his mouth. He does
this gently and his teeth have never so much as
dented the flesh of anyone, let alone broken the
skin. He took Krešimir's hand and held onto it as
we spoke. I've always read this behaviour in dogs
as friendliness, though of course there are those
people who are less comfortable with it. Now it was
my turn to pretend I hadn't noticed. 'How are your
plans coming along?'

'What plans?'

'To move to the coast. I hear the property down
that way is very expensive now, even more than
before. Very popular.'

Krešimir snatched his hand away from Zeka and
folded both hands out of reach over his chest. 'Yes,
well, I'll worry about that.'

'What about your own house? Are you selling that, too? Where will your mother go? How is she, by the way?' I was annoying him. When we were young I would find I'd suddenly stepped over some invisible line between his good humour and anger, without knowing what I'd done. Then he might sulk or even hit me. Don't forget how much taller he was than me. These days it pleased me to push Krešimir's buttons. I am still a great deal smaller than him, but he doesn't dare raise a hand to me. Krešimir looked at me. Though he'd crossed his arms to free himself of Zeka's attentions, he somehow managed to convert the pose into one of superiority; his face wore a sneer and he lifted his chin, exaggerating his need to look down on me. He was clean-shaven. Dark smudges on each cheek just below the bone. Lines travelled a curve from his nose to the sides of his mouth. He gave a phoney laugh. 'Very funny, Duro.'

I'd been wrong if I thought Krešimir could no longer get to me. I felt a trickle of anger between my shoulder blades. I shook my head and shrugged, whistled to the dogs and walked away from him. After a few seconds I heard the sound of his car door, the engine starting.

We were sixty, seventy metres or more ahead. Zeka had crossed into the field for one last rabbit run. We reached the gravel, just a few metres from the house, and Kos began to drift across the road towards the house, ready for her supper. As soon as I heard the speed of the car's approach I called Kos back. She hesitated, confused by a command that didn't make sense. As far as she was concerned we were home. Her hearing was going, she didn't trust it. Instead she obeyed her instincts and turned back

204

towards the house. And Krešimir, approaching, didn't brake. Kos's hip was struck by the Saab's front bumper. She was knocked up and sideways by the impact. For a moment she hung in the air, head skewed, then she dropped to the road.

14

The first shell lands on a house near the playground. No one is killed. The kids who were playing scream and flee, then return to stare in silence at the damage, as if they are worried they'll somehow get the blame. In the second week a shell blows one of my father's huts apart. My father is inside. Daniela is standing at the door delivering a meat paste sandwich sent by my mother. My father is fixing the roof, which will be blown away a few minutes later. Afterwards, in the other huts (where none of us had been allowed) we find broken coffee grinders, an inflatable paddling pool, electric bar heaters, a wooden clothes horse, pots without handles, a box of my old toys, two beehives and many pairs of old rubber boots. In the smallest of the sheds we find cardboard boxes of tinned food, mainly green beans, and sauerkraut. In another hut: car batteries, still serviceable. The last shed is stacked with wood: planks, sawn logs and kindling.

My father, who unknown to us was in the earliest stages of dementia, will thus spare us the worst of the siege weeks.

*　　　*　　　*

A Wednesday, I think, the days have begun to blend. All those things that once helped make one day different from the next: school, church, work, newspapers, the opening of a new film at the cinema, basketball games and football matches— these things can't be relied on any more. I am on the far side of the ravine. On the other side, above the woods, is the soldiers' camp. It is close to five o'clock in the morning and still pretty dark. At this time the soldiers are asleep in their tents. In a few hours: awake, shaved and breakfasted, they'll begin to lob shells at us, and we, on the cue of the first whistled warning, will run home to dive into our cellars. When I was a kid I kicked an anthill once and watched the ants, each carrying a glistening torpedo, scrambling to carry their eggs to safety. I watched and wondered if they could see me, the giant in the sky who'd just wrecked their world. These days whenever I see a woman running down a road with her child in her arms, I remember the ants.

Two pigeons tied to my belt. I must be back before the soldiers wake up. The sound of the shotgun doesn't bother them; so far Gost has offered little resistance, because all we have are shotguns and hunting rifles and they have 120 millimetre mortars, and because they are out of range and out of view, hidden in the trees in the old concrete bunker at the top of the hill.

A colony of crows is rousing, stirring and squabbling in the branches, a convention gathers on the grass below, thirty birds or more, facing west into the wind. I wait, wanting to make the best of a single cartridge. When one of the crows on the ground crosses in front of another, I fire. The flock take to the sky, two birds remain on the ground. Ten minutes later I leave the pigeons in a bag at my mother's door and head to the blue house. These days the door is sometimes locked, so I knock and after some minutes Anka appears. 'Hey, Duro.' She makes coffee as I set to work on the birds. She wears an old cardigan and has pulled a crocheted shawl from the back of one of the chairs around her shoulders; flat-footed, her face sleep-smudged, the imprint of the pillow on one side of it. She fetches two cups and sits at the table to watch me. I split the breast of each bird and pull out medallions of meat. The remainder of the carcasses I toss into the bucket by the door to boil for Kos. Meat is scarce. People trap rabbits, but the deer are too far up the hill, too close to where the soldiers camp.

'Only two pigeons today,' I said. 'I gave them to my mother. I'll bring you the next one.'

Anka smiles. 'Give your mother the pigeons. Don't worry about us.'

'She can only eat so much pigeon.'

'But we like crow. We love crow. Come over later. We'll have it with thyme and tomatoes. I don't understand why it doesn't catch on.'

'In Paris they ate elephant.'

'Who did?'

'The Parisians, during the siege. They ate elephant. They ate rats and cats, too. And dined on elephant steaks.'

'Liar. Where would they get elephants from?'

'From the zoo.'

'They ate the exhibits? What did it taste like?'

'I have no idea. Like pork, maybe.'

Anka pulls her chin in and tilts her head to one side. She draws the shawl around her shoulder and shakes her head slowly in disbelief.

'Where's Javor?' I ask.

She jerks her head towards the staircase. 'Asleep,' she says. 'We're only being bombed every day. Not enough to lose sleep over. I'm the one who doesn't sleep.' She laughs and I do, too. Javor always loved his sleep. At that moment he appears rubbing his head and sits down at the table. 'Talk of the devil,' says Anka.

'What's so funny?'

'Nothing,' she says and helps him to coffee, leaning into him as she does so, pressing her belly against his back.

'Hey, Duro, heard the one about the refugees and the dumper truck?' says Javor. He tells a story about a group of refugees from the east who fled in the back of a dumper truck. One of them was a pretty girl and the driver of the truck invited her to sit in the cab with him. The two got along very nicely. The driver impressed the girl with details about his truck, its size and load capacity, the purpose of various levers and buttons. At some point the driver made a piss-stop. He went to the back of the truck to open the tailgate so the people could get out. But he must have failed to apply the hand-brake properly because the truck began to creep forward. He called to the girl still sitting in the cabin. The girl, who had been paying only slight attention to the driver's talk, pulled the wrong lever: the one that operated the hydraulics to raise the dumping bed. She dumped the refugees on top of the driver.

You see, even then we could laugh, though my father and sister were already dead.

Anka says, 'I want grapes and cheese. Green grapes and Greek cheese.'

208

'Feta,' says Javor.

'Feta,' repeats Anka softly.

'Maybe I can get you some cheese, it will be just like feta, you'll never know the difference. We can ask Fabjan.'

'And grapes?'

'That might take longer.'

Anka throws her head back and groans. 'I'm sick of eating everything from a jar.' By now we've eaten the contents of our kitchen gardens, we are eating the bottled fruit and vegetables we have put aside for the winter. They'll last a good while, because in this part of the world we treat every winter as though it is the last.

In the evening I return with a bag of cherries. Anka is in the outbuilding removing a pot from the kiln. It is a deep bowl with an inwardly curving rim. The road south has been closed for weeks now; the trips she used to make to the coast in her Ficó to fill her orders with the tourist shops are no longer possible. There are no tourists. The coast is another country again. Behind me: stacks of wooden crates stuffed with decorated dishes, ashtrays, fridge magnets, all packed in straw. Anka has given up making these things. War has given her a kind of freedom and her work provides a place of refuge from the craziness. She sets the bowl on an old lead-topped table. When she sees me, or rather the cherries, she squeals and swoops, grabs a handful and rams it into her mouth. Juice spills from the corner of her lips; she looks like a young and healthy vampire.

'Oh Duro, where did you get these?'

'A wild tree.'

She stops and eyes me sideways with suspicion.

'No, Duro. I don't want them.' She picks up the bag and pushes it into my chest.

'Take them, it's fine.' I push the bag back at her.

'I know where they come from.' Takes a step back and wags a finger at me.

'Well then don't tell my mother.'

Anka laughs. She steps forward and snatches the bag, stuffs more cherries into her mouth. Afterwards she wipes her mouth and grows serious. 'You can't do this, Duro. You think I don't remember where the tree is? This is the last time.' Suddenly she hugs me. She smells of ceramic dust, vinegar and sweat.

'Where's Javor?' I say when she lets me go. Along with the other men of Gost we have joined the territorial defence forces. So far all we've done is show up in the school gym for nightly meetings. A representative from the Crisis HQ in the Town Hall informed us the new National Guard was handling the situation. They have taken up a position south of the town opposite the army in the north. In between lies Gost. The army want to reach the coast but we stand in their way. Each side has roadblocks you have to pass through, on the road north and on the roads south out of Gost. Same questions, but different answers for each.

'He'll catch you up.'

'Don't bother. We only want people who can shoot straight.'

This makes her smile. 'He's not so bad.'

'You were better.' I point to the bowl. 'This is good.'

'I'm going to decorate it.'

'I like it this way.'

'What does it matter? Nobody's going to buy it.'

'One day.'

210

'One day, sure.'

Duration, after all, is the whole point of a siege.

*   *   *

The storm over the town rumbles day after day. Some people have already left Gost. They left before dawn and after dusk, without telling their neighbours and they left their pets behind. How did they know? The rest of us didn't see it coming. Now it's impossible to leave. Too many refugees. There are the roadblocks and checkpoints. Both sides are happy to shoot you. A dog or a cat in the car is a sure sign you're getting out and that means trouble. The abandoned dogs sit outside their old homes waiting to be let in.

I borrow books from the library on the days it is open. I read about sieges. Constantinople. Delhi. Mafeking. Paris. Dien Bien Phu. Leningrad.

The siege of French forces by the Viet Minh in their garrison Dien Bien Phu took place in 1954 and lasted for exactly fifty-four days. In the middle of that fifty-fourth night the brigadier general in Dien Bien Phu radioed his commander and asked permission to surrender. You've done magnificently. Don't spoil it now by hoisting the white flag, said his commander, three hundred kilometres away. OK, replied the besieged man from his valley hole surrounded and overlooked by tens of thousands of enemy soldiers. I was only thinking to save the wounded. There were five thousand at that time, you understand. Well, see you soon, replied his commander.

French soldiers named their strong-points after women: Beatrice, Gabrielle, Isabelle, Élaine. The

211

men decided to hold off the enemy as long as possible and allow the men in Isabelle to make a run for it—they had the best chance, you see, but only seventy made it anyway, so it was for nothing. Ten thousand were taken captive, force-marched to prison camps across the country. Most of them died on the way.

Nobody had expected the Viet Minh to use nineteenth-century tactics.

In Dien Bien Phu planes dropped rations and the men crept out under the barbed wire into no man's land to fetch them and were shot to bits. The citizens of Paris ate the animals in the zoo: Castor and Pollux, the elephant pair, were shot through the eyes as nobody could lay hands at the time upon an elephant gun. Only the zoo's big cats were spared because of the difficulty of approaching them, also the monkeys: people thought they looked too much like humans. Parisians developed a taste for horse meat, which continues, as well as dog, cat and rat meat, which does not. Photographs of Paris during the great siege: people sitting in restaurants with napkins tucked round their necks, munching on rat *blanquette* accompanied by the last bottles of decent wine.

*   *   *

A heavy mist slides between the trees and across the sloping ground. The tree trunks are slick and black, thick odour of rotting leaves, and—mingled with the cold morning air and the sharp scent of pine—the snap of cordite. A deadly hush. I am alone. I tread with care, weight on the outside of my foot. The dampness helps, softens the ground; the heavy

212

air smothers small sounds. The deer are nowhere to be seen, but I sense them behind the mist, smell their moist breath, see the flash of a liquid gaze and feel a trembling footfall, twitching hide and hair, the quiver of a haunch. They are watching the shape-shifting patterns of mist. At the first tree I pause, wait and listen. I peer through the trees into the almost darkness. Forward, forward, step by step.

Minutes pass and still no sight of the deer. They must be retreating ahead of me, herding uphill. I stop and look the way I have come. The mist is beginning to clear in patches, here and there shafts of sunlight reach the forest bed freeing curls of vapour. Underfoot the ground is soft, springy and damp. The upper tree line is several hundred metres away. I'm closer to the soldiers' camp than I have ever been though still a good kilometre away and the wind is in my favour.

Out of nowhere a deer barrels across my path: a young male on the edge of panic, the smell of musk and fright all about him. He's there and gone. It gives me a jolt, a squeeze to the heart. I wait a minute or two before I begin to move steadily in the direction he went. A mature doe comes racing towards me, passing within metres, fleeing some threat, or she'd never come so close. Only a few times in all my years have I been so close to a live animal. Seconds later a group comes racing through the trees, a second group bolt past going the other way. I am caught in the middle of a stampede. There's something comic about it: the deer, their sudden leaps and graceless crashings, and when they stop they stand around as if they're embarrassed at their own behaviour, before the madness goes to their heads again and they're off, ricocheting through the trees.

Something has spooked them—not me, though by now they've surely scented me, which is no doubt adding to the general confusion. I wait in the shadow of a tree. There's no longer any point being here. Nothing can happen now, the deers' blood is up—I won't get close to the herd today.

Movement. There's another animal in these woods. Smaller, nearly as fast as a deer, a softer footfall. It scatters a group of deer and lurches round in a circle before heading back towards them. A dog: a youngster of two or so with huge paws, ears streaming behind him, tongue lolling, the thrill of the chase gone to his head; he races straight past me, the deer have his eye and he's heady with the scent of them. I don't recognise him as belonging to anyone in Gost and he doesn't look like a stray. A hunting breed, well fed, well cared for, totally undisciplined.

The sound of voices. Singing and shouting. Soldiers singing drunken songs. A late-night session has turned into an early morning hunt, but none of them is sober enough for it. The dog is out of control. This is bad for me. The big problem is the dog. At the moment he's too bound up chasing deer, but the minute I start to run or even move that will all change. If I stay where I am, which I don't have any choice but to do, he could still come back. I'm pretty sure he's seen me, he's just not that interested while there are deer to chase. I stand still and count my breaths.

Three, four minutes pass. I hear the hooves of the panicked deer, catch glimpses of them through the trees. The men's voices rise with the power of

214

the song, fade and start over. There are two, no, three of them, their singing so tuneless it's only on the second run I recognise the song as '*Hajde Da Ludujemo*'. Last time I sang it was at Javor and Anka's place after the party at the Zodijak. I think of how we used to all join in. I think about what would happen if I did so now. I smile.

And then the dog comes back.

This time he sees me, he's bored of deer he can't catch, he comes over. A nice dog, glossy and fit. I imagine one of them found him, or stole him somewhere along the front line, from one of the villages where some guy, who may be dead now for all I know, bred him and the rest of his litter.

I put out a hand to him, which is what he wants. Just to say hello. So long as I keep him quiet it can still be OK. Ignoring him will only make him more interested; anything as foolish as trying to hide would have started him barking. I stroke his muzzle and ears. In a quiet voice I tell him to sit. He sits and looks at me expectantly. I order him to lie down. He does. He waits, looking for his reward. When he figures it isn't coming, he looks around for an escape and then rises slowly, hoping I won't call him back. When he thinks he's clear he bounds away to look for his master.

The singing grows fainter. There are only two of them at it. Another song. They're moving away, heading to the camp, needing to get back in time to sober up, with a long day murdering civilians ahead of them.

When I judge it safe enough I move. I don't head back the way I came, but move diagonally downhill, taking advantage of the cover of the trees for as long as possible. It is later than I would like and there's too much light in the sky. This is a new danger. I have to get out of the woods and across no man's land without being seen. I start to jog, slowly enough to keep an eye out, fast enough to cover the ground.

I am still in the woods when I come across him. I stop and take cover behind a tree. Standing with his legs apart and his flies undone, pissing against a tree, unsteady on his feet, he sways forward and then back, holding onto his cock as if for balance and staring at the jet of piss. This guy is one of the drunk hunters who's been left behind by his friends. Only two voices where there had been three. My mistake. I'd assumed they were all still together, but no—here he is, number three, in my way, taking a leak while the sun climbs higher and higher with every second. Soon it will break the horizon. I feel a small jet of rage.

I am barely in his eye line, I move noiselessly until I am out of it. I am less worried about being seen by him than I was by the dog. The guy is dead drunk. I move behind one of the pines and wait for him to finish. He seems to take for ever. I lean against the tree and watch. He shakes the final drops from the end of his cock. I wait for him to zip his flies and stagger off, but he doesn't. He leans his back against the tree, standing in his own patch of piss, and begins to stroke his cock.

I wait and the waiting goes on, because the guy is drunk and his cock is stiff, but not stiff enough, so he rubs harder and harder but he still can't make himself come. He tugs at it a couple of times and stares as though his dick has never let him down this way before. I think he'll give up and stick it back in his pants but he doesn't. What is he?

216

Nineteen? Twenty? He can go on playing with his dick for hours. He changes hands. I think: Here is my enemy. I am watching my enemy masturbate.

The sun is rising. Above the horizon the sky is whitening.

My enemy. I could tell you I think about the shell that landed on my father's row of shanty huts; the explosion left him pumping blood when he should have been eating the meat paste sandwich carried by his daughter who is now lying on her back on the grass, the arms that carried the plate blown off. My father was killed at once. Daniela took five hours to go, her whole body shook in a long death rattle. The expression on her face was as if she had done something wrong, like an animal caught in a trap, crying without making any sound. I could tell you I think about all of that, but I don't. I think about the sun and the dawn which is almost over. I stare at this guy wanking in the forest. I have a silencer on my rifle. His friends will have reached the camp a kilometre away. I raise the gun and it's the easiest shot I have ever taken.

As for the soldier, he dies with his cock in his hand. I might have waited for him to have one last blast, but then, to be honest, I'd waited long enough.

15

The bowl I'd watched Anka take from the kiln days before is now a deep blue, the colour of sea when the water reaches a certain depth and the sun is high, when you sail over rocks. Fish of different sizes swim head to tail around the inside of the bowl, slender and pale. The bowl is like nothing I have ever seen Anka make, completely different from the thick, brightly painted pieces she makes for the shops. With the small tool in her hand, Anka scrapes at the fish and to each she gives gills, scales. An eye. Every so often she pauses to blow the dust out of the inside of the bowl.

I watch in silence. When she is finished I carry the bowl into the blue house for her. Cardboard and cloth cover the windows, the mirrors are taped across. The plates that used to be displayed on the dresser have been put away. On the table the blue bowl, looking suddenly immensely fragile.

Later in the day I ask Javor, 'How are the folks?'

'I was up there today. Roof needed some work. They're OK.'

'The house was hit?'

'Shrapnel.'

He worries about his mother who was due to travel to have an operation at the district hospital a while back. The hospital in Gost is too small. The operation had been scheduled and then cancelled when travelling became difficult. Javor's father is head of the post office. I told you this. A job he's been in ten or more years. I'd last seen him at my father's funeral five weeks ago. He'd brought Chivas Regal and said a few words in the church, the first time I'd ever seen him there, because the family usually worship at the Orthodox. My father had always thought he was about as decent as a boss could get. Too many people got their jobs because of who they knew. My father liked the fact his boss had once been on the floor sorting mail, just like the rest of them.

218

No post now for five weeks.

I've brought over a lark and a pigeon. Anka has stewed the birds whole, there is gravy dark with blood. Anka tells Javor not to put the prices at the Zodijak up any more.

'Tell Fabjan,' says Javor. 'He doesn't care. He says we sell *rakija* and beer, not baby milk.'

I'd been in the Zodijak just that morning. Krešimir had been there, too. He'd ignored my nod, as he does unless someone's looking. When he said goodbye to Fabjan he shook his hand, patted him on the shoulder. Fabjan is fast becoming an important person in Gost, it's as easy as that. Krešimir behaves with Javor as he does with Fabjan, but I've sometimes seen Krešimir give Javor the same low stare he gives me. And I never see Krešimir at the blue house. As far as I know Anka goes alone to visit her mother and brother at the house in town. Maybe this is the only way they have to keep the pecking order alive. Fabjan, who'd hardly bothered to look up when Krešimir left, asked me to help him heft some crates up from the cellar. Every bar in Gost is closed or on the point of it, and yet the Zodijak seems to have a limitless supply of beer, vodka and brandy. This fact I'm sure is connected to the soldiers of the National Guard who I see drinking there in the evenings. Fabjan keeps their glasses filled. When they leave he shakes their hands and this time it's Fabjan who pats the other men on their shoulders and tries to persuade them to stay, have another drink. One for the long road back to the checkpoint.

Javor and Fabjan are joint owners of the Zodijak but Fabjan takes all the big decisions and mostly this suits Javor just fine. Two things he hates:

219

conflict and hard work. Not that he's lazy, it's simply that he's never had to try too hard. His father is influential, his business partner has ambition enough for both of them. As a young man he walked a straight line from the love of his mother to the love of his wife. He does not lie, because he doesn't need to. He has never been betrayed; he has never been frightened.

In silence we sit at the table and pick the last shreds of meat from the hollow, ivory bird bones. Anka is thinner, the shadows under her cheekbones have deepened, her skin is pale even though it is summer. For all her outward robustness, there's a new delicacy about her. She is more beautiful than before. She uses her index finger to wipe the gravy from her plate and lifts it to her mouth. No bread for a week now. We dine on woodpecker and lark, like the kings of long ago, like the Parisians who dined on the elephant meat, on Castor and Pollux. Eating has become our only pleasure. We talk about food all the time.

'Asparagus, veal saltimbocca,' I say, describing the food in a hotel restaurant I worked in briefly. 'With mozzarella and ham from Istria.' The chef in that restaurant was an Italian and good, but it was attached to an ageing hotel whose corridors smelled of mould and toilet cleaner: the vast restaurant was more often empty. That nobody came to eat his food didn't seem to bother him in the least; he executed every order as though he were cooking for a duke. 'Once in pity I sent through a fake order. Nobody was in the restaurant and the manager was asleep in the office behind the front desk. I took the order, I served it to myself. I ate it. Veal saltimbocca. Asparagus. Another time he made

220

squid ink risotto for the two of us, he told me it was his signature dish. They made it in a lot of the restaurants I worked in but I never tasted it so good.'

As you see we did a good job of holding on to the lie of civilisation.

'You need a haircut,' I say to Javor. The soft brush of his hair has grown lank.

'I told him the same,' says Anka. 'You know what he says?'

'I grow it as an act of protest,' says Javor. 'When we are free I will cut my hair. I will also go to the movies, eat fucking maraschino ice cream and demand an audience with the Pope.'

While I listen to all the things Javor never knew he wanted, I look around. There is Anka's bra hanging to dry at the top of the banister, the picture of her grandparents on the dresser: her grandmother in mud-caked man's shoes, a wedding dress, her hair framed by the points of a star, on the couch a grey cat reaches out to touch the air with a single paw. 'Don't go,' says Anka, when I rise to leave.

'I need to, it's late.'

'To where? Stay.' Javor punches me lightly on the arm. 'It's dark. Not safe to be out.'

'As safe as staying.'

'True.' The window shutters, closed tight against the night, maybe even the dead eye of a rifle sight high in the hills. Javor stands to switch off the single light above the table before he opens the door.

I walk home slowly. Across the fields the houses of Gost are hidden by the darkness: not a single light, not a single sound, except the whisper and smell of the trees, no movement save for a pair of bats leaving their roosts. I walk on listening to the sound of my footsteps. I imagine the arc of a shell coming from the hills, the blue house blown apart behind me: the slender fish on the sides of the bowl, a golden star and the grey cat flying through the night sky.

*   *   *

I hold up the piece of mirror I use to shave and rub a hand over my head. Take the scissors and cut the hair blind, use a razor to remove the rest. All this by candlelight, some minutes past three, an hour and a half before the dawn. I dip my fingers into a jar of paint and draw two fingers across my nose and cheekbones, one side and then the other, and remember Anka's finger sliding across her plate last night, taking up the last of the gravy. Just like the old days when we went out before school: Anka, Krešimir, me. How I used to enjoy those early morning hunts.

I blow out the candle. Downstairs I pull an old woollen hat down over my forehead, from the rack I collect my rifle, the old 7.62 my father took such care of the years I was away. Outside Kos, in her pen, rises to greet me. I scratch the top of her head with two fingers and I promise to feed her when I get back. Today I'm hunting alone.

The morning air is warm and damp and the crickets have gone quiet. There will be a mist later, which is no bad thing. I breathe deeply, there's a tension in my gut. My heartbeat is slow and regular. My head is entirely clear. I leave the road almost immediately and duck into the long field, staying close to the hedge; moving at an easy pace I head straight uphill until I reach the pine plantation.

222

The last rows of trees mark an undeclared border between the people of Gost and the men in the hills. They don't drop below it and we don't rise beyond it. The two hundred or so metres of slope below the plantation is no man's land.

Moving from tree to tree, it takes me forty minutes to reach within half a kilometre of the old bunker where Krešimir and I used to play.

They've changed the position of the watch; it takes a few minutes to find him. He's awake, obviously exhausted, teetering on the edge of sleep. This is the worst time of the night for the look-out, standing alone in a dark forest, thinking no further ahead than the next hour, half-hour, fifteen minutes—the end already in sight. I see him check his wristwatch, flashing his torch on and off to do so. My watch, my father's watch which I've been wearing these past few weeks, is on the table by the side of my bed; on a morning as still as this one I might be given away by the ticking of the watch. It's early and I decide to have a look to see what's happening in the camp. I draw a loop around the guard and head uphill.

The smell of them: ashes and burned pine resin, earth, night breath, canvas and oil, underneath it all the sting of sweat and ammonia. With my next step I set foot on a firm crust of earth which yields to something softer. I ease my weight back off, too late. The stink floats upwards and clots in the back of my throat. I try not to breathe in. Along with their rations the soldiers are forced to swallow everything, all the boredom, anger, homesickness and frustration which comes with doing what they are doing; the brew curdles in their guts, their shit stinks of it.

Four guns. I am struck by the size of them. Even

223

though I was once trained to use these very guns, in my mind's eye they have grown to the size of howitzers, but really they are much smaller. The barrel reaches my shoulder, the wheels just above my knees, that's all. There's enough ammunition for more than a month. Probably there must be twenty men, asleep in their bivouacs.

In all their imaginings, this is probably not how they saw war: sitting on a hill, trying to frighten the shit out of people on their way to work and to school, blowing them apart. They start off being sickened by it, slowly become inured, and then bored, the resentment begins—that's when the fun starts. I saw it when I worked for a short time in a slaughterhouse. There were guys who in the first week could barely keep the contents of their stomachs down, a month later would be ramming the stun gun up the backsides of pigs and slitting the throats of lambs in front of the ewes. Not all the guys, just some of them. And maybe some of these soldiers have enjoyed it all from the start: look through the field scope and decide who to kill today. A man on a scooter. A couple leaving a café. A young woman carrying a meat paste sandwich to her father in a shack at the end of a garden.

The stink of them, I cannot stand it.

What are you doing? I stop moving. The voice, clear and loud, as only a sleep talker would speak, comes from inside one of the bivouacs. There's a stirring and grumbling, the sound of bodies turning. *I'm fucking your mother.*

Silence again.

Now it's time to choose. I can either go back for the boy down the hill, or I can wait for his relief. I think about it and decide to wait for the relief.

224

Today is the boy's lucky day. Maybe because he looked at his watch and maybe the watch was given to him by his father. Or because he doesn't look like the type who'd be out here willingly, doing this kind of work: he looked on the small side and quite young, difficult to tell exactly how young in the flash of light from the torch. Too young but old enough. Counting more than the minutes to the end of his shift, counting the weeks and the days until he can go home.

I change my mind back again.

A mist is coming down, as I knew it would, thickening around me. Soon enough I find him. He's sitting with his back against a tree, one hand on his upright rifle, head back, eyes closed. For a moment I think he's asleep, but he opens his eyes and looks around, peering into the mist. I am about a hundred metres away and I know he hasn't seen me or heard me: he's looking for the guy who's coming to replace him. He wants the hell out of there while he's still alive. The commander should put them on watch in pairs, but he doesn't want to lose face. As for me, I've tried not to be too predictable. But this guy, whose eyes keep darting in the direction he expects the relief to come from, well let's just say it would be a shame not to disappoint him.

I move closer. Seventy metres.

He cocks his head like a dog, turns from side to side. Then he yawns and even though he tries to control it, still it gives me the opportunity to move closer. Sixty metres. I have a clear line of sight through the trees. I raise the rifle to my shoulder and put my eye to the eye piece. In the grainy light of the new dawn I see him stare into the mist with the blank, wide-eyed stare of a person trying to stay awake. From a distance, the rustle of dead leaves. Now he's alert. This is it, he thinks, relief on its way or somebody coming to kill him. He's wrong on both counts. The sound is just deer moving through the woods, magnified by the mist, so that they sound nearer than they are. As for the person coming to kill him, I'm already here.

He has tightened his grip on his rifle and is looking around. He has that way of screwing up his eyes and sticking out his chin that short-sighted people do. He licks his lips and the corners of his mouth. The minutes pass. I place different parts of him at the centre of my cross hair, his left eye, then his right eye, his nose (which needs a wipe), his mouth. The deer move on. The man in front of me slumps, his shoulders and chest drop and his belly sinks, he loosens his grip on his rifle, he rolls back on his heels to lean his weight against the tree. He does something I've never seen a grown man do, he puts his thumb in his mouth and sucks.

Mist threads through the trees, water gathers on the branches, drops fall in patterns of sound. I let the minutes pass. I'm so close to him I can hear his breathing. Ten minutes or so later and the thing I've been waiting for happens. He yawns and this time he lets it go, taking short breaths and opening his mouth wider with each one. His eyes are closed tight and his head rocks back. He doesn't bother to cover his mouth.

Time now. I take a breath and exhale slowly. I think: Now that's a good way to die.

He is small, I was right. I pull off his jacket and use it to bind his head, to prevent a blood trail, because the back of his head is open. Then I hoist him without too much difficulty over my shoulders.

226

The body is warm and limp. When we reach the edge of the ravine I lower him to the ground and unwrap the jacket. His jaw falls open. I push it shut. He has a cleft in his chin and long, dark eyebrows. The jaw falls open again. I heft him over the side of the ravine. The body thuds as it bounces off a rock, a crack as it snags briefly on the branches of a small tree and then it's gone. A splash as he enters the swimming hole. The body lands face up and I watch while it gently corrects itself, spinning slowly in the current. I pick up both our guns and head home.

This is how it has been for a few weeks now. The first one, of course, the drunken hunter. There've been others. Three, maybe four. Once I left it too late and with daylight coming I had to string the corpse up by the ankles, hoist it into a tree and wait until later to come back. Some of the skull came loose and part of his brain slithered out and fell to the ground. I kicked earth over it. Later I worried the dog would find it, but that didn't happen.

All over the country the number of deserters is growing; the commander doesn't let his men spend too much time looking for the men who've gone missing. Does he even know they're dead? At any rate the dog has definitely gone, because there's been no sight of him, not even a bark or a whimper. Maybe he ran away.

*   *   *

September, a day passes without the scream and whistle of shells. I'd like to tell you we left our houses and wandered the streets shaking hands and gazing at the clear blue sky, but it wasn't like that. A month earlier the National Guard finally

227

lived up to their promises and began their offensive; they'd been waiting to be supplied with weapons and ammunition by the government. For months St Mary's Church survived the shelling. People said it was a miracle, but I knew, because I had read it in a book in the library, that artillerymen rely on spires and other landmarks to direct their aim. When, in the final days, the soldiers on the hill rained shells on us St Mary's Church was hit several times; this time they were aiming for it, something for us to remember them by. I pass by the day the shells stop and see the priest (he'd shown courage in the last months, leading the funerals to the graveyard): he is moving a large silver cross out of the way of the weather and thieves. In the street a dog stands on a low roof and barks at the heads of passers-by. The smell of scorched brick and dust mixes with the odour of oleander. For twenty minutes I help the priest shift rubble and broken statues, then I walk through Gost as I haven't for weeks.

Over the days that follow memorial notices are posted on telegraph poles and lamp posts throughout Gost, so that the poles and posts flutter with white paper like they do at carnival time; some notices are new and brightly white, others rippled and water-stained, streaked with ink. Some sheets of paper are blank, washed clean by the weather; announcements of new deaths are pasted over the old. I stop and read. Jelena Rukavina. I saw her, her face had been crushed by her own house, the cheek caved in and part of the skull. She looked exactly like a broken doll, as though her head was hollow inside. Joso Cacić. He burned. Gas from a pipe. He was trapped and he couldn't get away from the flames. We didn't get to him in time. Karlo

228

Klanac cracked jokes all the time we removed the bricks from on top of him. He died anyway. Smiling death, the doctors called it, something to do with the kidneys. Karlo Klanac went with smiles and bad puns. Bernarda Zorica. Shrapnel. Radmila Štimac. Shrapnel. Ivan Maras-Brico. I went to school with him. He had his head blown off. Miro's brother, digging up potatoes in his back yard, took a direct hit. Imagine what that does to a man. His wife, standing at the window, blinked and he was gone. Puff! Antun Ratković crashed his car driving home without headlights in the blackout.

Later I climb up to the old bunker, where the men had been camped. Bleached rectangles of grass, an old shaving brush and a pink plastic toothbrush with bent bristles, a lighter in the shape of a steamer ship, which no longer works, a penknife, the blade is rusty and the handle dew-stained but I keep it anyway, and a wallet empty except for a photograph of twin dark-haired boys. A pile of rubbish: empty tins, cigarette cartons and ration packs. And a cesspit full of shit.

*   *   *

In the third week of October the men arrive. The Mayor calls those of us who served in the territorials to a meeting in the school gymnasium, thanks us for our courage and dedication. We've been drilled in weapon use, though we all learned how to handle a rifle at our mother's breast. Mostly we cleared up after a shelling, hoisting corpses to the mortuary. We've attended nightly meetings. None of us has seen any fighting, which was left to the National Guard. Now the commander of the National Guard

229

stands beside the Mayor and afterwards shakes several of us by the hand and then shakes his fist in the air. There are a few cheers.

Standing either side of the Mayor are two of the men from the new unit. The Mayor introduces them by name. (Perhaps one of these names is familiar to you. For a while some seven or eight years later he was mentioned in the newspapers several times a week. One picture they used a lot. In it he wore a tall fur hat and a brocade jacket; probably it was taken at a wedding. By coincidence, I saw a picture of him in a newspaper just the other day. He was being transferred to an open prison for good behaviour, which is how seriously the government took his penance. He was sentenced to fifteen years, not enough, but still someone took the trouble to put him there. No, not enough, but enough to unnerve some people with secrets of their own. I looked at the picture for a long time: he hadn't changed much except that now he was bald. He is very unremarkable-looking, you would pass him in the street. You'll find the picture in the box with the other cuttings.) He has short dark hair, already receding into a sharp widow's peak, a nose with a cleft tip, grey eyes and heavy, pale eyebrows, which are at odds with the colour of his hair; he is dressed in fatigues, a peaked cap bearing the insignia of the new country and army boots, and stands with his legs apart and his hands behind his back, in the way that militiamen do. Everything in his manner gives the impression that here is a most resolute man, who knows exactly what he wants, down to his breakfast order. When he smiles he shows surprisingly good teeth. Next to him the Mayor in his nylon blazer looks grey and rumpled.

The Mayor tells us these men have been sent direct from Zagreb to offer us assistance. The one with the pale eyebrows steps forward and shakes his fist in the air. He cheers. His cheer contains the air of a challenge, so this time people cheer. He cheers again and we cheer back, once, twice, three times. By the third cheer the men are really roused.

The newcomers say they are here to protect us.

After the meeting a few souls wander over to the Zodijak for a drink. Fabjan is wiping down the pinball machine. No sign of Javor, who tends to stay away from the Zodijak a good deal of the time these days. I guess he and Fabjan must have decided it's awkward given the bar remains the favourite watering hole of the National Guard. Madness to turn down the money they bring. 'Business is business,' says Fabjan. So Javor concentrates on collecting supplies and bringing the books up to date. I've seen him sitting at the kitchen table working his way through the bound ledgers that contain columns of the Zodijak's profit.

We drink for an hour. There's talk, about the meeting and other things. Someone wonders out loud who the fuck these pansies are who turn up when the show's over, but they shut up quick when four of the same walk in: the two we have just seen at the meeting and two more. Fabjan goes over to shake hands and offer them drinks on the house, business first always. After he serves them he sits down at their invitation and from the bar I watch them laughing and joking, downing beers. Fabjan looks very comfortable: he's winning them over the way he wins over everyone.

By nine o'clock I'm drunk. The bar begins to empty as men leave for their wives and smashed homes. A couple more customers wander in, not a busy night. One of them is a distant cousin of Javor, looking for a drink because after all drinking is the only thing left to do. He nods to a few folk, including me, and leans on his elbows hunched over the bar. Fabjan, sitting with the new arrivals, sees Javor's cousin but he doesn't come and serve him. As for the cousin, he's in no hurry; he leans on the bar and kicks the floor with the toe of his shoe. After a while he reckons he's waited long enough and he wants that drink, he twists round to see what's going on. 'Eh, Fabjan!' Fabjan ignores him. The cousin calls again. 'Eh, Fabjan?' Again no reply, even though it's impossible for Fabjan not to have heard. So the cousin stands up straight and draws in his chin, the way people do when they think they are being insulted. He looks around, but nobody meets his eye. We are witnessing a show of strength and most people are not keen to get on the wrong side of Fabjan. In a situation like this timing is crucial. All it would have taken was for another customer to have ordered a drink, as little as that to bring Fabjan to the bar, to rupture the line, but the moment has already passed. And the reason why has something to do with the presence of the newcomers.

The man with the widow's peak and pale eyebrows lifts his glass to his lips and slowly drinks. He's watching, although his gaze rests on nothing in particular. He puts the glass down on the table, reaches for his cigarette in the ashtray and takes a puff, putting it back with the same deliberateness. He puts his hands on the table and spreads his fingers, the way people do in films.

Me, I stand there and watch. I am drunk, which

232

has slowed my responses. I've missed the moment too, and now it feels as if there is nothing to do but watch the thing unfold. I also want to know as much as anyone whether Javor's cousin will call a third time and demand to be served and if he does what Fabjan will do. But the cousin is no fool. He swears under his breath, pushes himself off the bar and leaves. Through the glass I see him gesture, more or less to himself, he sort of flicks his hand, as though there is something stuck to his fingers.

The man with the pale eyebrows and the widow's peak smokes his cigarette and orders another Johnny Walker. Fabjan takes his place behind the bar. The burning filter of the cigarette of the man next to me in the ashtray makes a bad smell until he finally notices and crushes it out.

By the next morning the whole incident is gone from my mind. Too much else to think about. I need to hunt, to bring some meat to the table. We have all been hungry for so long. When I see Javor later that evening the business with his cousin comes back into my mind, but there is Anka and in the moment I realise I am not sure what it is I am going to tell them. I say nothing. We talk about the food. I say nothing. This is the greatest mistake I will ever make.

16

First I dug a pit. I dug it at the top of the long field. A metre square, a metre and a half deep, because of foxes which as you know are relentless. Second I zeroed the sights on the .243. I have my own set-up at the far end of the long field, with a bench and target, and this was one time when everything had to be right. I spent half an hour up there, checking the alignment of the cross hair on the target, fractionally adjusting the sights. I set up the rifle in the place I'd chosen, then I measured a hundred paces and made a mark in the grass.

I lifted Kos from the blankets on the floor by the side of my chair where she'd lain for the last two days. There must have been pain, but she barely made a sound. Impossible to carry her all the way, so I laid her on an old trolley I had in the yard, the kind you get from railways, which is where I got this one in the first place. I'd used it to shift bags of cement when I was turning the old pig house into a home for myself eighteen years ago; in November of the same year I found Kos. In human years she would be a centenarian, so perhaps what we were about to do wouldn't be so far in coming anyway. I locked Zeka in the house, which is something I'd never done and would unsettle him, but was unavoidable. I gave him a piece of the fried liver I had in my pocket and set off with Kos, pulling her on the trolley first up the road and then carrying her from there to the top of the long field. I put her into the position and fed her some of the fried liver from my pocket. Kos lifted her head to take it from my hand, and nibbled it perhaps to please me for her appetite was pretty much gone.

After Kos was hit by Krešimir in his car, I had carried her into the house and examined her. Her hip was dislocated and although I had tried twice to push it back into place, it wouldn't take. I had to muzzle her to stop her biting me in the madness of the pain. After the failure of the second attempt I

234

sat back against the wall, then I released the muzzle and wiped the flecks of foam from the corner of her mouth. A third attempt would have been useless: at her age her chances of healing were already poor.

Now I put my lips to the top of her head, stood up and walked to where I'd set the rifle up an hour before. I could feel myself beginning to sweat, my palms were moist. I wiped them on my trousers. I didn't want Kos to catch the scent of my fear, I wanted her to die taking the trust with her. My father had put an end to our dogs, when the need arose, with a shotgun in the long field. He did it alone, solemnly, and never spoke to any of us about it. Sometimes, with a favoured dog, he would never mention the dog's name again. I'd thought through all the ways to kill Kos, to smother her perhaps. She would have let me put the pillow over her face, would only have started to kick when her instincts overcame her and died knowing she'd been betrayed.

As it was Kos was lying in the sun, in a place she knew. I'd positioned her with her back turned to me, not so that she couldn't see me of course, she was blind anyway, but because it made it harder for her to catch the smell of my fear and also because it presented me with the top of her head, which she raised briefly as I walked away. She was listening and waiting for me to come back to her. The sounds of the rifle—of the bullet dropping into the breech, of the bolt sliding into place, the click of the safety catch coming off—were sounds she had heard all her life, maybe they even brought back the memory of a hunt, if those were the last sounds she heard then that was OK.

She was lying on her side, one ear to the wind,

the cross hair was lined on the centre of her skull. My hands shook and I was glad I'd set the gun on a tripod. I'd taken care to fit the silencer, too. Nothing left to wait for and so I released the safety catch with my thumb, took a breath and slowly exhaled, I pressed the trigger and shot Kos through the head. Then I buried her in the hole I'd dug on the edge of the pine plantation. I went back to the house and let Zeka out. He circled the yard twice with his nose in the air and came back inside. I took a chair and sat at the table. For the first time in many years I didn't know what to do.

Fifteen, twenty minutes might have passed. I don't know. A knock on the door. I sat up, rubbed my face and went to answer it. Grace. She stood in the road, some distance from the door. She held out her hand with the palm up, a strip of braided thread lay across it. The events of the day, Kos, my mind wasn't working. 'What is it? What do you want?'

Grace smiled, maybe a little uncertainly because I'd spoken more sharply than I ever did; she raised her hand a little further. 'What is it?' I asked again, differently.

'A friendship band. I made it for you. To say thank you for helping me with the fountain.'

I took it from her. 'Thank you, Grace,' I said. I wanted her to go.

'Can I come in?'

'Not today,' I said. 'I'm busy.'

Grace's smile faltered.

I said, 'Thanks for this . . .' I wasn't really sure what it was. Before I could shut the door Zeka had appeared and pushed Grace's hand roughly with his nose, demanding to be stroked.

'Maybe I can take the dogs for a walk. If it would

236

help you. Where's Kos?' She looked past me through the door and began to call Kos.

'Kos is gone.'

'What do you mean Kos is gone?'

'Kos is dead.'

Grace looked up as though I'd hit her. 'Kos is dead? How come? What happened?' With every word her eyes grew brighter.

'It was an accident. A car.'

'Poor Kos. Duro, I'm so sorry.' Without warning Grace stepped forward and embraced me, an awkward embrace, I was standing on the step and she was several inches below me, she put her arms around my waist and pressed her ear against my chest. We stood like that for some seconds. I didn't know what to do, what I wanted was to be left alone. I patted her shoulder, I think. Grace sniffed and stepped back. She wiped her eyes with the back of her hand. I said, 'Thank you, Grace, very much for this.' I held up the coloured strip, stepped back inside and shut the door in her face.

The next morning I was up early. I made coffee and exercised, adding an extra ten press-ups, pull-ups and so on. I felt drained and heavy. I took Zeka for a walk in the hills. Dogs are slower to realise the fact of death than humans; of course Zeka didn't know Kos was dead, he only knew she wasn't there and he'd taken advantage of this by occupying all the best places to lie in the yard and in the house. But as we walked it became obvious to me that he was beginning to miss her presence. All his life they had moved and thought as a pair: running, trailing, routing. He'd been used to taking the lead in unfamiliar places and following her in familiar ones. Zeka bounded out of the house and across into the long field, but then all the rhythm was lost. He charged off once or twice at the scent of something, but lost interest. Again and again he circled back to me; by the end he had given up and trotted quietly by my side.

One thing I know, I have always been able to lose myself in work, so as early as was reasonable, I walked over to the blue house. As I turned the corner where the house comes into view I stopped to look at it. I was proud of my work: the gutters were cleared, the broken tiles of the roof fixed, the woodwork, windows and doors painted their original shade, the dead tree was gone, the stonework at the front was whitewashed. And of course there, restored, the mosaic of the bird. I'd never paid it much attention when I first saw it so many years ago. I thought it was just a bird, a whim of Anka's, maybe her way of making the house more her own, the fountain too. Now it seemed brighter, more splendid than ever before: you half expected it to take flight like a mythical creature out of the pages of a children's book that comes to life and flies over the hills and the roofs of the houses, breathing fire upon the townspeople.

Inside the house Grace was washing up the breakfast things. When she saw me she stopped what she was doing to come over and give me a hug. I sat at the table with the coffee she made for me, answered her questions and avoided her puddled eyes. Instead I talked about my plan for the day: to trim the trees at the front of the house and the hawthorn hedge at the back for which I'd brought the chainsaw along. Some sizeable branches needed to come down. I looked around the room. The interior had hardly been touched, though I'd

238

fixed the roof which would prevent the patch of wall getting any worse. I could do that later today or tomorrow. As for the rest, Laura talked about getting rid of the pine cladding and tearing up the floor tiles, she also wanted an entirely new kitchen and that was just downstairs. But I was in no hurry now, this was the house as I had known it and as I liked it, I could make sure the work was never done, especially if we began other projects, it would all go on the back burner.

Matthew walked in. As ever he appeared half-asleep and shuffled over to the fridge. He took a carton of milk and drank straight from the spout, then he slumped onto the table opposite me, his back to Grace, who, when she thought I wasn't looking, gave him a kick. Matthew looked up in confusion, first at Grace and then at me. He put the milk carton down on the table. 'Shit, man!' he said. 'I'm sorry about your dog. Jesus.'

'Thank you, Matthew,' I said.

Out of the tail of my eye I saw Laura appear at the back door, where she hesitated, paused for a moment and turned away. Matthew continued, 'Yeah, well like I said, when Grace told us . . .' He lost the thread. 'What was her name?'

'Kos,' I replied.

Matthew leaned across the table and patted me heavily on the shoulder. It was kind of Matthew, who hardly ever thought about anyone but himself. He sat back down, shaking his head as if making sense of the tragedy.

Later, with Laura, I discussed the height of the boundary hedge and which branches of the trees I planned to take down. After the moment when she'd turned away from the back door she'd eventually come into the house and behaved much as she was doing now. Her hands flew, her smile shone and her eyes slid over me. At lunch I helped Laura open a jar of pickled vegetables, for which she thanked me too many times. She offered me every item of food on the table separately, as if she was nervous, not of me going hungry but of leaving a gap in the conversation, into which something else might possibly slip. It didn't matter to me especially, you understand. That Kos was dead was a matter of fact, which couldn't be changed. I might even have thought Laura was trying to spare my feelings, if it wasn't for the way she avoided my eye as though pain was a disease she could catch.

Late in the day I went up to the hills with Zeka, spent too long up there and by the time I was coming down it was nearly dark, I was just below the lower tree line, not far from the place I'd first seen Laura's car drive into Gost. Just a little further on there is a view of the blue house and as it came into sight I thought I saw the figure of a man standing behind it, under the walnut tree and beyond the hawthorn hedge which I'd trimmed earlier that day. Now that the hedge was lowered you would have had a view to the back of the house, which I guess was why the man was standing there. My eyesight is good even in poor light, as I've told you many times, but now it was late and very nearly completely dark. I couldn't be sure. I stopped, waited and watched, keeping the figure in view and waiting for any shift or movement, and sure enough it came. There was somebody there and he had just lit a cigarette, taken the packet out of his jacket pocket, shaken it and put one in his mouth and then lit it. I had not much more than a view of his profile and a white smudge

240

of face, lit by the flare of the flame. He wore a pale jacket and dark trousers or jeans and stood smoking and looking into the back of the house, into the kitchen where I supposed the family was gathered to eat their supper. Upstairs a light went on and the man lifted his head towards the window on the upper floor. The light went off again and he went back to watching the kitchen window. He stood with his legs apart and one hand in his pocket, like a man on a street corner in any city in the world, casually lifting the cigarette to his lips and lowering it, watching passers-by as if he had every right to be there, not even bothering to look around or behind him. He might even have been waiting for the right moment to go and knock on the door, perhaps after he'd finished his cigarette. Or at least he would have if it wasn't for the fact he was standing in a field behind a hedge at the back of the house and not out front. The way he'd positioned himself was interesting: half hidden but in such a way as to suggest he didn't care whether or not he was seen.

From where I stood I couldn't see whether or not a car was parked anywhere near by. I moved closer, swinging back a little the way I'd come so that I approached from behind. The fact is I'd recognised him more or less at once, certainly by the time he lit his cigarette. Now he flicked the butt away with a gesture that was completely familiar. It wasn't Krešimir, who I'd also have recognised from his height and the slight curve of his shoulders. This man was stockier, heavier and a smoker, pale jacket and jeans. The jacket was made of butter-coloured suede and the car, wherever it was, would be a BMW. The man standing outside the blue house was Fabjan.

At a distance of one hundred metres I gave Zeka a silent command to lie down and to stay. At a distance of fifty metres I stopped and waited. Fabjan hadn't heard me, but as I say, everything in his manner said he didn't care if he was seen, in fact I'd go further and say it was almost as though he wanted to be seen, by the occupants of the house at least. He lit another cigarette, I watched him. He smoked it down, flicked the stub with his thumb and forefinger so it flew, a malignant yellow firefly, over the hedge and into the yard of the blue house. In all he smoked three cigarettes. He never turned. After the final cigarette he walked down the side of the house, where the ladder is. After a short while I heard a car engine and then a few seconds later came the headlights and the BMW drove past the blue house.

I called Zeka and went up to the hawthorn hedge, to where Fabjan had been standing and where, on the other side of the hedge, an ember glowed in the matted grass. For a minute I stood where he had stood, watching Laura, Grace and Matthew where they sat at table over the remains of a meal: a new Laura, with shorter, dark hair, a fringe and sun-tanned skin, a sweater over her shoulders, playing with the melting wax of a candle, her profile lit by its flame.

*   *   *

Sixteen years ago we endured months of candlelight. When it was finally over and we could turn the lights on, some of us were already used to the dark but for others nothing less than one

242

hundred watts would do. I've heard that over at the hotel the passing tourists complain about the lighting in their rooms, in the foyer, but most of all in the restaurant. They say it's too bright, they want something called ambience. The tourists can't understand and nobody wants to explain, so they lie and say that people here like to see their food.

*   *   *

Some people start to return to Gost, others leave. Javor's mother makes the journey north to have her operation. Javor puts her on the bus, which is packed with people. The family who owned the baker's shop up sticks and are gone. The shop is closed, the hatch through which they used to sell *devrek* and meat pies is sealed. Yesterday's bread still sits on the shelves at the back. Soon it is no longer yesterday's bread but three-day-old bread, last week's bread. There's no explanation, no note on the door, just an old notice in faded black felt tip stuck to the door which asks customers to make their orders for the next day by ten o'clock. Somebody crosses out the word *hleb* and writes *kruh*. Both of the words mean bread, but some people use one and some the other. The ones who start leaving are the *hlebs*. So now there is only one baker's shop in town. This inconveniences everybody, and yet it's also the way we want it. In the closed shop the bread behind the counter turns blue. I know the family, everyone does: the two daughters: the Mongol the boys at school used to follow and grunt at and the slutty one in the angora sweater. I'd often been to their house, my father and theirs were always lending and borrowing things.

243

Also the father used to supervise karate practice at the sports club, which I went to for a short while because my father thought it would do me good. In their front room they had a round rug, deep red colours, with a Persian-style pattern. I remember it well because I used to sit and stare at my feet and the pattern, embarrassed by the presence of the Mongol, while the red-haired mother offered me day-old pastries from the shop and the father went to search for whatever he was returning or giving.

So when I see a woman and a man, whom I also know, walking down the road with the very same rug on their shoulders, I know exactly from where it has come. The man strides forward and nods briskly at me but doesn't speak and looks me right in the eye for a beat longer than anyone would normally. Behind him the woman, his wife, who is still wearing her slippers (they are the kind with a small heel), totters under the weight of the thing. She gives me a sheepish grin, lowers her head and scuttles on. The husband's boldness stays with me for a long time. A pair of middle-aged thieves, challenging me to challenge them.

The door of the family's house stands open, a downstairs window has been broken. The television has gone already, and of course the rug. Over the weeks that follow the remainder of the family's belongings disappear into the homes of neighbours and former friends. I recognise their curtains hanging in the window of the deputy karate coach's house two streets away. Somebody drags a mattress from one of the upper floors, gives up and abandons it in the doorway. Someone else sets fire to it. A sticky little turd appears upon the scorched ticking. Stray cats move in and take over from the family's pet cat: the toms make mincemeat of him.

A meeting at the Crisis HQ, months, it seems to us, after our part of the crisis is over. Those of us who were in the territorials turn up at the Mayor's office to be told we're not needed and so we go away again. Fabjan though is invited, I pass him on his way in. The man with pale eyebrows and his cohorts are there too. I am on my way to the Zodijak when I see eight or so of the lads appear, the ones I told you about, who tinker with the engines of their motorbikes in the car park behind the supermarket and hang out by the pinball machine in the Zodijak. They're a bit like we used to be though Andro, Goran, Miro and I are thirty now. These guys are ten years younger. They look up to Fabjan. The meeting lasts three hours, I know because even though I have things to do I wait in the Zodijak the whole time and I'm there when Fabjan comes in and goes straight to the back room. A few minutes later the pinball boys turn up, only this time they don't stand around the pinball machine with their hands in their pockets, taking turns, comparing scores and sharing beers. No, this time they go straight to the bar where a few lean with their backs to the counter, facing the room and the street with a new assurance. When Fabjan comes out of the back room he pours drinks for the whole lot of them. In the days that follow I see them in the Zodijak a lot. Suddenly there's money about.

The National Guard leave. The boys from the Zodijak take over the checkpoints. There's one on the road between Gost and my house. The guys never check my ID, they always wave me through. Javor stops coming into town even the few times he did.

Days pass, not much changes. On roofs throughout the town the red of the new tiles stands out alongside the old faded red. The post starts again, letters from relatives in the city and overseas, some containing money. There are no new death notices, except of the very elderly, for whose hearts the whole thing had been too much.

The official start of boar hunting season. Usually that means visitors, men arriving from the city, groups of them, who stay for the weekend. This year that doesn't happen. On one of those October days Anka and I go up to the hills. We are alone. During the conversation on the way up to the pine forest she frowns and chooses her words carefully, as if she's worried about their effect, as if this thing, whatever it is that she's afraid of, which right now is made of smoke and dust, will crystallise and harden by being put into words, be made real, like an illness or a death pronounced by a doctor. There will be no going back. She chooses her phrases carefully: 'just a matter of time', and 'for now', and 'when things get back to normal'. A lot of people in Gost talk this way, if they talk about what's happening at all, but Anka does it because she's afraid she and Javor might need to leave, like the baker and his daughters, and she doesn't want to leave Gost because like all of us, like Javor, this town, these hills, the ravine and the pine forest are all she knows.

Later, alone on my bed, I think of Javor's cousin coming into the Zodijak on that day, which is now some weeks ago. I think of the sign on the door of the baker's, the *hleb* crossed out and replaced, in thick black marker pen, with *kruh*, how that word *kruh*, written in that way, takes on the weight of an

246

obscenity. I think of the thieving couple and the baker's rug, of how the man stared me down, daring me to challenge him and call him a thief. I don't know what it all means. I think about the pattern on the round rug on the baker's floor and how I used to stare at it as I sat in the front room of the baker's house, so that first the black and then the red stood to the fore, how shapes appeared and then receded, and how (if you stared for a very long time) the lines and dots seemed to shimmer and dissolve. Familiar patterns faded away, new patterns appeared where none existed before, only to disappear in the blink of an eye.

For three hours that afternoon all of this is forgotten as we hunt together for the first time since we were children. The air is warm, the trees heavy with fruit. Kos is with us and she picks up a scent almost immediately. By the time we reach the trees we've stopped talking, to give Kos a chance of course, and also because the conversation, so full of pitfalls and quicksand, frightens us both. So we let Kos take the lead.

Anka carries the smaller of the two rifles. I carry the one I once used to hunt soldiers of the National Army only a few months before. Anka is kneeling and I stand behind her. Kos has led us to a small bachelor herd of no more than ten. They are playing, making practice charges and trying to lock antlers. In a few years they'll be fighting for the herd and sometimes their lives. I remember once, out hunting with my father and his friends, we came across a big bull dragging the carcass of a second bull, almost as large as he was. Their antlers had locked during a fight, the dead buck's neck was twisted and broken; his opponent, unable to free himself, was faced with his own death. We watched as he pushed, dragged and tossed the lifeless body, finally standing still in exhausted bewilderment. The bullet, when it came from one of our group (it may even have been my father), must have been almost welcome.

Now there's a young buck whose antlers don't amount to much, no spread to the branches, each antler little more than a couple of spikes, the longer of the pair about fifty centimetres, enough to do damage without victory. In the long run he is more use to us than to the herd. I keep an eye on him and, when I look down at Anka, I see she's doing the same, waiting for him to come into range. Slowly she raises the rifle to her shoulder, she waits another minute, closes her right eye (I remember that little peculiarity of hers) and takes the shot. She is as good as she ever was, and briefly I wonder in that moment if she had been a boy, what would have happened then? Would Krešimir still have been Vinka's favourite?

We dress the buck there and then. Anka shares the work, pulling on the rope to hoist the carcass, which weighs about as much as she does. Unhesitatingly she draws her knife and slits the animal open from breastbone to belly. She is enjoying it, the physical work, the freedom which follows the months of confinement. With the back of her hand she wipes her brow and leaves a faint smear of blood above an eyebrow. She is smiling. I bury the spilled guts and wrap the heart and liver for Kos, cut the animal down and carry it on my shoulder. The three of us head back down the hill.

Anka sings.

From the blue house I head up to my mother's

house, carrying a haunch. Tonight we eat. My mother is pleased and begins to search her larder for what she might cook with the meat. Tomorrow, I say, as I kiss her. Tomorrow all of us, here for dinner. Me, you, Danica, Luka. She reaches up and places a hand on each cheek, kisses my forehead. I am not tall, but I feel tall next to her, who was never tall and now without my father seems smaller still. Her hands smell of roses and when I leave I carry the scent with me, in my nostrils, on the skin of my face. In the moment I decide to go into town and so I turn right and, as I cross the bridge into Gost, I see a man I recognise, he is an old colleague of my father's. I remember him from my visits to the post office and also from the funeral. He's a stocky man with muscular forearms and the rolling gait of the bandy-legged. He's walking along the road, quite fast, rolling a little which might be his legs or might be because he has been drinking, because behind him along the pavement there is a trail of letters leading back to town. The strange thing is that he doesn't seem to know they're there, or maybe he just doesn't care. He's walking along with his head tilted back; in his arms are bundles of letters, his pockets are stuffed with letters, his trouser pocket and the pockets of his post office uniform jacket, too. Every now and again one or several of the letters escapes at a time, adding to the paper trail behind him.

'Hoi,' I yell from the other side of the road. 'Mr Buneta!' (For that is his name.) I run and begin to collect the letters for him. What is he doing? What's he thinking? The man must be mad. I run back maybe one hundred, maybe two hundred metres, I don't know, gathering up letters. But he

249

doesn't seem to notice my efforts, certainly he doesn't acknowledge them, he doesn't even slow up so I can hand them back to him. I must pick twenty letters up off the pavements and even though I am the younger man by thirty years, what with so much stopping and bending the distance between us lengthens. Between letters I jog to catch up and flick through the letters I have in my hand. They are letters for people in Gost, with their names and addresses, postmarked and ready for delivery. But surely this guy doesn't think he's delivering them. There are a few for people I know. The baker, who has moved on, anyway, so there's no point delivering it. And Javor. Javor and the baker. Surely this is no coincidence.

Now I sprint to catch him up. 'Hoi!' I yell again, waving the letters. This time he stops and when I reach him, I see the man is crying, more than crying, bawling like a child. A big, bandy-legged, red-faced child. He drops all the letters he is carrying, balls his hands into fists and holds his arms stiffly down at his sides. He sniffs and sobs and speaks haltingly and I discover this: that the head of the post office, Javor's father, has been taken away by the men newly arrived in Gost. Buneta saw it, he jabs a finger at his own red and teary eye. He saw him being put into a grey van, inside which were other men: a restaurant owner, the director of the hospital, the bloke who ran the hardware stores. He saw what was happening, so when they wanted the post office records for the addresses of the others whose names were on their list, he had the idea of taking the letters, so they wouldn't be able to find them. His plan, as far as he has got, is to take as many letters as he can home and burn them.

All the people to whom the names belong are people who worship at the Orthodox church; the priest's name is on one of the letters. People who use the word *hleb* for bread. I bend down and pick up the letters, as many as I can. I force them into every one of my pockets and when they are full I gather an armful, run to the side of the bridge and throw them over the metal railing into the river. I have caught the man's madness and when I turn round I see him moving slowly away, with the air of a lost toddler.

And then I start to run. I run. Towards the blue house.

*　　　*　　　*

I shook my head. I turned away from the window. It was dark now, in my stomach a knot of foreboding tightened. I'd felt it all summer, but now, seeing Fabjan there outside the blue house in the half-darkness, I thought: It's already happening, things are changing. I am not a religious man, but it seemed to me Laura had been sent here for a reason. I'm not saying that was the case, I'm just saying that was how it seemed at the time, standing there on that particular night, in the place where Fabjan had stood. I could smell burned grass from his cigarette.

17

Laura arrived in Gost and opened a trapdoor. Beneath the trapdoor was an infinite tunnel and that tunnel led to the past. In the last days of the family's stay in Gost I seemed to have become trapped in the tunnel, somewhere between a time sixteen years ago and now. When I was a child I had, for a while, been fascinated by Greek myths as it seems to me every boy at some point is. The Minotaur, the monstrous beast created by one betrayal followed by another. Two betrayals: the King of Crete's betrayal of his god, when he refused to sacrifice the bull sent by Poseidon; the betrayal of the King by his own wife with the same bull, a betrayal which produced the Minotaur himself. So to hide their shame and guilt they built a labyrinth into which they confined the Minotaur. Sometimes I imagined myself as the Minotaur, roaming a maze of tunnels below Gost, the echo of my roars reaching the ears of those who lived under the sun.

* * *

I reckoned I had only a few more days' work on the blue house, it all depended on what Laura decided she wanted to do. A wasps' nest in the attic would have to come out. The dead tree needed to be cut into logs and they would see me through the winter, but I could do that anytime. Beyond that, the last remaining job was to fix the wall in the front room, everything else could wait. Matthew came by when I was on the ladder and asked if he could help, so

I gave him a job preparing the wall, tearing out the crumbling and broken plaster. Meanwhile I wandered out into the yard. Today was Friday, tomorrow it would be exactly four weeks since the family arrived in the last week of July. Such a short time. I stood at the outbuilding door and thought back to the day I'd first seen their car drive into Gost on the road that led from the coast, the way the vehicle seemed to hesitate before the turn, then later finding Laura in the road in front of the house looking for the water mains, our trips together to the swimming hole and to Zadar. The restoration of the mural and the fountain. Krešimir's rage. So much had changed over those weeks, and yet in many ways the change felt like a return to a past, as though Laura, Matthew and Grace weren't strangers newly arrived in Gost, but had in some way been here for a long time. They'd be going soon, in a week and a day to be exact. Laura had already begun to talk about how to secure the house when it was empty; I told her she needn't worry, I'd keep an eye on it. Laura leaned across the table and squeezed my arm and said something she'd said many times: 'What would we do without you, Duro?' She told me Matthew and Grace had to get back to school, both of them had important exams in the next year. For Matthew this would be his last year in school and then he'd be leaving home. She had talked about him taking a year off before university or college, to travel, maybe to Africa or India to help the poor.

Inside the outbuilding: the Fićo. The week before I'd managed a good number of hours on it. Then with the death of Kos I had briefly lost interest, but now I made up my mind to have the car working before the family left; I thought of it as my gift to Laura, and in the last few days I'd spent a lot of time thinking about this car and what it would mean to see her drive it.

I heaved open the double doors of the outbuilding. While Laura was out, I wanted to see if I could get the engine running. I'd given the car a thorough going over: cleaning the carburettor and the fuel system, I'd replaced the water pipe, the brake hoses and pads as well as the clutch cable and all the tyres. A new battery, that went without saying. I leaned through the window and released the hand-brake and pushed the car backwards into the sun. I slipped into the driver's seat, felt for the choke and pulled it out a little. I'd taken the key for the car from the hook beneath the shelf and I slipped it into the ignition lock and turned. A surge of life passed through the car and died. I tried again, pumping lightly on the accelerator, and this time the engine started up, the familiar sound all Fićos shared, the same pitch and whine as a coffee grinder. I gave the engine time to warm up and sat listening until Matthew rapped on the window.

'How cool is this fucking car?' he mouthed through the glass.

I wound down the window. 'Get in,' I said. 'Careful with the door.' I hadn't got round to oiling them yet. I reversed the car over the grass towards the track at the side of the house which led to the road. I took the car up the road, the one that led away from the main road towards the old farm buildings. It drove OK, the engine sounded a little rough and juddered slightly, a couple of things still to smooth out, but I was pretty pleased. At the end of the track I stopped and turned to Matthew. 'Do you want to drive?'

'I don't know how.'

'Time you learned. I'll show you.' I climbed out and Matthew scrambled over into the driver's seat. 'OK,' I said. 'Remember how I asked you to put it into gear the last time.' I talked him through the rest. He stalled three times before he got going. We drove in second gear towards the farm buildings; before we reached the hamlet four or so kilometres on we switched places and I turned the car round. I let Matthew drive back to the blue house. 'Drive into the yard. I need to check something and then we will put it back. We can make it a surprise for your mother if you don't tell her.'

With Matthew's help I put the car back in the outbuilding, covered it up and closed the doors. I needed a little time to tune the engine, check the contact breakers which I thought were probably the source of the shuddering, after that the car would drive perfectly. By tomorrow, I thought. I lowered the bucket into the well, drew it up and took a long drink of water. The next day was Saturday. A good day, Gost would be full.

* * *

Next morning as soon as I'd eaten and exercised, I went over to the blue house. As usual the family were sitting outside over coffee and the remains of breakfast, sleek as a family of otters basking in the sun. Laura was still in her night-clothes, Matthew was bare-chested, wearing a pair of pyjama bottoms, only Grace was dressed.

'Hello, Duro,' said Laura, shielding her eyes from the sun as she looked up at me. 'Have a coffee, there's more in the pot.' She hadn't yet brushed her hair (her newly dark hair) and her face was bare of make-up, her slanted eyes were half closed against the sun and her robe had slipped to reveal the strap of her nightdress, her bare legs were stretched, toes pushed deep into the grass.

I sat down. 'Thank you.'

As soon as I appeared Matthew slipped away. When he returned he'd changed into a T-shirt and jeans, in his hand he carried Laura's blue shawl. He winked at me as he slipped it over her eyes. 'What's this? Matthew?' Laura put her hand up to the blindfold, patted her son's fingers.

'We've got something to show you.'

Laura, completely obedient to her son, offered no resistance. Instead she held up her hand for him to take. That Matthew hadn't said anything to Grace either was obvious by her expression as she stood up to follow; she looked from Matthew and Laura to me and back. I shrugged as though I had no idea what was happening either. Matthew led his mother through the house and into the courtyard. She said, 'Hold on, I don't have any shoes.' Grace kicked off the pair of flip-flops she was wearing and slipped them onto her mother's feet. Pretty feet with painted nails, the second toe slightly longer than the first. Laura felt for the step, Grace picked up her mother's foot and placed it so she could feel the edge. 'Hold on! Don't move. Stay there.'

Matthew and I opened the door to the outbuilding, which swung open with a great deal of creaking.

'What's going on?'

'Hey, I said don't move,' called Matthew. He took the key to the car from the hook and went over to his mother, lifted her hand and pressed it into the palm. She fingered it, like a contestant in a game show.

'Well that's easy enough. It's a key.'

'You can look now,' said Matthew.

Laura pulled the shawl down from her eyes, frowned and peered into the darkness of the outbuilding. Matthew and I each took hold of one end of the cover of the car and slid it off. Grace clapped a hand over her mouth. Laura took a pace forward. 'You mean to say it's ready?'

I said, 'Yes, it's ready to drive.'

The three of us stood back and watched her as she walked towards the car very slowly, as though it might just disappear in a puff of smoke. Carefully she opened the driver's door and stroked the cover of the seat; she climbed in, felt for the ignition and slotted the key inside. When she hesitated Matthew said, 'Go on. I've driven it.'

'Have you?' She looked up at him.

'Sure, Duro let me. Yesterday.'

'You two have been planning this?'

Matthew smiled.

'Well, come on!' Laura patted the seat next to her and Matthew opened the door and was about to swing himself inside but stopped. He stood back.

'No, take Duro first.'

'Of course. Come on, Duro,' called Laura.

I sat in the passenger seat. Laura turned the key in the ignition and the engine started. I would have preferred to warm it myself beforehand, but that would have spoiled the surprise. She eased the car out into the courtyard and the sunlight and then into the track at the side of the house. Matthew whooped and ran after the car for a short distance, to be left behind as we picked up speed. I listened to the engine, and was satisfied. I wound down my window and dipped my hand into the wind, I turned to look at Laura as she adjusted the driver's mirror and she caught my glance and smiled. 'Are we going for a spin, then?'

I nodded. 'Turn right here.' I directed her out towards the main road, the one that heads north. A blue butterfly flew in through the open window and danced for a few moments in front of the windscreen and our faces. Laura slowed until I had time to catch and release it; she said it was beautiful. She began to sing and tapped the steering wheel lightly. She drove well, without hesitation, except once to look for the location of the indicators, and so I leaned across to show her. And she drove barefoot, Grace's flip-flops kicked under the seat, feeling the pedals with her toes, like she was pushing them into sand, down on the accelerator. We were out on the main road, the warm wind on our faces.

'How fast can I go?'

I didn't answer the question. I leaned back and closed my eyes. Not so easy to relax in a car this size, you can imagine, all the same I did feel relaxed. I listened to the whine of the engine as it responded. I remembered the smell of the car, the way you could feel each rut and wrinkle in the road. Everything felt good. For the first time in many years I felt something like happiness. We did not speak, until Laura said, 'Duro, I think we're going to have to go back.'

I opened my eyes. 'Why?'

'Because I'm still wearing my night-clothes.' And she looked into my eyes and laughed.

258

Later, after Laura had dressed, and after first Matthew and then Grace, and then Matthew again but driving Laura this time, had all ridden in the car, Grace and I were left alone in the yard. I turned to Grace. 'Where's the hat your mother bought in Zadar?'

'Dunno. Why?'

I said, 'Isn't it the same colour as the car?'

'Oh yes it is. Red hat, red car. Hang on. I'll go and find it. Good idea. Mum will love that.'

*   *   *

That evening (because I had an idea about what might happen) I went to town for a drink. I've told you people no longer walk out in the evening, things have changed, but still there are a good many people around on a Saturday evening in Gost. Women doing last-minute shopping before the shops close on Sunday. Men sitting outside bars. Lads riding their scooters around the supermarket car park.

Plenty of people in the Zodijak. Fabjan was there. I nodded to him and said hello to the girl who took my order; I noticed she no longer greeted every customer with a smile. After she'd delivered my drink she went back to playing with her hair at the bar, pulling it out strand by strand from a patch at the back of her neck. I went to sit at Fabjan's table; I wanted a ringside seat. Last time I'd seen him he'd been standing outside the blue house looking over the hedge at the family inside. He barely greeted me and nor did he offer me a seat (not that he ever does). He was smoking and reading a paper. I sat with my back to the bar and stretched out my legs,

259

watching the street, and when I finished my drink I called for another one. Today I had all the time in the world.

Some time ago Fabjan had installed a satellite dish, quite likely illegally. Since the days of the pinball machine there had been continual upgrades at the Zodijak. On big-match days the place was packed. Today CNN was on: fires in Greece, the government has declared a state of emergency. Fifty-three people missing. Pictures of burned-out villages, burned-out cars, all of which looked very familiar. Evacuation helicopters. A statue of a winged god or perhaps an angel, blurred by smoke, flames visible in the near distance. There followed a feature about a member of the Ku Klux Klan convicted by a Mississippi jury of kidnapping and killing two black teenagers. The murders took place back in 1964, when the state was segregated, three years after I was born. James Ford Seale. On the screen a photograph of him as a young man, movie star handsome. Pictures of him being led into court: orange jumpsuit, wire-framed glasses, age spots. Happy black folk outside the court waving a placard: *Forty Years On*. The brother of one of the murder victims, according to the words running below the pictures, was the one who had tracked the old man down.

I sipped my wine and checked the football scores on the back of Fabjan's newspaper until he put it down, possibly to spite me. I made some conversation about the football. He was no more in the mood for talking than on any other day. He answered me in monosyllables as he went through receipts in his wallet. I sipped more of my wine and counted the minutes.

260

This is what happened:

Some time between six thirty and seven Laura drove by in the Fićo. One or two people noticed the car, I've already told you they are quite rare these days. Even I can't remember when I last saw one on the road. You see them dumped outside people's houses, all rusted up. But also, and I've told you this too, in some quarters the cars were gaining a little cachet. So when Laura drove right through the middle of town in the Fićo some people's attention was caught by the small red car. In the Zodijak a man at the table behind me said to his companion, 'Would you look at that?' (The guy from the municipal offices again.) His companion twisted round to see what he was talking about.

'Now I had one of those. My first car. Loved it like my life.'

'I had one. My brother's first. He gave it to me when he went abroad.'

'Mine was white, I put black stripes on the bonnet, like in that film *The Italian Job.*'

'Those were Minis.'

'I know.'

'Had to keep the back open to stop the engine overheating.'

'Drove it everywhere. Reinforced the roof to take more weight.'

The girl, who was serving them beer, said, 'My uncle had a car just like that. He lived in Novigrad.' Some of the other drinkers started talking about the cars: the limited choice of colours, advantages over the Fiat 600 and vice versa, the eighty kilometres per hour top speed. Someone claimed to have made eighty-six in theirs. Not a single person had not, at one time or another, owned or known one of

261

these cars.

Fabjan looked up from the contents in his wallet. He turned his head to see what people were looking at, his great bull neck made it a slow movement. Laura was parking the car on the opposite side of the road. I kept a silent eye on Fabjan who watched with nothing more than casual interest much in the same way the two men and the waitress did.

Maybe if it had not been for what happened in K— just a couple of weeks before, which had everybody talking, already thinking the thoughts they tried not to think, that and the restoration of the mosaic and the fountain. Word had got around. The nerves of the town were close to the surface. The waitress was the only person to whom none of this meant anything and I wonder to this day what she thought about the way all the men around her went silent and stared at this woman in a red hat, stepping out of a small red car. This woman who was at least twenty years older than her, with short dark hair, the men were staring at her as if they'd never seen the like. The waitress, pretty and blonde, glanced around at the men and at Fabjan who was sitting with his hand (holding a receipt) frozen in mid-air and flounced back inside to the bar. Finally, Fabjan swallowed.

What stillness that evening, it lay over the town. All that moved was Laura, trailing a storm in her wake. Imagine: Laura in her red hat and the sunglasses she wore against the low evening sun, moving through the town, visiting shops to pick up whatever she'd come into town for. Did she even notice the long looks? The exchanged glances? And if she did, did she ask herself what it was all about? I don't imagine so: knowing Laura, she would have swung through the town thinking only about what she had to do, crossing the errands off her list and enjoying the evening sun on her face.

*   *   *

In the bakery (which opens for a few hours on a Sunday) all talk was of the night before. I'd made sure to stop by for a pastry for my breakfast, something I did occasionally. Those who had seen the woman in the red hat who drove the little Fićo told those who hadn't all about it. Details were added: the woman wore a necklace made of pottery beads, she spoke English but something in her accent made it sound as if this wasn't her native tongue; it was as if she understood what people around her were saying. It was the same woman who took over the blue house a month ago now; it wasn't the woman who had taken over the blue house, though she looked like her, this was a different woman. The woman was in her thirties; the woman was in her forties. It was claimed she asked directions to a house in Gost. Descriptions of her outfit varied: some said she was wearing a smock, others jeans. I know that Laura was wearing her denim skirt, a blouse tied at the waist and espadrilles, because it is my favourite outfit of hers.

Three details remained consistent: that the woman had short dark hair and wore a red hat. That the car was a red Fićo.

Later that day I was having a drink in the Zodijak. Perhaps I should have avoided the place for a while, but I was enjoying the atmosphere in town since Laura's jaunt and I wanted to savour it. Anyway, it was Sunday and Fabjan was with his family, at least

I assume he was. I bought a glass of wine and sat at the front of the bar; the evening was pleasant, cooler than it had been. The sky was filled with starlings the way it had been the evening of the day I first met Laura. You remember I'd stopped for a drink there and then seen Krešimir passing by with his shopping and invited him for a drink. I mention the starlings for no reason except that they were there, carving patterns in the sky as they so often did. It meant a hawk or a kestrel was somewhere around. I was watching them much the way I did the time before and when I looked down I again saw Krešimir, only this time he wasn't walking past on the other side of the road carrying his shopping home, this time he was storming across the road towards me. It gave me a thrill to see him so angry; my heart quickened because Krešimir in a rage is capable of anything. I curled my fingers around my glass of wine.

'What the fuck do you think you're doing?'

I stayed calm. The stakes we were playing for were rising and I needed to keep sight of the end game. I looked at him, I didn't answer, though I may have blinked, with a kind of surprise. 'What the fuck do you think you're playing at?' He was practically foaming at the mouth. Nobody looked up. Around us the other drinkers stared into their glasses, or at the street ahead, or up at the television above the bar.

I said, 'I don't know what you're talking about.'

'You'd better put a stop to this shit, all this shit. I'm warning you.'

'What shit are you talking about?'

'That fucking woman, that fucking house.'

I said, 'You mean the blue house, the one you

264

sold to the woman from England?'

You'll guess that the way I said woman from England and not Englishwoman, *Engleskinja*, was deliberate. Woman from England—the words left space for doubt to creep in and where doubt existed there was the possibility of something else: the dark child, scratching against the walls. Now I had the attention of everyone in the bar. They were all listening, even though some of them were still pretending not to. I stood up to face Krešimir because he was towering over me where I sat and I felt disadvantaged. I considered putting my glass of wine down. 'What is it you think I am doing?'

'You know exactly.'

'I've done work on the house. I need the money. So what?'

'Trying to stir things up, cause trouble.'

I raised my voice to be sure I was heard. 'You're the one who is causing trouble, you did it the day you sold the house. You had no right. No right. That house was never yours to sell. It's you who has brought the strangers here and you who brought this whole thing down on our heads.'

By now the other drinkers were listening, making no pretence at deafness. Hardly a person in Gost didn't know what we were talking about. This was good, but I'd had a bellyful of Krešimir. I said, 'I think you need to calm down, Krešimir,' and took a step back when he lunged for my throat. One of the men who had been watching stood up and put himself between us. He was broader than Krešimir by a hand-span. He didn't say a word, he looked at Krešimir and tilted his head towards the street, showing him the door so to speak, obvious too from the way he stood he was confident he had the rest

265

of the bar at his back. Krešimir, for all his bluff, is a coward. He took a step back, shook himself off and disappeared. I nodded to the man who'd just saved my skin and he nodded back. We did not speak, we resumed our places. I took a sip of my glass of wine and returned to watching the street and the patterns of the birds in the sky.

18

We were petty thieves, smugglers and black-marketeers. We kept illicit stills, we hunted out of season because we could. We hated to pay tax, we did deals on the side and took cash whenever we could; we were the kind of people governments don't like: bullet-headed, obstinate, as hard to control as it is to herd cats. It turned out we were the sort of people who would steal from the houses of those who had fled, which we did, without shame.

I see Goran's wife in the street and she is wearing a long leather coat I've never seen her in before. Bicycles for Andro's two boys, there's a swing chair on the front veranda that wasn't there before. Miro drives a different car, a car I recognise and I know doesn't belong to him. So, he shrugs and asks me what's the difference? If they come back he will give them their car, of course he will, otherwise it just sits there outside the house or somebody else takes it. He used to sell dirty videos to make a bit of cash, but he doesn't bother with that any more. He has a house full of second-hand items for sale: everything from kitchen clocks to candlesticks.

Yes, we are petty thieves, smugglers, black-

266

marketeers, we are makers of moonshine and tax dodgers, we fiddle the books of our businesses and peddle porn, and when our neighbours' houses are empty we steal from them.

One thing we are not is killers. We hate to be governed, we are unruly, headstrong, we govern ourselves and all that governs us is the weather, the changing of the seasons, the land.

So what we lack they send to us.

They arrive and what they find is a bunch of petty crooks and boys who race their scooters up and down the supermarket car park, with moustaches of soft sparse hair, bitten fingernails and acne scars: boys in love with their cocks, who think themselves men.

Soon there is a list of names, drawn up from the post office records. People are told to report to the Crisis HQ. There are arrests, the new authorities insist these are not arrests but detentions in the name of security. Two students shop their teacher, who gave them poor grades. A farmer, mad with jealousy for ten years, exacts revenge on his wife's old lover. Grudges are reckoned. Greed grows. People denounce their neighbours to the new authorities on the quiet, with an eye on the couch, chest freezer, televisions always. Others give names in exchange for cash. 'Daddy's hiding in the attic,' says a small boy to the men who have come to take his father into custody.

The grey van does the rounds. Around and around.

*   *   *

Javor moves into my father's sheds at the bottom of my mother's garden. The people who know he

267

is there are: my mother, Anka, me. Anka visits him every day and sometimes stays over; the nights are still warm. They eat with us in the house and at night retire to the shed. One day the grey van visits their house. Anka is there. She tells the men Javor has gone hunting, it's the best she can come up with. They tell her to ask him to come down to Crisis HQ, nothing serious—in regard to his father. For a moment we forget and laugh about this, because Javor is a terrible hunter. I feel sorry for Javor, he is scared, he asks me to find out what has happened to his father.

I ask Fabjan, because Fabjan knows everything and everybody. I don't trust him, but he is Javor's partner and friend. He promises to investigate and he acts like he's taking it seriously. A day later he tells me not to worry, to tell Javor not to worry: his father will be released in a few days once the authorities are convinced of his loyalty. It's all connected with his job, which is after all an important one, a lot of people with his kind of background are going through the same thing. There won't be any problem. He even tells me where the detainees are being kept: in our old school. 'I mean,' he says, 'they're keeping them in kids' classrooms, not the police station. A baby could break out of there.' He shrugs and picks up a glass to begin polishing it. 'The whole thing's fucking crap, but tell Javor I'm here minding both our interests. The only thing to do at a time like this is make money. People turn into arseholes. Fortunately they turn into hard-drinking arseholes.' He puts the glass down. 'So where is Javor?' he asks, picking up another glass.

'At his house,' I say and shrug, like the question

268

means nothing, though my heart beats a little faster. I keep my eyes on the counter in front of me, but I watch everything he does, for a sign, for a hint.

Fabjan polishes the glass very carefully. 'Sure,' he says and sets it down. For a moment neither of us says a word. Then Fabjan starts to tell me about an idea he has for pond-raised catfish, he saw it on TV, wonders whether it would work here.

Parked outside the school is an old-fashioned grey van. Nothing looks very changed, there are a couple of guys, the ones from the Zodijak, cleaned up and given caps. Hardly Fort Knox, I say to Javor and Anka later. Anka watches me and nods without smiling. 'OK,' says Javor in answer to each new piece of information. 'OK, OK, OK.' He is sitting with his legs crossed, hunched over himself as though he is very cold, sucking smoke through a rolled cigarette; he used to smoke occasionally but now he smokes a lot. The foot of the crossed leg flips up and down, all the while he is staring at me very intently. I wish I could offer him more; I can't tell whether he is satisfied with what I am able to tell him; he just taps his foot and jerks his head forward, blinking, a woodpecker searching for grubs. 'OK, OK.'

'Is there anything you want from the shops?' I ask, getting up to go.

'You can ask Fabjan for my share of the profits. We need money. Anka hasn't been selling. Fabjan knows that. Tell him I just need enough to get by for a few days more.'

'No problem. Anything else?'

Javor smiles and throws the cigarette stub out of the door of the hut. 'Get me some fucking ice cream.'

Anka gives me a lift into town in her car. We pass the Crisis HQ and Anka looks at the building, which was once a municipal office where some works of minor bureaucracy were achieved. Now it is everything. Anka is going to visit her mother. I tell her I have some business to do, there is work around for someone like me, although rates are low. Still, work is work, I'm in no position to turn it down. After that I'm going in search of ice cream, whatever I can find. Maraschino. And if I can't find that, I'll buy a can of condensed milk and a packet of wafers which is the next best thing.

Some say October is the best time to visit these parts, after the rush, but when the sea and the air are still warm. There is a low sun. Anka takes her time gathering her things together before she steps out of the car. She places her basket on the car roof while she searches for something in her handbag. At the last minute she looks up and waves at me. She's wearing a red hat, the one she wore the summer before and earlier this summer, before the bombardment began. For a few months nobody wore colours, nothing that might risk turning you into a target and certainly not a red hat. But in recent weeks she has taken to wearing it again. A small act of defiance.

*   *   *

What memories of people you keep with you. I remember my father polishing the lenses of his black-framed glasses and peering through them before he placed them on his nose. I remember that he did it, of course, but each time I remember it, I remember the one particular time he did it

270

just before he opened a book of birds I'd brought home from school with me and began to name each species without reading the captions. Greenshank, redshank, sandpiper. I remember the smell of him at Christmas and weddings, his citrus aftershave. I remember Danica being stung twice by bees during a family picnic. My mother rubbed crushed parsley on my sister's arm. I remember my mother with a pair of secateurs in her hand, tapping the glass of the kitchen window at a cat about to defecate among the herbs. Most strongly I remember, again, the smell of my mother: her rose hand cream. When she'd been cooking she smelled of sweat and onions. I remember Anka standing on a rock, one leg stretched out behind her, a pointed foot. Anka shooting a rabbit. A coin flipping across the knuckles of her right hand. Picking a drunk Javor from the floor. Once again the strongest memory is a smell: of Anka's vinegar-clean hair the day she hugged me and pressed her nose into my face as she kissed me, the day I came back to Gost. That smell. Maybe the memory of the physical senses, those of taste, touch and smell, is stronger than the memory of images or sounds. I don't know. Maybe it all depends on the person. Whatever, the memory of the sight of Anka in her red hat, with her red car—was never one of the ones I kept—not until a summer sixteen years later brought it sharply back. It wasn't my last memory of her.

My last true memory of her was of another time, not long afterwards.

*　　　*　　　*

Once, long after we were lovers and had already

271

become friends, Anka told me that her favourite place on my body had been the back of my neck. I was sitting at the table in the blue house, the table I made, cutting a piece of lino with a sharp knife. She passed behind me and touched it with her forefinger. 'The way the hair grows,' she said. 'And the skin is very soft. You grow rough all over, except here, in this place,' and she tapped the top of my spine, 'nothing changes. You are all still boys. Yours looks exactly the way it did when we were still children. If I took a photograph and showed it to somebody they wouldn't be able to tell me if you were a girl or a boy.' It was perhaps the only time she ever referred to the fact we had once been more than childhood friends. That evening I held up the piece of mirror I used to shave and tried to see the back of my neck in the reflection of the window.

Two years later I am standing at the door of my mother's house watching Anka wash her hair at the well. She's not doing it well. At first she scoops palmfuls of water from the bucket over the back of her head. When that doesn't work, she tries to pour water over her head by holding the pail at an awkward angle, elbow in the air. The water rushes out and swamps her. From the kitchen door I laugh. 'Go shit in a lake, Duro,' she says through her hair.

Where was Javor? Still asleep in the hut. She doesn't want either to wake him or to leave while he is still asleep and so she goes out to wash her hair by the well at our house, even though she has a well and a bathroom at home.

I come down to help her, taking the pail. I am eating a carrot and I bite a piece off and give her the rest. She stands up to eat it, flipping her hair back over her head. She is facing the sun and the

272

light catches her cheekbones. In her eyes the pupil and iris are separate, two distinct colours, where usually they are almost the same. Her beauty changes depending on the time of day, the quality of the light. She laughs and takes a bite of carrot and chews it carelessly with her lips slightly apart, so that occasionally there is a faint glimmer of a tooth, a hint of orange. She swallows the last of the carrot, bends and flips her hair over her face.

I sit on the edge of the well and pour water in a thin stream so that it slides over her hair. She takes a bar of soap (shampoo is scarce) and rubs it into her hair and I watch the motion of her fingers and the magic of the rising froth, not listening to what she is saying until the fingers of the hand which isn't holding the soap grope round and catch hold of my wrist. 'Stop, stop!'

'Sorry.'

'Wait. I'll tell you when to start again.' While I wait I fold my arms and stare at the hills. My mind moves away from the hair-washing and the well water and I wonder where we are heading. Nobody dares think more than one day in advance, can imagine a place in time as distant as next week, next month, next year. Nor is anyone thinking about war, or using the word. Not the newspapers, not the drinkers in the Zodijak. War is far too big a word.

'Duro, pour!'

I begin to pour again. The water is cold, very cold indeed. I can see it in the pinched, pale ends of Anka's fingers. For the first time I notice the back of her neck and realise that this maybe is the only time I've ever seen it, at least since we stopped being children, because usually this part of her is curtained off by her hair. I remember not so long

273

ago when she talked about the back of my neck. Now here is hers, pale as the moon, the hairs raised on tiny goose pimples. I reach out my fingers and touch it. She lifts her head slightly. 'What?'

'Nothing. A bit of soap.' I pour more water and when I look up, Javor is standing at the door of the outbuilding where he sleeps, barefoot, wearing a pair of jeans, smoking a rolled cigarette. Just watching us, without anger. I hold out the bucket to him and he stubs his cigarette out on the side of the flimsy building, steps forward and takes it from me. He tips the remainder of the water onto Anka's hair and she sees it's him, reaches behind her and briefly clasps his ankle with her fingers.

I go into the house and come back with my mother's bottle of vinegar.

Afterwards Anka rubs her hair with a towel and leaves it to dry in the sun. The nape of her neck is back behind its veil. I go to fetch coffee and when I come back she is sitting on the edge of the well, where I had sat; Javor is behind her. He is playing with the hair at the back of her neck and occasionally, idly and without thinking, he strokes her neck with his thumb. When I hand him his coffee he removes his hand from Anka's neck to take the cup. I don't envy him. These people are as dear to me as they are to each other. Javor and Anka. My friends.

The image I best remember from that morning is only this, a single snapshot: Anka, bent forward, her neck exposed to the light, the filaments of fine hair standing upright on their tiny goose-pimple hillocks.

*　　　*　　　*

274

A day later I go to town, to the Zodijak, sent by Javor. When I arrive, there is Krešimir, standing in the office talking to Fabjan. The door has been left slightly ajar. I wonder if I should come back, but at that moment Krešimir leaves. He passes me at the bar. Usually Krešimir ignores me but this time he smiles, nods and asks after my mother and sister. I tell him they are fine. He leaves. That's it. All of this is unusual, but not enormously so. Krešimir doesn't like people to know of his dislike for me so he greets me when he sees he has no choice, this time because Fabjan has come out of the office and is standing right behind him. Krešimir likes to impress Fabjan, I've told you this. Maybe he wants Fabjan to back some business venture of his. Krešimir was meant to make money but never really has, well not a great deal, not as much as was always supposed, despite his job at the fertiliser factory and all the opportunities that must offer. I think it is because Krešimir is afraid of risks, would rather hang on to what he has, like all good misers. Fabjan, on the other hand, could never be accused of being afraid to take risks. Fabjan is all about business. All the same there is something about Krešimir's smile that makes me wary, as his smiles always do.

Fabjan nods at me and goes behind the bar. I take a coffee, there are other customers in the bar. I wait for the place to empty and then I give Fabjan Javor's message about the money. Fabjan doesn't look up from what he's doing, which is jabbing the buttons of an outsize calculator with his finger, but he nods as if he is listening and jabs some more. He stares at the numbers on the screen. 'Tell Javor I'll have something for him tomorrow. How much does he want?'

I say enough to last until this is over. I name a sum.

'Tell him I can do better than that. The way inflation is going, he'll need more than that. But he'll need to hold on a few days: cash flow, you know. It'll be sorted. How's he doing?'

I say he's fine. His mother left for her operation, which she'd had to put off but couldn't any longer. She'd gone to the district hospital.

'Tell her to take her time coming back. You know what I mean?'

I tell all of this to Javor later. He presses his lips together and nods, frowning. He's worried about his father and wants to try to see him. I say I think that's a bad idea, but I'll go. Anka and I walk back down the road, she to the blue house and me to my place; Anka is quiet and restless at the same time. She tells me she and Vinka had argued on her last visit.

'Over what?'

'She's drinking more. She gets into rages. I'd asked for a little money, just until Javor gets some in. She started on Javor. We argued. No, she argued . . . I tried to explain the situation. I didn't want to argue.'

'I can give you money.'

'It's fine. Krešimir gave me some. It'll be sorted soon. Fabjan knows.'

'Krešimir was there?'

'Yes. Krešimir was there.'

*　　　*　　　*

The rain comes down suddenly, though the sky stays bright. It feels like a summer storm but it's a bit late

276

in the year for that. I am on the mountain above the tree line. The rain is so heavy that, despite the light, I can hardly see where I'm going. It's like looking through a waterfall. With the lightning I change my mind about going back through the plantation and head in the direction of Gudura Uspomena.

Earlier the same day, as well as visiting Fabjan at the Zodijak to ask for Javor's money, I had also been to ask after Javor's father. The school looked just the same as before, the grey van parked outside. I approached one of the lads outside, I recognised him and he knew me by sight. He told me visitors weren't allowed but said he'd take a message. I thanked him. I told him I'd wait in case Mr Barac had a message for me. The lad shrugged, please yourself he said and disappeared inside. About fifteen minutes passed and just when I was about to go in search of him he came back and said, 'Barac has been released.'

'Are you sure?'

'Isn't that what I just said?' he replied cockily.

'Yes, and I asked if you were sure.' I stared him down.

'That's what they told me.' Surly now.

So then I went by the Barac house and found it closed up, as it had been ever since Javor's mother travelled to have her operation and her husband was taken away. I've checked on it at intervals, to make sure it doesn't get looted. So far nobody has dared. I banged on the door for the sake of it. A woman passing by watched me out of the corner of her eye. At the end of the street she stopped and turned to look. At first I ignored her but then I stared back at her and after a while she shuffled off, though not immediately. At first she met my gaze for a full four or five seconds before she gave a little smirk, dropped her chin and turned her back to me. Nobody had dared to steal from the house just yet, but that didn't mean they wouldn't. What was it they were waiting for? I wondered. Was it merely a matter of time, or was there some other signal? I went back to the school, to the same guy I spoke to half an hour before, and waved at him from a short distance. He looked up but didn't wave back. He ground out the cigarette he'd been smoking and was about to duck back inside when I caught hold of his arm. I told him the house was empty.

'So what? What's that got to do with me? They said he'd been released.'

'Who?'

He jerked his thumb in the direction of the school building.

'Well someone's made a mistake.' I let him go.

Something like twenty minutes passed before he came back out. He mumbled and I couldn't hear.

'What?'

'Deported.'

Javor's father had been deported, but how do you deport someone from this country? 'To where?' I asked.

Javor's father had wanted to join his wife and gone to the north.

'You just said he'd been deported.'

A minute ago he wouldn't look at me, now he looked up, lip raised above yellowish teeth, like a cornered rat. 'That's all I fucking know,' he hissed.

'Did they say when he was let go or taken there or whatever?' asked Javor when I told him.

'No,' I answered. 'Your mother hasn't called?'

Javor shook his head but determined to remain

278

hopeful. 'She's been in the hospital. It hasn't been long, a few days since he was taken into custody. Maybe there's some kind of transit centre ... paperwork.'

I had forgotten. It felt like we had been in this new world far longer.

Here up in the hills the rain washing down my face feels good. I lift up my head and open my mouth and let the water in, it is sweet, pure and sweet. I shield my eyes and look in the direction of the town, invisible behind the torrent of water. Let it run, I think, through the streets, down the gutters, into drains until it is carried away by the river. Let it wash away the shit and the pus and the blood, the things that can be washed away. But let it also wash away the fear and the malice and the spite, the things that are harder to erase. I wish these things that are happening right now weren't happening to us, I wish they were happening to someone else, somewhere else. I didn't care who. I clenched my fist. Leave us alone.

The rain makes Kos mad: she runs in a loop with her head down, and races through puddles with her head held high, letting her tail and backside drag through the water.

As swiftly as it came, the rain clears: the drumming slows and the threads of rain thin and lift. The air is scentless, pure. When it is clear again the sun shines strongly. The roofs and roads of Gost glitter and wink, the heat draws out thin drifts of steam from the tiles and stone. Between where I am standing and the houses of Gost the ravine yawns and stretches out, like a sleeping dragon whose tail begins at Gost and whose body lies to the north. The trees that fill the upper banks are just beginning to

279

change their colour. Opposite me the clouds have moved behind the hills, dark-centred clouds with gleaming edges, and through the gaps between them slanting columns of light fall, radiating out from a hidden sun, lighting parts of the hills and the fields, a roof here and there.

My father used to call this god light.

On a tree on the edge of the ravine a colony of crows shelters and with the end of the rain they become twitchy and raucous, hopping along and between branches, others hunched and watchful sit facing the ravine. Forty, fifty of them. Not so long ago I hunted these birds for food. For no reason, except that I feel like it, I lift my rifle and send a shot into the sky. The air vibrates with movement. I lower the rifle. A stupid thing to do, but who cares. Something about them bothered me. Perhaps they reminded me of the woman earlier in the day, hovering around the Barac house, waiting for something, for a death. And yet they are beautiful birds: the intensity of their colour: black beak, eye and feather; when they stand and tilt their throats to the sky, they look noble in their own way. As a child I collected every feather I found, examined one under a magnifying glass: the filaments and threads, all the varieties of blackness. Even now I find it hard to pass a crow feather and not bend to pick it up, just to hold it for a few moments before giving it to Zeka who loves to play with them and carry them to his bed. The farmers hate the crows and trap or shoot them, hang the corpses on the fences to rot, as a warning to others. A time-tested method, the birds' bodies rotate in the rain and wind, their heads flop on the ends of their necks, execution victims. The ends of their feathers lift and flutter like the clothes of hanged men. And yet were it not for the crows the roads would be littered with road-kill carcasses and the woods, fields and hills with the rotting corpses of every animal that ever died. I watch as the birds hover overhead, circling in the currents of air over the ravine. In less than a minute they're back, every single one of them. There must be something in the ravine, a deer that's fallen over the edge maybe, possibly still alive and the crows holding on until it's too weak to fight before they stab at it with those murderous beaks. I put my gun on my shoulder and move closer to the edge. Kos, by my side, swings into the lead, because now we are doing something interesting.

Within a few metres of the edge the smell starts, unmistakably a decomposing animal corpse. High, strong and sweet, it has a quality about it I can only think to describe as alive. It seethes, enters your nostrils like a swarm of tiny insects. The rain had cleared the air and now the heat of the sun releases the stink, along with the smell of earth and rotting leaves and something else, wet ash.

Autumn rains have left the ground soft. The earth gives way beneath my boots. There are tyre tracks. Someone has been up here, hunting from the back of a pick-up truck, dazzling the deer with the headlights and then chasing them down, possibly to their deaths over the edge. On the grassy slope which borders the steep edge of the ravine a couple of rocks have come loose and rolled away, leaving streaks of earth. A crow swoops and another: defending their find from me, this intruder. I expect to see a buck with a broken neck, but there is nothing. In the place where the ravine shelves less steeply some of the topsoil has washed away. I

281

climb down, it's easy enough and Kos outpaces me. Her fur is raised and her nose is down, suddenly she's very interested, zig-zagging, sniffing the ground. Whatever is there has been buried and the foxes have got to it, and now the rain has done the rest. Kos barks. She barks and bounces the way she does when she has found something and wants my attention. I know because of the pitch of her bark, which is both a call and a warning: she has found something she either cannot handle alone, like a large boar, or else cannot understand.

A human body. Wearing a blue wool sweater, a polo-neck stained with what at first looks like earth or blood, but is actually scorch marks. I squat down to take a closer look, to check the unbelievable truth of what I am seeing. The face has been burned away, the nose is gone, the nostrils are dark holes, the lips are no more, the gums shrivelled and the teeth are bared like an animal's and black in places. Reddish, singed hair, like doll's hair. Fingers curl around a handful of soil. Candle-coloured fingers. A woman sprawled and stiff on her back, legs open, knees bent.

Everything else disappears.

I stand up. My heart is beating wildly, the blood rushes to my head. I try to call Kos but my throat has closed and my mouth is dry, I can hardly make a sound, much less whistle. I step forward and yank her collar. I look around, but there is nobody watching us except the crows. For a moment I feel dizzy, the periphery of my vision is closing in black. I have stopped breathing and when I begin again I breathe hard, inhaling the awful smell deep into my lungs. The thoughts come fast, as I try to rationalise what I am seeing. I even think that perhaps this is some kind of overflow from the cemetery, where at one time the burials had become too many. Rogue gravediggers, perhaps, disposing of bodies they are paid to bury. But I know better, I know evil when I see it, the smell of it.

I was right about the foxes. There are more bodies, buried less than a metre down and they have been unearthed by animals and the elements. A short distance away an exposed shin, partly eaten, I can see the teeth marks, the torn flesh and gnawed bone. There is clothing: shredded and burned. I pick up a stick and use it to turn over pieces of a garment: denim, a jacket perhaps. It too is partly burned.

The bodies haven't been here for very long. My stomach bucks and the bile rises. I bend over and retch, drily save for a string of yellow. I have a terrible thirst. I pull the collar of my shirt across my mouth and poke in the earth with the stick, the wet leaves and ash with the stick. A twisted leg. The heel of a trainer. A yellowed hand, bent sharply at the wrist. Beneath the fingernails there is dirt. Dark unravelled entrails, strewn about by the birds, I suppose, caught in the low branches of a bush. The belly itself is a dark, gleaming hollow and the flies, chased away by the rain, are returning in their scores, bluebottles buzzing loud as bees. Every few seconds I have to stand to breathe, there's a light wind that comes from the west. I turn my face into it until I can bring myself to look again. I have a duty. I count. There are at least five people, though there could be more.

A crow swoops down and rises back to the branch with a coil of intestine in its beak. The sudden movement makes me start and straighten. I lose my grip on my rifle and it lands on the corpse with the open belly. As I reach for it my hand touches the cold flesh and I snatch it back, I fight the urge to flee. I wonder again if I am alone here, whether I am being watched by whoever did this. I stand there, listening, holding my breath, but there is no sound. I am alone, standing on the edge of a ravine: the landscape I know so well is suddenly a new danger. Now the silence is terrifying. I turn and run. Once away from the ravine, under the cover of the trees, I stop. Up in the trees the other crows start to squabble over the piece of entrail. I try to think what all of this means. Of one thing I am certain: these are not the men I killed and threw into the swimming hole. Those men, the soldiers, are long gone. I have dealt with death. I dealt with the deaths of those men, disposed of their bodies. But these deaths are different. These are different people. These are people I know. One of them, the one with red hair, is a woman.

I think I know who she is: the baker's wife, mother of the Mongol daughter. Perhaps the Mongol is buried there, too, the whole family. I don't know.

I don't know.

19

Things in Gost had begun to get to some people.

Grace, the first to see the damage, was red-eyed with crying. Laura stood with her hand over her mouth and her arm around her daughter. Matthew was sitting at the outside table, sleep-slow, his mind fractionally behind his body. He'd been woken up by Grace's shouts.

Paint all over the mosaic: white gloss paint. Loops of it cover the rising bird, sliding immensely slowly downwards. Clots of paint lie under the water on the mosaic of fish and weeds. A trail of white between the wall and the fountain. No sign of the can. Whoever had done this had brought the paint with them, because it wasn't mine. The gloss paint I'd been using was locked away in the outbuilding and anyway was blue. It must have happened the night before or very early in the morning, while they were all asleep. Not one of the family heard a thing.

'How could this happen?' asked Matthew.

'You wouldn't have woken up anyway,' said Grace. 'Maybe none of us would.'

'I mean there's no one else around here. They'd have had to come in a car or else it's a very long walk.'

'Probably they parked somewhere and walked the rest of the way,' I said.

'Yes,' said Laura. 'That would figure.'

'But why?' asked Grace. She rubbed an eye leaving a streak of white across her cheek. Paint on her face and hands.

'They're louts. Too many young men who don't want to work and then don't like it when other people have some money,' I said quickly.

'We're going to have to go to the police,' said Laura. 'I mean, this is awful.'

I doubted, I said, they'd be moved to mount much of an investigation, though I could be wrong. It would be very interesting to see what they would do, certainly nothing that they thought would be bad for tourism. It was an idea in which people had never lost faith: the hordes of tourists who would

285

one day return to fish and cycle and hike in the hills, transform the grey fate of towns like Gost. On the other hand they would want Laura to feel they were taking her seriously. They would make a show of investigating, but they had no interest in actually finding the culprit.

'How do you get this stuff off?' asked Grace.

'We'll do it. Easier before it dries too much.' I touched the paint lightly with my forefinger. The skin was still quite thin and the paint was wet beneath, meaning it hadn't been thrown all that long ago. If I'd gone up into the hills that morning, as I so often did, I even might have caught them in the act. Because so many of the tiles were glazed the paint wouldn't be too hard to get off. On the whitewashed surface of the wall, white on white, it barely mattered.

'What about the police? They'll want to see it,' said Laura.

I said most likely a photograph would do and so Grace went to fetch her camera.

A few hours later you could hardly tell it had happened. I fetched some soft rags from my house and we wiped away the worst of the mess. On the glass and glazed tiles the paint hadn't taken. Worst affected were the cream-coloured tiles that made up the background, which were some kind of soft stone. For those we had to use stripper, trying not to do too much damage to the surface. I only had a third of a can remaining and so I left Grace at work while I headed into town to pick some up.

In town I went to the hardware shop (the one which is not part-owned by Fabjan, of course) and on my way back I caught sight of Krešimir. This time I made sure he didn't see me: the last thing I needed was a repeat of the other day when he'd lost his temper with me at the Zodijak. Most probably he was going home for lunch. He was dressed for the office in a jacket and trousers, a pair of loafers. I watched him for a while, more or less to enjoy the sight of him. I wondered how he was feeling. The talk and the rumours slid through every street and house in Gost and, whenever the blue house was mentioned, so was Krešimir's name. Krešimir Pavić. People would fall silent at his approach and drop their gaze, begin to talk again once he was (almost) out of earshot. They'd be enjoying it. Of all of this I was certain. He walked like he was in a bit of a hurry, with his shoulders square and his chin out. To look at him you'd think everything was fine. But I know Krešimir like nobody else. He hates to be shown up, he hates it. So he puts on a bit of bluff, meaning the more confident he looks the worse it is. At the door of the house he stopped and searched for his keys, but not finding them he rapped on the door. I expected to see his wife, but when the door opened there was Vinka, her black hair pulled back in the style she'd worn all the time I'd known her; from where I stood I could see the sharp divide of colour at the roots. Her face was skeletal, skin like uncooked fish. She was without lipstick but her eyebrows were crayoned sloppily and comically high on her forehead. Unsteady on her feet, she almost fell out of the door as Krešimir shouldered past her and would have, but for the fact she managed to catch the doorframe. Unseen, I watched as she turned to follow Krešimir, patting her hair like a faded belle and closing the door behind them.

*   *   *

287

I fried sausages and onions for my supper and peeled and boiled some potatoes. It occurred to me I would miss Laura and the family when they went. In four weeks I'd grown used to having them around. That moment I decided to call my mother and Danica. My mother had finally moved into her own flat, the years on the waiting list had paid off. All the same it was she who picked up the phone when I telephoned Danica and Luka's place. Over the sound of the television in the background she began to complain. 'The bedroom's damp. It makes my legs hurt.'

'Won't the social housing people come to fix it?'

'They say they will, but they make me wait. If you were here you could do it for me.'

'I could, but then so can Luka.'

Silence. Then, 'I don't like to ask. He's busy.'

I said, 'Let me talk to him for you.'

'Thank you,' said my mother, not really satisfied. She'd never stopped asking when I was coming. To stop her doing so again I asked to speak to Danica. Danica came to the phone. I heard her telling my mother she'd take it in the bedroom.

'She's watching her television programmes. Those Brazilian soaps.'

'How is she?'

'Getting older, she misses you.'

I didn't reply and when Danica didn't say anything either, I said, 'She says there's damp in the bedroom of her new flat.'

'I know she does, but the flat is fine. I think she's lonely there on her own.' She paused. 'I was going to call you. There's something I need to talk to you about.'

'Well here I am.'

'Luka and me, we've been accepted to go to New Zealand.'

The news winded me. Danica told me the application process had taken a year, but they had almost reached the end now. All they were waiting for was the official letter.

'When will you go?'

'Before Christmas.'

'And Mother?'

'She wants to come with us. She's a dependant, so she's allowed so long as we take care of her. A lot of families have moved to Auckland. She'll probably even know some people.'

I was silent. Down the line I could hear Danica breathing and, faintly, the sound of the television in the other room. Then she sighed. 'Life goes on, Duro.'

After the phone call I ate the food I'd cooked and tidied up the house. I found the strip of braided thread Grace had given me the day I killed Kos. I put it in a drawer where I saw the green and blue tiles I'd brought from the blue house. I thought about the attack on the mosaic. For all that I disliked Krešimir it would be too easy to blame him. Krešimir's methods are far more underhand. He likes anonymous letters and poisonous words. Though I was not at all tired, for some reason I remained ravenously hungry even after I'd eaten. I fried more sausages and drank several glasses of wine. I tried to read the newspaper, but I wasn't really in the mood, I was restless. I turned on the television and let the pictures and canned laughter blot out my thoughts. I ate the sausages with my fingers straight from the pan, sitting in front of the television. I flicked channels. A re-run of *'Allo 'Allo*, which had been one of the most popular television programmes in the country twenty years ago. I watched it for a while and even laughed, helped by the wine. Also now for the first time I could understand the joke of Officer Crabtree's accent. 'Good moaning,' he says to René. 'Good moaning.' I laughed, but the joke quickly wore off. I switched channels, pressing the remote control over and over, until the television stopped responding. I still didn't feel the least bit tired but I could think of nothing I wanted to do, so I prepared to go upstairs to bed and a night of sleeplessness.

Before I went I opened the door and stepped outside. The night was warm, the air that slipped past me into the room brought with it the scent of the night, clean and fragrant. A light wind was blowing, dry from the desert. Down on the coast it carried a red dust that coated your skin, and sucked the moisture from everything, even the fruit on the trees. The last strip of light lay across the horizon. Whirr, whirr. Pat, pat, pat. Whirr. The nightjar. I closed the door and slid the bolts.

I climbed the stairs, washed and got into bed, between clean sheets that smelt of nothing. I lay for a while staring at the ceiling and then, though I hadn't thought I would, I went to sleep after all, a half-sleep, patterned with dreams. I dreamt I was eating a fine meal, soup and meat, surrounded by people who knew me. Even though it was a dream I could taste the food, even the texture of the meat. The dream switched. I was in the woods following a great boar. The boar was unafraid of me, as I was of it. He walked ahead and I walked behind at exactly the same pace. I wasn't carrying a gun, just walking through the plantation in the same direction. Zeka started to bark and I shushed him, but he disobeyed me and went on and on. And then I heard the sound of a girl calling me . . .

I surfaced like a man who has nearly drowned. Outside Zeka was barking. My chest heaved and my heart was beating hard, my neck was damp with sweat. I lay still and listened. A banging on the door. A voice calling my name. Grace. I pulled on a pair of jeans, ran down the stairs and opened the door. Grace's face was round and pale in the darkness, her eyes wide with fright. She was wearing nothing but a nightdress. She said, 'Oh Duro, you have to come. There's a man in the house.'

'A man? Who is he?'

'I don't know who. He said he wanted to talk to Mum, and I was frightened so I called her. Now he's got her and won't go. I think he's drunk and he seems very angry about something, but she doesn't know what he's on about.'

'How did he get in?'

'The door wasn't locked.'

I went to the back door and picked up a shotgun. 'Stay here,' I ordered Grace. I was without shirt or shoes, the gravel sharp beneath my bare soles. In less than a minute I reached the blue house. I ignored the front door and skirted round to the back; barefoot and on the grass now I made no sound. Inside, a single light from a table lamp and Laura, sitting on the sofa. She was wearing a robe; the family had evidently been in bed when the intruder arrived. She was sitting up very straight on the sofa, as if to attention, expressionless, her hand at her throat like she would strangle herself. I couldn't see any sign of a man, but Laura's posture was enough to tell me of the threat in the room. Whoever was with her was hidden by the angle of the wall. I listened: the rumble of a male voice. Krešimir?

A movement. A man's hand stroked Laura's hair. Laura flinched and leaned away, she put her own hand up over her hair to cover it, but the man's hand pushed Laura's out of the way and carried on stroking, picking up strands of her hair and letting them fall. Laura skewed her neck away, I saw her mouth open in protest, but if she said anything I couldn't hear her.

I pushed down on the handle of the back door and stepped inside. Laura turned to me, clearly with no idea what to expect; when she saw me she closed her eyes, breathed out and let her shoulders drop. I walked into the room.

Fabjan.

Sitting next to Laura on the sofa. At the sight of me his hand froze. He lowered it, though only as far as Laura's shoulder where he let it rest, like a man with his hand on a dog's head. He sat with his legs apart, looking like he did every day, wearing his butter-coloured suede jacket, a pair of jeans (the belt cutting into his gut, faded patch around his balls), loafers without socks. His eyes were narrow and puffy, his lips moist and red, a day's growth of stubble shaded the lower part of his face. He'd been drinking, though he was far from drunk, just drunk enough to be dangerous. He smiled and said in English, 'Ah, Duro. The hero. Welcome. Come in.' I took a few steps forward. His eyes darted to the gun. 'So you've come armed. What are you going to do, shoot me?'

'If I have to,' I said in Cro. 'Take your hand off her.'

Fabjan lowered his hand with a slow insolence.

'What are you doing?' I said, again in Cro.

'Well—and not that it's got anything to do with you—I'm paying a visit to this lady, who's a friend of mine. Right?' He looked at Laura, who didn't answer. Her hand was back at her throat and her eyes fixed on a spot on the floor.

'Speak Cro,' I said.

'Fuck off.'

I jerked the shotgun upwards. Fabjan's eyes followed it, so did Laura's. 'What do you want?'

'I told you. I'm visiting a friend.' He leered at Laura a second time, let his eyes travel down the front of her body. She lowered her hand from her neck and pulled her dressing gown further across her breasts. Fabjan pushed his face close to hers and flicked his tongue against the back of his teeth in a suggestive manner. 'What's it to you? Unless you're fucking her. Or maybe you just want to.' He no longer spoke in English, he turned towards me.

'She doesn't want you,' I said. 'So what *are* you doing here?'

'I've come to find out what the fuck's going on.'

'Meaning?'

'I want to know who's playing games.'

'No one's playing games.'

'Yes, they are. And people are talking. And they're talking now about this house, about the red car. About this stupid bitch. Because of this stupid bitch.' He swung his head round to look at Laura. This time she flinched and looked at him and then immediately back at the spot on the floor.

'Don't look at her,' I said. Then in English, 'Laura, go to my house. Grace is there.'

Laura rose and left the room, pulling her dressing

gown tightly around her, her head down. She went
without a word, as though she was afraid of being
called back. Once outside she began to run, I
listened until her footsteps faded. I reached for one
of the kitchen chairs and sat down, the gun between
my knees.

'Put that thing away, would you?' said Fabjan.
'You're not going to shoot anyone.'

'No,' I said. 'Not if I don't have to. But I'm close
enough here to take your foot off. Or blow away
your face. Have you ever seen a gunshot wound?
Probably not. I forget you don't hunt. You were
never in the Army either, of course. Well, at close
range the pellets haven't yet fanned out, they
enter the flesh in a wad. The cartridge opens like a
flower, it's made of plastic, you know. The cartridge
follows the shot into the flesh and it leaves a wound
the shape of a flower. Very pretty. It would kill you
of course. But then I wouldn't shoot you at close
range, nothing to make it worth going to hospital
for—what with all the explanations about what you
were doing here. No, you'd prefer to ask your wife
to pick pellets out of you for the next week.'

He looked me in the eye, some seconds passed.
'This is crap,' he said after a bit. 'I'm fucked if I
know what's going on.'

'You know.'

I didn't say anything else. The years of silence
spoke. Fabjan half opened his mouth and stopped,
his narrowed eyes held my gaze. He didn't want to
risk saying anything else. He shrugged as if nothing
mattered. 'If you say so.'

'Go,' I said. 'Don't come back.'

Fabjan rose and walked towards the door,
stopped, his hand on the door knob, and turned to

me. 'What do you want anyway?'

'Krešimir says he's leaving Gost.'

Fabjan was silent. He pursed his lips. 'So?'

'I'll miss him,' I said. 'And so would you.'

For a few seconds Fabjan considered my words. He didn't add anything. We understood each other.

*   *   *

When Fabjan had gone I sat for a few minutes and thought about what to tell Laura. A sound made me turn. Matthew: standing on the stairs. I'd completely forgotten about him. 'Duro.' He rubbed an eye. 'What are you doing here?'

We walked over to my house. I boiled water, made coffee. I told Laura that Fabjan was a businessman with many interests in Gost, a thug who operated outside the law. He and Krešimir had a falling out over money, I said. Krešimir owed Fabjan money and Fabjan wanted to be repaid from the sale of the house. I said I didn't know more details but I supposed that's what it had been about. Fabjan was used to getting what he wanted with threats. Laura didn't pretend to understand; she was still stunned. If she had questions they'd come later, by which time I would have thought up more answers. For the time being the explanation I'd given was good enough. Matthew had slept through everything and his questions about what had happened prevented the need for further analysis, rehearsing the sequence of events from Grace being surprised by Fabjan when he walked in without knocking, frightening the life out of her where she stood in the kitchen, to Laura coming down the stairs in answer to her daughter's call, Grace running to fetch me.

I walked them back to the blue house and stayed there the night. I lay on my back on the couch. I thought about Fabjan's question. He asked me what I wanted, a question to which he already knew the answer and had known it for many years. It was why we were still here, we three in Gost, when so many had left.

I wanted everything the way it had always been.

*   *   *

Along the edge of the field: a dense scattering of pink pimpernel, the flowers came up at this time of the year in the farmers' fields. The day was hot, cloudless, the trees shimmered behind currents of air in which a pair of kestrels hovered. The heron passed overhead on its way to the river. No wind. Dust in the air. The darkness of the trees came abruptly and I had to slow down until my eyes adjusted to the change. I'm getting old, I thought. Once or twice I heard the sound of other living things in the woods, but I hadn't come to hunt, I'd come to escape the house. I carried nothing and had left with no particular destination in mind, but now I found myself headed for Gudura Uspomena.

In Gost talk about the blue house continued. People knew about the paint attack, though not about Fabjan's visit. I imagined eyes following Krešimir wherever he went. I didn't go to the Zodijak, I thought I'd give Fabjan a day or two. Anyway his car wasn't parked outside. When I went back to the blue house the doors, which had stood open so much of the summer, were closed and Laura answered my knock warily, her hand at her throat as it had been last night. Inside the house was slightly altered: no vase of flowers on the table, the throws on the chairs, the cushions, these things were missing. Put away, I supposed. Laura was preparing to leave. We drank coffee at the kitchen table and she said she'd spoken to Conor who'd offered to fly out, but she'd told him they were OK. He'd asked her to give me his thanks. It seemed to me the full extent of what had happened the night before was just beginning to be felt.

'What about the police?' I asked Laura.

'Conor says we might have to stay on if there's an investigation.'

I told her that was likely to be true, that I was there if she needed me. 'But he won't be back,' I'd promised her. 'He was drunk. It's over.'

Below me the water level in the swimming hole was low and the water barely moved. Shades of green, white rocks visible beneath the surface. Downstream the waterfall had narrowed to a spout, which spilled evenly into the pool below. The sound rode upwards through the still air. For twenty minutes I stood and stared at the view. I'd known it all my life and it changed every hour of every day.

A noise behind me made me turn. Something moved in the trees. The footfall, too heavy for a deer, belonged to a person. I waited with my back to the ravine. A figure appeared: Grace. She walked towards me, the sweat shone on her forehead and she was breathing heavily. A few metres out of the trees she stopped, looked at the sky and then out across the ravine, shading her eyes. She came over to where I was standing. 'Isn't it amazing? You never brought us up here. I found it by myself.'

I turned away, to look out over the ravine. 'What do you want?'

'I wanted to talk to you about the man who came last night.'

'His name is Fabjan.'

'And he runs the café where Matt went to use the Internet. Mum told me. She couldn't remember his name. Is he a friend of yours?'

'No,' I said.

'Do you have any friends?'

'Not really.'

Grace was quiet. She chewed her top lip. 'But you used to.' She said it as a statement, not a question.

'Yes,' I said.

'So what happened to them?'

I shrugged.

'You knew the people who lived in our house before, didn't you?'

'Gost is a small place. I live a few hundred metres away. How could I not know them?'

'Yeah but.' She raised her hand to shade her eyes as she turned to look at me, I had my back to the sun. 'I think you knew them quite well.'

'So I did. So what?'

'Mum hasn't figured it out because she doesn't care to look. It's how she is. She sees the world the way she wants to see it, and then she believes that's the way the world actually is, if that makes sense. And Matt, well you know Matt.' She stopped and smiled at me: a sweet, small smile. 'But it's not that hard. Remember you told me how Kos found her way around? The places she knew by heart, you'd never know she was blind. Then other places, I remember you said she'd rely on Zeka or sometimes you'd have to call to her.'

'Yes,' I said.

'So Kos knows our house . . . I mean, she knew it.'

298

Grace paused. 'She knew where the doors were and where to lie down so she was out of the way without anyone having to tell her.'

I shrugged again.

Grace went on, 'Also the way you touch the table. I've seen you do it. Of course, you knew the mosaic was there all along. I worked that out ages ago . . .' She stopped talking and bent to pick a blade of grass and smoothed it between her fingers. 'So I think you knew the people well and you used to visit there a lot. Before us.' She sat down on the ground and began to chew the end of the blade of grass. 'It's OK. You can tell me. I want to know.'

20

I discovered the bodies at the ravine.

On the way down the hill my head and heart pound, there's a metallic taste in my mouth, also bitter bile. I am suddenly cold. And thirsty, desperately thirsty. I find a stream and drink from it, the water tastes of rotten leaves, I gulp it down like a man who has been lost at sea. The stink of the corpses is in my nostrils, my clothes, my hair. When I begin to move again I don't run, I drag myself through the woods. What slows my pace is the immensity of the crime and of what it required for those bodies to be there: dumped in the ravine and raked over. How many people did it take? Who else knows about this? How many people in Gost are part of it? At times I imagine I'm being followed or watched and that somebody will challenge me. Once or twice I stop and listen. The further I get the more the idea of the bodies being up there, carelessly buried, nobody to guard over them and left to the animals, seems impossible: the baker and his family and their Mongol daughter. Who else has been killed and discarded? I think of the others who have gone, the empty houses. I think of my father's colleague from the post office, whose boss is Javor's father—walking along with his pockets stuffed with envelopes. What was it he knew or imagined? He was a man in his sixties, who'd seen more than I ever had, who may even have fought a war. I wonder at the fate of Javor's father. I walk on, my mind becomes clearer. First, Javor. Javor must get out of Gost. I start to think how this might happen, I don't trust the roads: full of checkpoints, militiamen and soldiers. Maybe through the mountains. Javor is no outdoorsman but I could go with him. Winter, when the passes became snowbound, is still some way off. There is fighting further north, which is where it moved after it left Gost. To the coast then. Across the plains, by foot. The hardest thing would be to stay out of sight. My thoughts loop back to leaving by road, of what it would take to smuggle Javor. Who could I rely upon? Now and with this new knowledge, how do I know who to trust?

I pass nobody. The light is going. At this hour people are at home, especially these days when people spend a lot more time shuttered indoors. I think about them, huddled over their plates of food: cans of potatoes and meat taken from their neighbours' larders, wearing their neighbours' clothes, maybe even burning wood from their neighbours' woodsheds in their stoves. No sight of the moon. A wind from the north brings more wind and with it a light rain, which as I walk begins to fall more heavily, gusting across the road. I wipe the water from my eyes and carry on. At the bend in the road I take the short cut which leads to the back of my parents' property, behind my father's shanty town. There, standing at the back door of the house, I see my mother. She isn't wearing a coat or holding an umbrella, she's just standing holding herself, allowing the rain to soak through her clothes, looking in the direction of the road. On the road, just pulling away, is the grey van. I recognise it immediately: the grey van with the old-fashioned shape, I last saw it parked outside the school. I've only had the knowledge for a short while and I'm already too late. Javor! Do I shout his name? I don't know. I see my mother turn in my direction and raise both her hands, one in my direction and one in the direction of the van.

I thought I had seen the worst, but worse is to come. I have been wasting time.

Now I run. I cut back out to the road and follow the van. Like a delivery van which has collected a package it isn't moving especially fast then after a short while it begins to gather speed. It's headed downhill towards the blue house. I can think only: Anka. I keep running. Briefly I'm aware of my mother's call. I run through the long field, slash through wheat ready for harvest, releasing clouds of insects. To my left I can see the headlights of the grey van sweeping away from and then back towards me as the van rounds the bend and even though I have been able to cut the corner, moving as fast as I can, I am being left behind. The van is gathering pace. This gives me hope and sure enough the van passes the blue house. I begin to slow down. Saliva

301

floods my mouth, and again the aftertaste of copper. I have sprinted for almost a kilometre. A pain in my side makes me twist. I bend over, my knees crease and I go down. For a few seconds I remain on all fours; I smell flowers, wet soil.

I walk the rest of the way. I think they must be taking Javor to the school building. There may be time yet, something we can do. My mind races through possibilities, turns again to who might help, but no names come to mind. In the last few months everything and everybody has changed. People you thought you knew. There's Danica and Luka, I trust them, of course. Anka and me. But what can any of us do? Fabjan is the only person I know who might have influence. Fabjan knows the militiamen, they drink in his bar, he buys them rounds. They supply him with black market whisky. I reach the blue house. Fabjan's car is parked outside. For a fraction of a second I am relieved because Fabjan is already there, ahead of me, but before the whole thought is even formed I know I'm wrong.

Fabjan has known about this all along. He is part of it.

The door of the blue house opens. There is Fabjan now. And there is Anka. He is holding her, fingers closed tight around her upper arm, hurrying her towards the car. Holding the back door open is a man in uniform, one of the new arrivals. Next to him is the young man I spoke to at the school; he wipes his nose with his fingers, his head low while he watches Fabjan with Anka. There is something feral about his posture, that stare. Anka is tying a scarf around her head, she is hurrying. What is she thinking? That Fabjan has come to help her, take her somewhere safe, or maybe somewhere where she can talk to someone who might be persuaded to let Javor go? She has put her trust in him and there's urgency in her movements, such that she doesn't seem to notice the grip of Fabjan's hand on her upper arm.

I'm running again. With two hundred metres between us, I call Anka's name but the wind, the rain, the cloth of the scarf she is tying around her head blot out the sound. Fabjan, though, hears something. He raises his head sharply and peers into the gathering darkness. I can see him, but he can't see me. He gestures to the two men, says something to Anka, pushes her along. Now they're getting into the car. The doors slam. Fabjan guns the engine.

*   *   *

Time passes.

I stand in the rain outside the blue house and when I start moving again it's at a steady jog. I am wet through, but I feel nothing, just a pulse in my forehead, the beat of my heart, the butt of my rifle hitting my shoulder. By the time I reach the school building it is dark. No lights, no grey van, no sign of Fabjan's car either. I walk back the way I have come. I have only one idea, which is that they might at some point take Javor or Anka or both up to the ravine and that if I can do nothing else I will go to the ravine and wait. Kos is still with me, keeping pace, the run has scarcely put her out of breath. I have a growing sense now of what I must do.

The door of the blue house is locked. I find the key and let myself in. All is darkness, the smell of cooking and pottery glaze, on the table a pair of

303

freshly glazed dishes. I pick up a cloth lying there, one I've seen Anka use to wipe her hands. On the back of the door are scarves, jackets and coats. I take a scarf belonging to Javor. On the counter in the kitchen is the heel of a loaf of bread and a couple of apples, which I stuff into my pockets. I find a piece of salami and take that too. I fill my water bottle from the tin jug of well water in the corner.

On the way back up the hill I run to a slow rhythm, one I maintain until I reach the lower tree line. Only there do I stop for breath. No sign of either the grey van or of Fabjan's car. I can hear nothing beyond the rain and the wind. I stop and crouch down next to Kos, I talk to her until she is still. One after the other I offer her the things I have taken from the blue house: first the cloth, then the scarf. Again, the cloth and then the scarf. I give her a small piece of salami and shove the rest back in my pocket. I stand, sling my rifle over my shoulder again and we press on, Kos with her nose to the ground. The woods are dark; the only separation between the trees and the air is a difference in the density of the darkness. The trees are a solid black. The air shimmers, is speckled black and grey.

Kos sweeps her head from left to right across the ground and occasionally lifts her head and tilts her nose to the sky. The rain, though heavier now, for the most part fails to break the canopy. The sound of drops hitting the branches creates a white noise that absorbs everything else. We head steadily uphill. All the time I am listening for sounds, of men's voices or a truck engine, looking for the light of torches between the trees. Although the temperature has dropped and my clothes are soaking I feel neither cold nor hungry, nor thirsty as I had before, instead I feel alert, alive. I have slipped the rifle from my shoulder and now carry it in one hand, my fingers grip the stock. I try to work through events and possible outcomes in my mind, but I can only think of one. The way seems longer than it ever has and when finally I reach the edge of the ravine all is silent. The sky is dark. The moon, in its last quarter, has not yet risen. A scattering of stars and the lights of Gost. There is nothing and nobody. I think about what to do next. I sink to my knees and press my forehead against the barrel of my rifle. Impossible they could have got there before me, without me seeing or hearing them. Kos had picked up no scent. She stands next to me patiently waiting to be told what to do. But I have no other plan.

I have no other plan.

This is it.

After a while I stand and go to wait inside the trees, squatting with my back against a trunk. I'm not hungry; I eat an apple for the energy I may need. I eat it all including the core. Then I kick over the sodden pine needles at my feet and make a place for myself and Kos among the dry ones. I sit and listen to the rain. I tell myself nobody can get past me to the ravine. I wait. From time to time I stand up to stretch my legs. The moon rises. The rain eases off. Perhaps I doze; I am not aware of dreaming and yet it seems as though I am, as if everything that is happening is taking place in a dream. I pray for it to be so. I wait, adrift in time and space.

The hours pass and nobody comes. It's well past midnight when I head back down the hill with Kos

305

at my side. We go back down through the woods, cutting across the hillside. The thoughts fly, of what I will do next, I don't yet know but I am no longer in the same state as when I found the bodies, ran through the long field to the blue house. Then the fear had been at my heels. Now it is curled around my heart, my heartbeat has slowed and my mind is sharp and cold.

We have almost reached the bottom tree line when I become aware of a shift in Kos, a new tension. She trots ahead and begins to loop, running in circles and swinging her head from side to side. She is breathing heavily. I go to her and offer the cloth and the scarf one more time. She sets off, running in circles and figures of eight, and then she stops, sniffs the ground and heads unhesitatingly in the opposite direction from the one we have come in, uphill away from the ravine. Her pace gathers, her nose is close to the ground. I run behind her. It's hard going, my legs are heavy, my boots soaked. Kos never stops, except once when she loses the scent and doubles back on herself a short way to make sure, then follows the same line. She leads me straight uphill towards the old concrete bunker. A few hundred metres from the top tree line I see the beam of torchlight stitched through the trees. I slow down and stop and put out a hand to touch Kos, who slows too. I make her wait as I go forward.

*   *   *

A group of people. I count four. There is Fabjan and the two men I saw with him earlier. And Anka. The first thing I notice is that she no longer has the scarf she was wearing when she climbed into his car

306

and I wonder what happened to it. Another thing, she is barefoot. Why is she barefoot? Where have they been all this time? What has Fabjan done to her? The thought fills me with rage, I come close to rushing at him. Was Anka Fabjan's reward for a job well done? It cannot be, and yet what else could account for the missing hours?

Anka. What has he done to you?

I look to the left and to the right. Nothing. I move forward until I am level with the last line of the trees. I can hear them talking. I can't catch the words, but they are spoken in an ordinary tone as though they are trying to decide on something. Nothing from Anka. Then an exclamation from Fabjan: 'Jesus!' He covers his nose with his hand. A gust of wind brings with it the stench of the pit latrines. They start to move further on, away from the smell. The youth moves Anka on by pushing her in the back with his elbow. How full of swagger he is now. I follow them, moving parallel to them, soundlessly, behind the line of the trees.

Another hundred metres on they stop. The rain has started again and is growing heavier, the moon risen to its full, faint strength and the light catches the slanting lines of rain. Now that there is a little more light I can see the two men carry rifles; the youth's is an old hunting rifle with a wooden stock, the uniformed man is carrying a military-issue rifle and has a pistol in his belt. Fabjan appears unarmed, instead he stands before Anka revealed in all his true nature. And Anka stares at him through the rain. It's hard for me to see her expression. There's fear, yes. But it seems to me, as far away as I am and as little as I can see, there's puzzlement too. People who find themselves about to be killed, for no real reason, must wonder how it came to this, when they have hurt nobody, done nothing to deserve it. She must have thought Fabjan hated her and wondered why. But what Fabjan has for her isn't hatred, Fabjan doesn't hate, he doesn't need to hate to do the things he does. This is what you have to understand: for him, people like him, it's not difficult.

He simply wants what he wants.

*　　　*　　　*

'Go on,' said Grace.

*　　　*　　　*

I must kill them first, before they kill Anka. But they are three and I am one. Though Fabjan appears unarmed, he might easily be concealing a pistol. It's a risk I have to take. But before I kill Fabjan I must kill the men who are clearly armed. Which one first? I can try for them both in quick succession, the group is so tight, but of course with the first shot everything will change. These are the split-second calculations I'm making as I hide in the line of trees. A fresh thought comes to me: Anka's arms aren't bound. Because she's an unarmed woman, they don't see her as a physical threat. When the shooting begins they probably won't concern themselves too much with her in the first instance, they'll save themselves. Perhaps I can lead them away, give her the chance to escape. It's now almost completely dark. I look at the curled strip of the moon: there's a wisp of cloud across it which will clear in a moment and the small amount of extra light will help me with the shot. I raise my rifle. I decide to take the uniformed man, reckoning the youth probably is the lesser shot.

But something happens first. Anka lunges at Fabjan. If she is to die, she wants to show him what she thinks of him: spit at him, hit him, anything. There is a struggle, the youth loses his grip on her arm, she manages to break free and runs a short way. Anka slips and falls into the mud and comes up more furious. Fabjan is hit in the mouth, perhaps by Anka, more likely by the butt or barrel of a rifle. He swears and I see his hand go to his mouth. He spits something out: saliva and a fragment of tooth. The struggle lasts a very short time and then it is over. The youth is holding onto Anka, like a dog waiting for the command from its master. I shoot him in the forehead. He stands for a moment, teetering, dead on his feet. Then he falls forward onto his face. The uniformed man is the first to react, he shouts and he and Fabjan run for the cover of the trees. I follow right behind them; more than anything I want to kill Fabjan.

They split up and head in different directions. I chase the one I am sure is Fabjan, I can still see well enough. Without his torch Fabjan blunders and crashes through the trees and more than once trips and falls. I'm gaining on him when the first shot comes. Two shots from the militiaman's pistol, he doesn't care much if he hits Fabjan. I go down, I keep still. I think of Anka up by the bunker, she will have run. I need to give her more time. I can't let them have her. I have killed a man and I will kill again if that's what it takes to keep them away, but now it's too dark and I've lost track of them. So I fire once into the trees, so they know I'm still out here and to keep them on the move.

I wait for minutes, listening. No more shots come, no sound of boots; later I hear an engine. I leave my place and begin to make my way back up the hill. I call for Kos and a few minutes later she is by my side.

There is the dead youth. I turn him over: one eye is a bloody hole, the other sightless. Of Anka there is no sign, which is as I would have expected. My plan now is to follow her and to catch her up, to take her to safety. But the rain and the mud have made things difficult for Kos. During the scuffle the scent lines became tangled, now they cross and recross each other and Kos doubles back on herself trying to follow a single line. We branch out in several different directions before I give up, too dangerous. At any moment the militiaman could come back for me, could bring reinforcements. For Anka, too, who along with me is a witness to all that has happened. As I pass the dead youth I think of disposing of his body the way I disposed of others, over the ravine and into the swimming hole. I have my hands under his arms, I let them drop. What does it matter? Instead I look for his rifle. It is missing.

I stay away from the ravine and the woods for a week or more, two weeks. When I finally go back up there, the bodies have been moved, the earth turned over. Just a few scraps of singed denim.

*   *   *

'I thought she would find a way to come back. To my house, to my mother's house. To those people who loved her and would protect her. Or to send

310

a message at least. But she never did. She decided to rely only on herself. She went. There was a moment, after I shot the youth. I remember how she stepped back, she never screamed, simply stepped backwards into the darkness, turned and fled. For a long time, as I waited for her to return, I believed she knew I was there behind the trees and that this was my doing. That she knew I would come. For who else could it have been?'

'Do you think she will come back one day?'

'If she survived, if maybe she headed south and not north. But they would have been on the lookout for her. She would have had to circle back on herself. Cross the ravine. And if she forgives us, if she ever forgives us.'

'What about Javor?'

'The authorities found Javor, his remains, long after the war, many kilometres away. The militias had begun to transport people to be killed. Then came more wars, so many wars, it took years to find them. We were just the beginning, you see.'

Together we looked at the houses of Gost down below. I said, 'You can never tell anybody.'

'Why don't you go and live somewhere else?'

I shrugged. 'Why should I? And anyway where would I go? When you've seen it and you know nothing is going to change that, you get used to it, like an aftertaste of something rotten. You get used to it, because you have to. Gost is my home. I live here because it's what I want.'

'But then you're reminded, every day.'

'Yes,' I said simply. 'But I like to remember. Not just the bad times, but the good ones too.'

'And that horrible man, Fabjan?'

'I like to be sure he remembers too.'

311

21

Summer is nearly over, that time of year again. Here at the Zodijak it's still warm enough to sit out and will be for some time. At this time of day the sun is low, it dazzles the drinkers who sit out front. I was in town running my errands earlier in the day, have stopped by as is my habit. The new girl has gone of course, decided life in Gost didn't suit her after all. On the coast the restaurants will be closing up for the season: umbrellas stowed away, chairs turned upside down on tables for the last time. In the restaurant where I once worked with the Italian chef there was a tank in which hundreds of fish were kept alive. At the end of the season we had to catch all the fish so we could empty the tanks. I've been back to the coast. Sometimes I wonder what took me so long. I went to Pag, I drove across the newly renovated bridge, I even found my old hut, which has been done up and is rented to visitors. Wild bees had made their home in the old hives. Sage still grew everywhere. I understand why Krešimir had a dream of a life on the islands: I did once and it was a good life. But Krešimir won't be going. Krešimir is staying in Gost; we are all staying in Gost: Fabjan, Krešimir and me. We three.

In the last days of their stay I tried to make sure that Laura and the family had a good time, to repair a little of the mood. I told Laura again that Fabjan had been drunk and there would be no repeat of his behaviour. I'm not sure how convinced she was, but later in the same day we shared a glass of wine outside the house and, in discussion about some fittings for the house, she said she'd look in England and bring them out *next time*—so that's a good sign. The wine brought some colour back to her cheeks and we talked about the first time we'd met, when I found her looking for the water mains outside the house, and she blushed and laughed. I could still tease her, see.

I want them back.

The last thing I did was take Matthew hunting, as I'd promised. He didn't do badly at all: more nerve than I'd given him credit for, though he flinched at the last moment and we ended up trailing his animal a short way. Zeka did well, considering it was the first time he'd worked alone; his confidence is building. I haven't started another dog yet, but I will, perhaps in the spring so I can use next year's hunt season to bring her on. For now Zeka and I, we manage on our own. We miss Kos still. Grace, once I had taught her how to tread more lightly and not to alert every beast for two kilometres around to her presence, turned out to have the eye and the steady hand of a marksman, the ability to concentrate, to go straight to the zone. I'd seen it in the way she worked to restore the mosaics, everything she did from examining a dragonfly's wing to baking a cake, weaving friendship bands, so I fetched mine from the drawer and let her tie it round my wrist. In the woods, I watched her: the way she cradled the stock, you'd never believe it was the first time she'd held a gun. I thought about Anka and I felt the ember of hope that has burned inside me for years, that Anka is out there somewhere, that she took the boy's rifle and used it to stay alive, that one day she'll come back to Gost.

There are people like me all over, the ones who

want to remember, like I told Grace, different from the ones who want to forget. Every time a DNA test comes up with a match, something is quieted, a hope is doused. I wonder if Krešimir and Vinka check with the authorities. Krešimir told Fabjan where to find Javor, I saw it in his eye that day at the Zodijak when he stopped to greet me. I knew it then. It was in his smile, in his voice and in his tread as he left. He'd found a way to avenge himself on all of us. Once, blind drunk, I banged on the door of their house. Krešimir was out but Vinka, equally drunk but better used to holding her liquor, flew into a rage in defence of her son. 'He did his duty. It wasn't his fault.' And maybe Krešimir never imagined it would go so far. Probably he was moved by nothing more than a low spite. It was all the same to me: Vinka never cried for Anka and neither did Krešimir.

The family had been gone about three weeks when the graffiti appeared. It was painted on the bridge in an uneven hand, slashed strokes. It said:

We are all Krešimir Pavić.

It remained there for a whole day before the town authorities had it cleaned off. The paint must have been oil-based, black, hard to remove, the ghost of the words remained visible.

I didn't see the graffiti when the paint was fresh, I hadn't been into town for a few days. Still so much work to do. Up in the attic I cleared the wasps' nest. Wasps are master builders, their intricate hexagonal homes, comprised of thousands of identical cells, are extraordinary. They are hunters too, though most people consider them nothing

314

more than scavengers and nuisances. I have seen a wasp alight on a fly and sever its wings, carry the maimed creature away to feed its young. I removed the nest with care, handling it with respect, as one must. Next I need to finish splitting and stacking logs—the dead tree, hours of work there to be done before the *bura* begins to blow and the sea freezes over.

The next time the graffiti appeared it was on the wall of the railway station. *We are all Krešimir Pavić.* Talk in the bakery, in speech comprised of half-sentences, gestures and looks. The dark child is scratching on the walls, the scratching is becoming louder. In the Zodijak, a heavy silence. Fabjan sits surrounded by it. The words on the walls hold different meanings for different people, but nobody will say what those meanings are. People in Gost look at each other, mistrust seeps through every conversation. For days, it seems, we stand on the edge of something. *We are all Krešimir Pavić.* On the door of the empty Orthodox church. But who is responsible?

From the Town Hall the authorities have reacted furiously: with detergents and solvents, scrubbing brushes and high-pressure jets. It is laughable. They worry about the tourists, but the hunting season has started and tourists are even scarcer than the wild boar. Warnings are posted, of the penalties for defacing public buildings—the first time such a step has been taken, after all there is graffiti all over Gost. Krešimir, who is at the centre of it all, doesn't know what to do. In the absence of the culprit being caught, he is taking the brunt of it. His swagger is all gone. Fabjan has had a word with him, advised him to keep a low profile, no sudden moves, that sort of thing. Too many people out there who might still be interested, journalists and the sort. Better not bring any more down on our heads. You can rely on Fabjan to get his point across. So Krešimir has decided to stay on in Gost.

Lucky for him the graffiti stopped. The authorities at least seemed to be on Krešimir's side. As quickly as it went up, out they came with their hoses and rubber boots. So in the end whoever was responsible gave up. For two weeks nothing. The talk began to subside, the silence at the Zodijak to lift.

And then this afternoon, in town running my errands: a new blade for my saw, mousetraps for the blue house. I make sure I take a look in at least once a week, to check for leaks, that the window seals are sound, that no animals have gained entry. I like to walk through the rooms, you can imagine. Strange to be in there alone; in all the years I have known the house, there was always someone: first the Pavićs, then Javor and Anka, the family over this last summer. Today in town I passed by the Orthodox church and there, sprayed on its double, metal-studded wooden doors, massive: a rising red bird, with outspread wings of blue and a crown of gold, trailing a red and yellow tail. From its uplifted beak came curls of gold breath. It flew straight upwards into the sky.

Ah, but here is Fabjan now, parking his BMW. I am sitting at his table, so he has no choice but to come and join me. Probably you wonder how we all stand each other as I do sometimes, but the truth is we have no choice. In towns like this there is nothing to do but learn to live with each other. I must live with Fabjan, as he must live with me. I'll ask him how his tooth is and if he intends to hire another girl next summer. He'll have to sort something out in the long run. There are after all, and as Laura said, so many summers.

Acknowledgements

Thank you to:

Igor Zvonic, who shared his memories of life in the former Yugoslavia in the 1970s and 1980s, patiently answered all my questions and helped with translations, also Boris Bošković for his help with details of the text. To both for talking to me about the war in the former Yugoslavia.

Sam Kiley for his knowledge of the war in the Krajina and memories of reporting from the region for *The Times* in the early 1990s.

Igor Zvonic, Boris Bošković and Sam Kiley, also Michael May, Gertrude Thoma and Simon Westcott who took the time to read *The Hired Man* in draft and shared with me their comments and observations.

Simon, companion in life as well as during my research trips through Croatia and the part of the country that briefly became known as the Republic of Serbian Krajina.

Charles Perry, of the UK National Rifle Association, who taught me about guns and how to shoot them. Corrine Edwards gave me an insight into the ceramicist's art.

Writers Slavenka Drakulić, Dubravka Ugrešić, Josip Novakovich, Ivo Andrić, Aleksandar Hemon, Misha Glenny, Laura Silber and Allan Little, Rory Maclean—authors whose work was most informative in researching this book.

Feral Tribune, Croatia's all-too-short-lived satirical magazine whose reporting of and investigations into war crimes led to prosecutions of several of those responsible.

David Godwin: rock steady friend and so very wise.

Michael Fishwick, for his company and counsel on our journeys together through the place he calls 'Fornaland'.

Everyone at Bloomsbury, in particular Alexandra Pringle, Anna Simpson, Holly MacDonald, Mary Tomlinson and Jude Drake.

Mo.